THE

PERFECT VICTIM

TEMPE BROWN

DEDICATION

I dedicate this book to my best friend, Vivien Weller, now in heaven. She was an encourager extraordinaire; one of those beautiful souls that made you feel that you were worth more than you thought you were, and that you could do more with your life than you ever thought you could. Thanks, Viv, for pulling out of me the gifts that only you saw, and made a believer out of me.

See you later, my friend.

TEMPE BROWN

ACKNOWLEDGMENTS

My heartfelt thanks to Shirley Moran, the inspiration for this series. You are undoubtedly one of the hardest working human beings I have ever met, and you get very little appreciation for it. The transportation industry is tough; it is a business where if things go wrong, they can go very wrong. You pay close attention to every detail to keep your clients safe and happy. I'm grateful for your good heart and for letting me work with you to get a better feel for this series and for being my pal.

~ ~ ~

A huge thanks to my good friend Lonny McClung, Capt. USN (Ret.) for his incredible advice and help with this project. Lonny is an aviation consultant. During a 30 year career as a carrier-based fighter pilot, he logged over 7,000 hours, more than 1,000 carrier landings, and over 250 combat missions in Vietnam. He served on both coasts and was Commanding Officer of four different aviation units: Fighter Squadron 51 (F-4's); Fighter Squadron 124 (F-14's); and Navy Fighter Weapons School (TOPGUN), all at NAS Miramar, San Diego; plus Training Air Wing TWO at Kingsville, Texas, training Navy Pilots who manned carrier-based fleet tactical jet squadrons. Thanks, Lonny, for helping me with a wild white-knuckle ride!

~ ~ ~

Many thanks to my longtime friend, Nabil F. Warsal, MD, for his help answering some medical questions. Dr. Warsal is a General Surgery specialist in Newark, Delaware. Having over 55 years of diverse experience, especially in General Surgery, he is affiliated with many hospitals including Christiana Care Health Services, Inc.

I can't thank you enough for taking the time to give me the advice, for your expertise and for your, Donna's and Jonathan's great friendship and support over the years. I am one blessed lady to know you and call you friend.

TEMPE BROWN

Other Books by Tempe Brown

The Seed

The Little Dirt People
What it Means to be Born Again

The Payback Game
Sixteen Days of Terror

CHAPTER ONE

Near the end of June at three o'clock in the morning, due to a combined temperature inversion with a stubborn high pressure, humid air began to move over the surface of the city causing a thick cloud of fog to settle itself for the night along the Potomac River. Soon it would slowly crawl over the banks of the historic waterway and into the streets and wide boulevards of its namesake, Foggy Bottom. Its denseness would veil the famed buildings and monuments, causing them to appear otherworldly.

Two shadowy figures, dressed in black and wearing ski masks, hunched behind thick bushes across from a nondescript storage building and watched and waited. A camera was mounted over the door, accompanied by a single light. When he thought it was safe, the taller of the two raised his Ruger 22/45 Lite, muted with a silencer, and shot out the light. The sound was no more than a muted thud. Breaking glass scattered in splinters and fell onto the ground below. The two waited several minutes, watching and listening in case the sounds had aroused attention to cause someone to come to investigate. Security was nowhere in sight. This was going to be easy.

They picked up two large objects and advanced toward the door. With no light, it would have been difficult to maneuver, but they were equipped with night vision goggles making their task much easier, but they had to work quickly before the fog reached them. Night vision goggles didn't work well in fog.

The keyhole was found and the door opened with little sound. They each picked up their load and, once inside, set them down again and carefully closed the door behind them and locked it. It was pitch black inside. The shorter of the two quickly pulled out a flashlight, located the blinking red light, went straight to the alarm pad, hit a few numbers and disarmed it. Careful not to leave fingerprints or footprints, they wore gloves and thick cloth coverings over their shoes.

Aiming the flashlight straight at the camera to "blind it," the taller one reached up and pointed it sideways away from the site where they would be working.

They removed the night vision goggles and followed the flashlight beam toward the back of the narrow room, passing several stacks of boxes, fold-up tables, and old file cabinets. The storage building smelled musty and immediately attacked the sinuses of the shorter one. A few steps further, they found what they were looking for. There were several crates stacked five high. Giving a satisfied nod to each other, they lifted two, set them aside and replaced them with two identical ones.

Their task complete, they took the crates toward the entrance, now their exit. The tall one carefully repositioned the camera; the shorter skillfully reset the alarm. They picked up the containers, opened the heavy door and cautiously looked around. The dense shroud of mist had reached their location. It was the perfect concealment for them. The one with the key set his load down and quietly closed the door behind him. He took off his glove, dug around inside his pocket for the key, found it, and felt around the metal plate in the dark for the keyhole. After a few seconds, he found it, inserted the key and locked the door and pocketed the key. He then pulled a handkerchief from another pocket, thoroughly wiped off the plate, careful to leave no fingerprints, returned the handkerchief to his pocket, picked up his glove and put it back on. At that point, they knew that their night vision goggles would be mostly useless. The two felt around for the stolen crates, picked them up and silently disappeared into the fog.

CHAPTER TWO

The streets of the capital were decorated with blinking Christmas lights and wreaths of greenery. A twenty-foot-high Christmas tree graced the entry of Georgetown's posh Sequoia Restaurant located at the National Harbor.

The distinguished Maitre'd greeted Sabyl warmly with a lilting non-descript accent. "Ah, Ms. Martin, so good to see you again."

"Thank you, Alfred. You as well. There will be three of us for brunch."

He bowed slightly, like a man thoroughly accustomed to the etiquettes of the perfumed elite, picked up three menus and smiled. "Of course, right this way."

Some of the faces she passed were familiar to her; most were not. She recognized Senators Locklear from Oklahoma, Senator Gerald Stewart from Idaho, Congressman Bradley Stovall from Tennessee, Deputy Mayor Sheryl Dalton and a smattering of assorted media types.

Men and women alike watched her stroll gracefully across the spacious room. Her closest friend, whom she was meeting today, Rebecca Carriere, a best-selling author and former columnist for the Washington Times, once told her, "You walk like a model."

Sabyl wore a double-breasted charcoal-gray belted coat with a mandarin collar and black wool pants tucked into her ankle boots. Her honey-colored hair fell loosely from beneath a beret she bought at the Charles de Gaulle Airport on a layover on her way to one of her trips to Italy.

Alfred led Sabyl to her favorite table by one of the floor-to-ceiling windows that overlooked the harbor. He helped Sabyl with her coat.

"Thank you, Alfred." She sat down, and he handed her a menu and laid the other two on the table's edge.

He smiled, bowed his head smartly and said, "Enjoy."

She looked out the window at the expansive patio with its blue umbrellas tied firmly closed, standing at attention like royal guards. If not for the cold weather, they would be open with the tables filled with numerous tourists and Washingtonians.

Sabyl looked forward to seeing Rebecca. On those rare occasions when they had a little extra time, they might be found browsing the small mom and pop bookstores in Bethesda, eating at one of the abundant ethnic restaurants around DuPont Circle, perusing the shops and small galleries along the canal in Georgetown, or an escape into history through the endless corridors of museums. But Sabyl's work was her greatest delight, although it was not without its challenges. If she didn't have at least a dozen brush fires to put out in a day, she felt something was amiss.

The worst nightmare of her career was the night of President Stanton's inauguration five years ago. She had subcontracted sixty-four limos out of New York; half the drivers got lost or lost their clients. Added to that, some of Stanton's friends from his home state of Alabama didn't hold their liquor well and barfed all over the backseats before the gala night was over. She was glad the new administration was mostly teetotalers.

The harbor water glinted brightly in the strong sunlight, a welcome sight after a week of rain. Sabyl's long, thick lashes shaded her soft hazel eyes. Had it been a few degrees colder, the streets would have frozen overnight and would have been a nightmare for her thriving limousine company.

Having grown up in Pennsylvania, Sabyl was used to cold weather, but looked forward to spring and the warm fresh air; especially to her biannual trip to Italy to escape the pollen of the cherry blossoms. Otherwise, her voice would sound like a cat with a fur ball stuck in its throat for a solid month. She sighed at the thought of Italy, her beloved second home. She would love to stay there for more than two weeks at a time; in fact, if she could, she would stay two months, but that was impossible. Owning the most lucrative transportation business in Washington kept her tethered to the nation's capital. It was one industry that when things went wrong, they went very wrong. Dealing with top government figures, and some of the most successful and powerful people in the world, meant having to stay focused on every detail, small and large, until the clients were finished with their business in Washington and were safely transferred back to their destinations.

Early on, it didn't take her long to realize what a cutthroat business the transportation industry could be, but even with all its headaches, Martin Transportation had been very good to Sabyl. Success had not come easy, but then it never does. Many of the other limousine companies dealt with their clients like a catalog of numbers, seemingly clueless that pampering went a long way in this business. They were apparently in it just for the money. Although she loved to please people, she was no pushover. She was tough and knew how to hold her own.

There were cultural differences that she soon learned to deal with. Some Middle Eastern clients were, at first, offended by the idea of a woman being in charge of their transportation and telling the drivers and security details what to do, but upon seeing how carefully and meticulously she ran her business, many of them were won over.

Limousines were as common as lawyers in D.C., yet business was seldom slow. But if things did get slow, she would allow her drivers, who mostly owned their own cars, to take an occasional wedding, but never proms or stag parties. Those were left to the smaller companies with their white stretch limos.

She liked working with the government, or at least with their transportation people. They were easy to deal with, mostly cooperative and efficient in every detail. Other government agencies were a different story. She often wondered how anything got done in the District. If there was anything Sabyl disliked, it was dealing with people who were inept. Over the years, she found there was a lot of that disease in D.C.

Over the years, through hard work and sheer determination, she had landed numerous notable accounts, including Destry Oil, Vostra Faccia Cosmetics, dozens of powerful CEO's, movie director, Austin Fleming, the great classical guitarist Juan Montez, the Latin idol Roberto Enrique, Worldglobe Bank, wealthy sports figures, and the *Kennedy Center*, just to name a few. And, of course, countless government contracts.

Although she was raised in a small town, she loved Washington, especially the history. On one of her many trips to Italy, she spoke with pride of the history of her nation's capital. Her friend Gianni countered, "Il Mio Caro, I have faucets older than your country!"

As soon as Sabyl got settled in her seat, she saw Rebecca heading her way with a man in tow who looked to be in his fifties. She wondered if he was her latest boyfriend.

"Sorry to be late, dear," she said, leaning down to give Sabyl a kiss on each cheek. Her blonde hair was pulled back and fastened with a clasp, enhancing her elegant features. Her face was classic Grace Kelly, the kind artists love to paint. "Parking was grisly," she said as she pulled off her gloves. "I want you to meet a friend of mine, Professor Paul Larson. He teaches law at American University. Paul, this is my dearest pal, Sabyl Martin."

He extended his hand. "Ms. Martin, so happy to finally meet you. Sorry, my hands are cold."

"Not a problem. So are mine," she said. "A pleasure meeting you as well."

He helped Rebecca with her coat, revealing a muted green cowl-necked cashmere sweater with rows of silver chains cascading over it.

Paul pulled out her chair, she sat down and folded her gloves and placed them in her pocketbook.

The professor pulled off his coat and sat down. "I've read a lot about you in the papers, of course. This country owes you a great debt."

"No, please . . ."

"Oh, come now, you're a national hero."

Sabyl put up her hands in protest. "Honestly, I'm no hero, and that was over a year ago . . ."

Rebecca turned to Paul. "Understandably, she doesn't like to talk about her run-in with the terrorists."

Paul was not deterred. "So the bad guy—what was his name—Endicott?"

Sabyl gave a frustrated nod.

"John Endicott was just one of his many aliases," Rebecca interjected. "And just one of many bad guys."

"Right," Paul continued. "Didn't Endicott hire one of your limousines and do his dirty work from there?"

Sabyl shifted her weight. "Well, sort of . . ."

Paul pressed on. "So tell me about this Endicott character."

"Rebecca can tell you more about him than I. She did a lot of research on him to write about him."

Rebecca crossed her arms and leaned forward. "He was a cold fish," she said flatly. "His father was British, his mother from Croatia. When he was nine, both were killed in an automobile accident in London. His maternal grandmother brought him to live with her in Croatia, but she died of cancer a year later. Having no other known relatives, he ended up in an orphanage, and after a few weeks, he ran away and lived on the streets. Oddly enough, he was taken in by the Croatian Mafia."

Paul's brow furrowed. "Oh, wow!"

"At the age of eleven, they taught him how to handle a gun. He killed his first victim at the ripe old age of twelve. When most kids that age were playing ball, he was planning his first hit."

She looked at Sabyl and then back at Paul. "Of course, with our nation under attack, a lot of journalists wrote about him and his hideous schemes. He brought a lot of grief to our country." She reached over and gently squeezed Sabyl's hand. "But after he targeted my best friend to be murdered, it got a little more up-close-and-personal, so I decided to do a little extra research and write about him."

Paul shook his head. "What a nightmare those two weeks were!"

Sabyl nodded and thought, Sixteen days, to be exact.

Paul asked, "So why did he target you? How did you wind up on his hit list, Ms. Martin?"

She folded her arms and leaned back. "The morning of his arrival at Dulles, Endicott had lost a small black book in the back seat of Rudy's car."

Rebecca cut in, "Rudy is Sabyl's first driver. He's been with her from the beginning. He's like family to her."

Sabyl smiled. "That's right. So, after Rudy dropped him at his hotel, Endicott realized the little book was gone. He immediately taxied over to my office and asked to hire the same car and driver, hoping to find it in the back seat of Rudy's car without anyone being the wiser. He hired him for two weeks and said he had an important meeting to attend. Once in the car and the divider up between them, he searched the back seat for the little black book and not finding it, he questioned Rudy about it. He told him he had found it and tossed it in the lost box. It was written in Arabic and Endicott knew Rudy was from Egypt and could read Arabic."

"And had he read it?"

"No, but he somehow concluded that Rudy had read it and probably saw something in it that could tie him to what he had come here to do. I guess he thought he might have discussed it with me."

"Which placed both of them in the crosshairs of the assassin," Rebecca interposed.

"So he broke into your home in Pennsylvania and tried to. . ?"

"He sent one of his operatives," she said, wishing they could change the subject.

"How ghastly! You lead an exciting life, Ms. Martin."

"A little too exciting, I'm afraid. And please call me Sabyl."

Rebecca reached over and rubbed Sabyl's arm. "We'll change the subject, dear. I'm sorry."

A young man approached the table and greeted them warmly. He took their drink orders and announced, "Your server will be right with you."

They thanked him in unison.

To lighten the mood, Rebecca opened her menu and, without looking up, said, "So, Sabyl, have you looked at the Sunday buffet or are you going to order from the menu?"

"I think I'll do the menu," Sabyl said.

"I think I'll do the menu as well."

A few minutes later, a young man brought three goblets of ice water. "Hi, my name is Lee, and I'll be your server. Are we ordering from the menu or doing our brunch buffet?"

"I think we're all ordering from the menu," Paul answered.

They each ordered, he gathered up their menus and scurried away as though on a mission.

Rebecca looked out the window. "Isn't this sunshine divine? I'm so weary of all the rain."

Paul agreed. "Yes, even though it's still cold, I see the tourists are out in full force."

"As I came in, I noticed several senators and their families are here today," Sabyl said.

The professor took a sip of water. "Wonder why they're here so late. I thought Congress would have gone home long ago."

"I guess it depends on what's on their plate," Sabyl said.

"Some may be here to pick up their kids from college before they head out for Christmas vacation," Rebecca assessed. "Or maybe they just want to hang around town. There are so many wonderful events here at Christmastime."

"True."

Rebecca squinted, her eyes trying to see across the room without her glasses. "Paul, isn't that Professor Hickson?" she asked, nodding toward a square-shouldered man with graying hair, his arm around a tall, shapely blonde with large, round eyes. They were waiting to be seated.

"Yes," Paul said. "Brilliant man. Teaches computer science at AU. He's mentored a lot of the students. He even helped one of his graduates, Derrick Blake, start the Tech Center on the east campus at AU."

Sabyl took a sip of water. "Tech Center?"

"Yes—kind of a store for software and electronics of all sorts. Blake runs it. Seems he's a bit of a genius himself."

"I thought I recognized that name. Derrick Blake built my website. He's dating one of my reservationists, Jenny Wong."

"Really? I'm surprised he dates at all. He's sort of a loner. Guess those quiet types will surprise you."

"Jenny seems quite taken by him. Calls him her geek."

Rebecca asked, "Who's that with Hickson?"

Paul unfolded his napkin and placed it on his lap. "His new girlfriend."

"My goodness, she's gorgeous. I thought he was married."

"He is." Paul shifted his weight. "Story has it that they met in New York at a conference where he was speaking. I guess they hit it off and the next thing I heard, he was getting a divorce and she moved in with him."

The trio watched as Professor Ted Hickson helped the woman with her coat. She sat down, and he politely pushed her chair up to the table.

Sabyl cleared her throat. "Guess we shouldn't stare."

Rebecca asked, "How do his colleagues feel about it?"

"The faculty at AU is not very happy with him. He's asked his wife for a divorce. Apparently, he's going to marry that woman."

Sabyl took a sip of her water. "What's her name?"

"Eva Thorn something. Thornburg—something like that. His wife's a lovely person," he said shaking his head. "Too bad. Seems to be happening a lot these days."

Rebecca smiled wryly. "Tell me about it."

"Is that what happened to you, Rebecca?"

"Yes, but I'm over it. Life's too short to let another human being ruin it for you."

"True. What about you, Sabyl? Are you married?"

"Um, no."

Rebecca whispered sympathetically. "Paul, Sabyl's a widow."

"Oh, I'm sorry."

Sabyl looked down at the ice in her glass. "It was a long time ago."

"But she has a new love," Rebecca said brightly.

Sabyl smiled, "Not so new . . ."

"Wonderful! Tell me about him," Paul said.

"Well," she said beaming, "His name is Scott Terhune, and he works for the Department of Homeland Security."

Rebecca leaned toward Paul and lowered her voice for effect, "He's a Secret Service agent, and he is gorgeous!"

"That he is," Sabyl answered.

The server brought their lunch and served it graciously.

They chatted amiably as they ate. Suddenly, a cacophony of cell phone tones began going off all over the restaurant. People immediately started calling for their servers.

Sabyl remarked, "What on earth..." Her phone chirped in her pocketbook. She quickly reached for it and answered, "This is Sabyl." Her face grew ashen. "What? Oh, no!"

Rebecca whispered, "What is it?"

Sabyl closed her eyes as if in pain. "Okay, thanks for letting me know, Frank."

Paul frowned deeply. "What's going on?"

That was my day dispatcher. "Two planes have crashed. Eyewitnesses to both of them said they exploded in midair."

"Oh, my God," Paul and Rebecca said in unison.

"Two? Where?"

"One went down over Kansas, and one near Kearney, Nebraska."

"Paul exclaimed, "Two planes exploding? That's no coincidence. That's terrorism!"

Sabyl closed her eyes and exhaled, "Not again."

More cell phones began going off as others received the news of the explosions. News spreads as quickly in D.C. as in a small town in the Oklahoma panhandle. Several people, including senators and members of the press, quickly paid their bills and hurried out.

Sabyl, Rebecca and Paul waited for their check in stunned silence. After paying, they said their quick goodbyes, promising to keep in touch, and went their separate ways.

CHAPTER THREE

Monday morning, Sabyl pulled into her private parking space, got out and opened the back door for her four-year-old standard Beagle Beau. He jumped out, shook vigorously, rattling his stainless steel tags, and headed for the door.

It was a known reality that Beagles should never be allowed to roam free without a leash, as its nose is sure to get it into trouble. But Beau, curious as he was, never left Sabyl's side. Fiercely loyal and protective of her, he would only leave her company when at the office, where he loved to hang out with the drivers in the lounge area in the garage.

Dotty Stevens, Sabyl's secretary of ten years, opened the door for them.

Sabyl let Beau go in ahead of her. "Thanks, Dotty."

"Morning, boss." Dotty leaned down. "Hey, Beau! You want a treat, huh, boy?" Beau's tail swished back and forth like a windshield wiper as he followed her into her office. It was located next to Frank's, across the lobby from Sabyl's office.

Sabyl looked to the right and waved at her head dispatcher, Frank Lauriette. He was on the phone and waved back without looking up.

Sabyl walked into her office and dropped her heavy leather pocketbook on the floor and sat down in her comfortable antique desk chair that allegedly came from the House of Representatives, with the seal still on its side. She found the grand old chair at one of D.C's better flea markets.

Her office was not large but adequate. On her desk were stacks of files and phone memos, a flat screen computer sat on one corner, her multiline office phone next to it to her right. Heavily draped floor to ceiling glass windows overlooked the brick circle drive. Two overstuffed leather chairs sat across from her desk. Behind her was a built-in wall unit of shelves burdened with books, framed photos of some of her most noted clients, and Awards of Excellence from the *National Limousine Association* (NLA). Beside her desk to her left against the wall was Beau's doggie bed.

After giving him his treat, Dotty followed Sabyl into her office and helped her with her coat. "What do you make of these plane crashes?"

"It's absolutely horrible. I can't imagine how those bombs could have gotten past security."

Dotty hung up Sabyl's coat. "I know! Somebody's not doing their jobs keeping us safe!"

Sabyl punched the button on her computer to start it. "For sure."

Sabyl admired her secretary and friend. Dotty was in her late forties, a bit stout wearing her ever-present sweater. She had thick, short dyed-brown curly hair and inquiring blue eyes. She was a cancer survivor and had come through an abusive marriage like a champ. At one point, her wealthy executive, albeit alcoholic husband had knocked her down the stairs in their home when she was pregnant with their daughter, Mary, causing Dotty to give birth to a child who was born brain damaged. Dotty sued, got the house and a significant settlement, and was set for life financially. She didn't have to work, but she was never one to sit around doing nothing. Her rapier-sharp wit kept everyone in the office on their toes.

After agonizing over Mary's need for special care, Dotty found an excellent facility on Maryland's Eastern Shore that specialized in the kind of care and attention she would need. Mary had the mental capacity of a seven-year-old. Now twenty-one-years-old, she had grown into a happy, lovely young woman. Sabyl loved Mary and always planned something delightful for her when she came to town.

Beau, having finished his treat, ambled past Sabyl's desk and dropped into his bed and let out a big sigh.

Dotty shook her head. "Two airplanes exploding on the same day sounds like terrorism to me. What does Scott think?"

"I haven't had a chance to talk to him. He left a message on my phone that he would be pretty tied up."

"Yeah, I can imagine! I hate to say it, but I wonder if we'll be getting a lot of calls for—you know—funerals."

Sabyl leaned back in her chair. "It's certainly possible. Seems like we're reliving the attacks of last year."

"Yeah, only instead of targeting our top leaders one-by-one, it seems they're going after everyone."

Frank took off his headset and walked into Sabyl's office. He rubbed the back of his neck. "Guess you've heard about the plane crashes."

"Who in the world hasn't heard about them, Frank?" Dotty asked wryly.

"Yeah."

Frank was six-feet tall, forty-five, black, and wore horn-rimmed glasses. He was a recovering alcoholic and in better health than he had been in years. Sabyl had fetched him out of the drunk-tank more than once. He was one of the few detainees who, when bail was met, was driven away in a limousine. She had stuck by him when most employers would have fired him for some of the mistakes he had made while brain-dulled from hangovers; errors that cost her some significant clients. When he realized how much pain his drinking was causing her and how much stress he was putting on his marriage, he finally got into AA, and he's been sober for four years. He would do anything for Sabyl.

Frank laid a stack of papers on her desk and sat down in one of the leather chairs. "Those are the latest transfers to the airports."

Sabyl picked up the papers and looked at them.

"I heard this morning that one of the passengers aboard that flight heading for Sacramento was a senator," Frank offered.

Sabyl looked up. "Who?"

"Senator Martin Lyles of California. He was heading home for Christmas."

Sabyl shook her head. "How awful!" She swallowed hard. "I feel for all the families…"

Dotty thought, *of course, you do. You know exactly how they feel.*

Frank asked, "What does Scott think?"

"I haven't had a chance to talk to him."

"Yeah, I imagine he's pretty busy."

Dotty's eyes widened, "I'll bet people are pretty nervous about flying right now."

Sabyl nodded. "I imagine so."

Frank stood up. "Guess I'll get back to work." He stopped and turned. "Hey, you've got a flight coming up pretty soon, don't you?"

Sabyl looked at him sideways. "Don't remind me."

"When are you going?"

"The twentieth. Maybe this will all be over by then."

Giving Frank that "you idiot" look, Dotty quickly changed the subject. "Uh, Sabyl, when are we having our office Christmas party? We need to pick a date. Time's going pretty fast."

"Let me get settled in and then we'll look at the calendar. I'll need to see what the reservationists have cooking, and then I can give you a definite date."

"Okay." Dotty headed for her office.

Frank followed her out and asked, "Hey, Dotty, what about your floors? We had a pretty good rain last night."

"Water flooded my dining room again. It always comes down that hill behind my house and right into my French doors. All the parquet tiles are curled up—my floor looks like a tray full of party mix."

"Again? I thought those drainage people were going to fix that."

"Yeah, me too. I need this like I need my wisdom teeth."

Frank fumed, "You just had those floors replaced. Your insurance company needs to make those drainage people make this right!"

"I know. It's the pigs. I can't believe I have to deal with this again. If they don't fix the drainage problem, it's just going to keep on happening."

"So the drainage people haven't come out at all to deal with it?"

"Nope. I called them and gave them an earful this morning. Again! They said they'll be out sometime today."

"So what company are you using?"

"CFIC."

"CFIC? What does that stand for?"

"Capital Flood Inspection Control. As far as I'm concerned, it stands for CFI care!"

Sabyl walked out of her office and headed for the coffee pot in the foyer next to Dotty's office.

Frank leaned against the wall with his arms folded. "It seems to me they're getting the cart before the horse if they're not dealing with the drainage problem first before they put your floors in."

Overhearing the conversation, Sabyl frowned sympathetically. "I'm sorry you're having that trouble again."

"Yeah, me too. Oh, well. That's life in the big city."

"Gotta get back to work," said Frank, as he turned to go to his office.

Dotty sat down at her desk. "I'm going to get on the horn right now and call my insurance guy."

Sabyl said, "Good idea. If you need me, I'm going to the garage to talk with the guys."

"Okay."

Sabyl poured herself a cup of coffee and headed for the garage, Beau trailing behind.

Seven of her small army of drivers, George, Burt, Rudy, Ricko, Stubby, Maurice and Lawrence, were watching the latest news reports.

George Parker, the garage manager, had been with Martin Transportation for nine years. His square features were fairly nondescript except for generous laugh lines around his eyes and a Santa-shaped nose. His graying hair was receding, much to his chagrin. At five-feet-ten, he was more muscular than stout with massive biceps that strained the seams of the arms of his blue work shirt. When he wasn't working, he and his wife, Betty, enjoyed perusing the multiple flea markets on Saturdays on Wisconsin Avenue. One of Betty's favorite things to do was to find deals on domestic items such as flatware, dishes, kitchenware, bedding, and children's clothing to donate to the various women's shelters in and around the city to be given to the victims of abuse to help them get back on their feet. Their Jack Russell terrier, Elvis, usually accompanied them. They would leave with a trunk load each Saturday, head home to clean up the items to make them like new and then she would distribute them to the shelters on Monday morning after George left for work.

Burt Hastings, a former Greyhound bus driver from South Carolina, and a huge Clemson fan, was a chain smoker with yellowing teeth, a long, face, droopy blue eyes and a glass-half-empty outlook on life. His wife Phyllis nicknamed him Eeyore. Burt hated D.C. traffic, the many traffic circles, and had been the beneficiary of a half-dozen parking tickets from the D.C. Metro Police, which he lamented often. When he saw Sabyl approaching, he quickly snuffed out his cigarette.

Ramose Abana, whom she nicknamed "Rudy," was her first driver when she started her company fifteen years ago. A large, gentle man with copper-hued skin, large brown eyes and coal-black hair, Rudy was born in Al-Kosheh in Upper Egypt, which, puzzlingly, is south of Lower Egypt. Ancient maps were drawn with South at the top until the standard of North at the top of maps and charts became universal after Columbus' voyages.

Rudy and his lovely doe-eyed wife, Layla, came to the U.S. nineteen years ago, and after five years, had proudly obtained their American citizenship. Their son, David, a medical student at Johns Hopkins University in nearby Baltimore, had earned a full scholarship. No parents could be more proud.

Rudy's seventy-five-year-old father, a Christian minister, was still preaching in Al-Kosheh. The increase in Christian persecution in much of the Middle East and the eradication of Christianity in its region of birth was of great concern to many. Rudy worried about the safety of his father and prayed for him daily. He had begged him to come to the security of the U.S., but he would always gently decline saying, "My calling is here, my son."

Often, while waiting for a client, Rudy would be found quietly reading his Bible, praying or listening to a tape of one of his father's sermons on a small battery-operated cassette player that he bought on eBay.

Sabyl looked to Rudy's quiet strength and often counted on his prayers, especially through her twice-fought battle with breast cancer. He was more like a brother than an employee.

The drivers had been watching the game between the Steelers and the Carolina Panthers until it was preempted by the breaking news of the downed airplanes. They were in the spacious lounge on the street-level floor of the garage that housed the sedans, stretches, SUV's, minibuses, and nine-passenger sprinters that made up Martin Transportation. They watched silently as ESPN brought the latest news as it came in.

Stubby Jones, a former New York City cop, sat with his hands tucked under his armpits, his chair pushed back and balanced on its back two legs.

Ricko Garcia was finishing cleaning out a large pot in which he had cooked his famous chili with meatballs, better known by the drivers as Gut Grenades.

Maurice DeLorian, one of Sabyl's veteran drivers, stood when Sabyl walked in.

Stubby brought his chair down on all fours and leaned forward, his beefy arms resting on his thighs.

George stood and quietly welcomed her. "Hey, boss."

The others greeted her, their faces grim with the recent reports of the downed aircrafts.

Always the gentleman, Lawrence Washington, the tallest and oldest of the drivers, with a strong resemblance to Morgan Freeman, stood and offered her his seat. She thanked him and sat down. He asked, "Sabyl, what does Scott think about these bombings?"

"I haven't had a chance to talk with him. He's been pretty busy, and I don't imagine he would be able to discuss it with me if he did have time to talk to me," she said with a note of sadness. "How are you guys doing? You need anything?"

"No, I think we're good," answered George for the rest of them.

She looked at the large screen TV that covered a good part of the north wall. Leaning down to rub Beau's velvety ears, she asked, "Any more news?"

"No," reported Lawrence. "They're just showing the same pictures over and over of the wreckage."

"And that," offered Burt, pointing at the screen showing the grief-stricken family members who had been waiting for the arrival of their loved ones. "Hard ta' take," he said, his brow in a knot.

"Yes, it is," whispered Sabyl. She stood up and said, "Well, just wanted to say hi. Come on, boy." Beau wagged his tail and followed her as she turned to go. "See you guys," she said and headed out the door toward her office.

"See what you did, you bonehead," said George.

Burt shrugged his shoulders sadly, remembering how Sabyl had been through the same thing when her husband and son died in a plane crash in Colorado. Burt hung his head and said in a low voice, "Aww, I didn't mean nuthin'."

CHAPTER FOUR

In the beginning, the intimidating presence of dozens of Secret Service agents on campus was met with a mixture of resentment and awe. The president's daughter, Allyson Anderson, was a freshman at American University. At first, the students stared when she and her protectors moved about the campus, but now, four months into the school year, she was mostly sympathetically ignored. Most of her classmates shied away from her, but a handful befriended her. One of them was a handsome young man by the name of Jeremy Stallings. He wasted no time making her acquaintance and after a few awkward tries, asked her out. Of course, four strapping Secret Service agents accompanied them. The six of them have been going out ever since.

The AU campus was now nearly deserted. Most students had packed up their belongings; things that would be needed for the time spent away from the famous university. Only a few remained, putting together their last minute items in small suitcases and backpacks, trying desperately to pack so they could keep their luggage down to a reasonable size to be admitted as a carry-on when nervously but bravely boarding the various airlines that would hopefully take them to their destinations and away from the world of academia.

Allyson, Jeremy and the ever-present Secret Service agents came to gather up the rest of her things before heading off for Christmas break, or winter break for the politically correct.

Kyle Sloan sat on the steps of the tech center and opened his sandwich bag and took out a pastrami on rye and a small bag of chips. The cowlick in his dark hair was starting to spring back up. No amount of mousse or blow drying helped for very long. Kyle was a senior, carrying a 4.0 average in Computer Science with a special interest in Computer and Information Security. Computers had been his life since he got his first one as a Christmas gift from his parents at the age of ten. He was especially adept at hacking.

Sitting a few feet away, his boss, Derrick Blake, was his usual guarded self, which Kyle noticed had grown increasingly worse over the last few weeks. Anxious to finish the inventory of the tech center that he basically founded and managed, Derrick's dark eyes squinted under his aviator sunglasses as he watched the Secret Service agents moving about.

Kyle took a swallow from his water bottle. "Sure would like to meet Allyson Anderson."

Derrick glanced at him sideways. "Why? Looks like she's already got a boyfriend."

"Yeah. Just thought it'd be cool to meet the president's daughter."

Derrick sat quietly, chewing a bite of his sandwich.

"How much longer before we finish up our inventory, do you think?"

A dark cloud passed overhead, bringing a cold wind that blew across the campus.

Derrick slid his sunglasses to the top of his head. "We should be done in another couple of hours."

"So, what are you doing for Christmas?"

"Nothing."

"You're not going home?"

"I am home."

"I mean—you know—to where you're from in Ohio to visit your mom. I mean, won't she be alone?"

"No on both counts. My sister will bring her to her house for Christmas."

Kyle wadded up his sandwich bag. "She still living in that nursing home?"

"Assisted living. It's hardly the same thing."

"Right." Kyle stretched and yawned. "So, whatever happened to that program you were working on?"

Derrick's jaw tightened. "None of your business, dude."

Kyle frowned and put up his hands in mock surrender. "Okay. Whatever," he said and looked away.

He's really in a foul mood, Kyle thought. He watched as Allyson, her boyfriend, and their luggage were swept into a black Suburban and then it drove off.

"I wonder where they'll spend Christmas," Kyle thought aloud.

Derrick took a swig of his water, screwed the lid back on and ignored him.

Across the east campus, Professor Ted Hickson and a blonde woman drove up in front of the building where the Computer Science Department was housed and parked. Hickson got out of the silver *Mercedes C-Class Cabriolet,* walked around and opened the door for the woman.

Kyle watched as her long, shapely legs gracefully unfolded.

She stood, straightened her belted coat and took the professor's arm. Hickson closed the door, and they walked toward the newly built structure where he and hundreds of other teachers and staff members had moved their departments into their new "digs." Hickson was proud that he had taught at the university for the past twenty years. But an early retirement looked more and more promising.

36

Kyle whistled softly. "That Mercedes hers or his?"

Derrick stared straight ahead. "Don't know—don't care."

Kyle let his eyes slowly tour her curves. "Nice," he whispered to himself. "So that's Hickson's girlfriend. He turned to face Derrick. "I thought he was married."

"He is," Derrick sniffed.

"Too bad. His wife seems nice. She used to come into the tech center when it first opened, remember?"

"Yeah."

"What do you think of these plane crashes?"

"Obviously terrorists."

"Makes me not want to fly ever again. Glad I live nearby. Not that I'm going anywhere for Christmas…"

Derrick wadded up his sandwich bag and drained his bottle of water. "Life goes on, dude."

A few minutes later the pair came back out, the professor carrying an expensive looking leather satchel. He opened the door for the statuesque woman. She slid in and arranged her legs. He closed the door and went around to the driver's side and got in. The engine started with that sound exclusive to high-priced, high-powered cars. He backed out and exited onto New Mexico Avenue.

Kyle watched them drive away. "The dean and the other Profs know about this?"

"Don't see how they could miss it." Derrick stood and tossed his lunch bag in the trash bin and walked up the steps of the tech center. He turned and said through clenched teeth, "He'll get his."

CHAPTER FIVE

The nation was in shock, having been thrust once again into the cauldron of terrorism. Homeland Security worked the phones attempting to allay the public outcry of yet another attack on American citizens.

Ron Keefer ran a tight ship as Special-Agent-in-Charge (SAIC) of the Washington field office of the Secret Service Agency. The forty-three-year-old black Penn State graduate leaned forward on his elbows and looked into the eyes of his two best agents, Scott Terhune and his partner, Lou Martz.

Scott graduated from Florida State with a bachelor's degree in Criminal Justice and a master's in Computer Criminology with a 3.8 average. The Secret Service was his goal, and they accepted him eagerly. He had completed his required six years in the field office in Richmond, eight years on protective detail with former President Stanton and now in his fifth year at Headquarters in D.C. where he had been a part of the Electronic Crime Special Agent Program (ECSA), training agents in computer networking and digital forensics. He worked with local law enforcement on computer crime investigations handling internet fraud, network intrusion and destruction, and identity theft. But his specialty was cyber-forensics and computer/network security issues. With the attacks last year, and a greater need for protection of the top government officials, he found himself back and forth between the office and temporary protective details.

Scott noticed the tenseness in his bosses' face.

Keefer began, "I called you in to tell you that I just returned from a meeting with the President and the Secretary of Homeland Security, John Killian. A special investigative unit is being formed comprised of two of the best men from each of the following agencies:" He quickly rattled off the initials of the departments involved: DHS (Department of Homeland Security) DoS (Department of State), DoD (Department of Defense), ITA (Office of Intelligence and Threat Analysis), NSC (National Security Council), NTSB (National Transportation Safety Board), NSA (National Security Agency), JTTF (FBI'S Joint Terrorism Task Force), CTA (Counter Terrorism Agency), CIA (Central Intelligence Agency), NTAC (National Threat Assessment Center), DIA (Defense Intelligence Agency) and, of course, our Agency and their National Response Team (NRT).

"We've got to get to the bottom of these bombings. It's time these agencies learned to work together. To quote the president, 'This territorial crap has got to stop.' I happen to agree." He leaned back and continued. "The head of each agency has been asked to choose two of their best out of each agency and, I might add, the president emphasized that those chosen must be fair-minded, of excellent morals and specifically non-territorial—not apt to be a James Bond-type loner, especially after the recent scandals involving the heads of certain agencies, but a team player." He leaned forward again and looked at the agents in front of him intently. "I've chosen you two to represent the Secret Service."

Scott and Martz looked at one another and looked back at their boss. "Thank you, sir," I guess, Scott wanted to add but didn't.

Martz mumbled "Thank you," with a tinge of skepticism.

"We'll have our first briefing this afternoon at 2 p.m. The location is on the folder in front of you."

The two agents looked through the file. Scott looked up. "You're heading this thing up?"

"I am," Keefer said flatly.

Scott and Martz blinked in amazement, knowing that the Secret Service Agency was Keefer's life. "Congratulations, sir. Is this a permanent position or just for…"

"Depends on how well it works. I'm sure everyone will be a bit leery because it's been tried before and it didn't work out very well, but sometimes it takes a tragedy to get us moving."

"Pain causes change," Martz offered.

"Exactly. In truth, the idea has been in the President's mind since he took office last year after the attacks on our leaders. He feels this is the time to implement it. After Nine/Eleven, it became obvious to everyone that there's a real need to make some major changes, and that if there were to be another terrorist attack, the territorial governmental agencies would possibly respond no better."

"How is it going to work?"

"Each agency will continue as they are but the agents on our team will have at his or her disposal the full resources and information of their respective agencies and any information that may be pertinent to the bombings will be shared. Hopefully, things will move along at a much faster rate in the investigative process."

Martz cleared his throat. "What happens if someone in one of the agencies withholds vital information?"

"I'll have their butt in a sling."

Martz exhaled loudly. "Right."

"Sounds like there are going to be a lot of muscle in one room," Scott remarked.

Keefer smiled. "I know what you're thinking; too many chiefs and not enough Indians."

"Yeah, something like that," Scott admitted.

40

"They'll have to check their egos at the door."

Martz scratched his cheek. "Who's going to take our workload here—and yours, for that matter, if I may ask?"

Keefer looked at his watch. "I'm meeting with my assistant Marion Stanley in a couple of minutes to turn my duties over to her, and I'm recommending Bill Archer and Clorissa Littlefield to take your cases. If you have objections to these choices, I want to hear them now."

Scott shrugged. "I've no objection."

Martz nodded. "Excellent choices."

"Then I suggest you brief them within the hour. Then clean out your desks. We're moving to a new location up the street. Keep your items few. This agency will be lean and no-nonsense. You'll have the opportunity to ask more questions in front of the other agents when we meet with all of them. If you have something you don't want to put forth there, ask now or forever hold your peace."

"I have one . . ."

"Okay, Scott, shoot."

"Will we still be able to work in the field? I mean, we're not going to be sitting behind a desk all day, are we?"

"I asked for the best men—and the best means the best in hands-on investigating. You'll be in constant contact with me as will the other agents and we'll do this unusual thing called communicating."

Scott and Martz nodded.

"Each agency represented will also have some serious technical help. You'll see all the latest gadgets that will be at our disposal." He stood up. "I don't have to tell you to keep this under wraps for now. We've got a lot of work to do, and we don't need the press shoving microphones in our faces." He gathered up his papers. "Oh, and the name of our unit is Unified Agencies Task Force. UATF—with the emphasis on Unified."

~ ~ ~

Sirens, a typical sound in the nation's capital, shrieked on the street below the small apartment in northwest D.C.

A single bed, neatly made, sat in one corner. A small, round ornate rug lay beside the bed. A chrome gooseneck lamp stretched over the edge of the bedside table. The apartment was plainly furnished and neat. Against the north wall were shelves sagging under the weight of thick books, most of them about computers. Across the room was a makeshift desk composed of a door that lay across two small file cabinets. A laptop sat open on top.

The dusty plastic blinds were closed, and a small flat-screened TV set on the weather channel droned softly in the background.

He turned on his computer and sat back with his hands folded like a schoolboy and waited. As soon as the computer finished booting up, he put in his password and then opened a website, scrolled down and looked at the airline schedules. "There it is," he whispered to himself. "Flight 84 out of Reagan National. Departed on time at 8:10 a.m. heading for New York." He looked at his digital watch and smiled. Good. It's halfway there. He got up, walked over to the remote that was lying on the coffee table, and changed the channel to CNN. He then returned to his desk, bent over and turned off his computer. He yawned and stretched and went into the tiny kitchen, took a plastic bottle of water out of the refrigerator, closed the door with his foot and unscrewed the lid. After taking a swig, he went back into the living room and sat down on the small flowered sofa, rested his ankle on his knee, turned up the volume and waited.

~ ~ ~

George came out of the garage into Sabyl's office. "Hey, boss."

"Hi, George. Is Rudy back yet?"

"He had a transfer from Reagan National. Should be back in about a half an hour. Want me to go get your Starbucks?"

"No, thanks. Rudy will bring one. He always does."

"You sure?"

"Yes, I'm sure."

"My wife and I saw a sign the other day at a flea market we like to go to. I should have gotten it for you. It said, 'Give me coffee and nobody gets hurt. She almost bought it for you for Christmas."

Sabyl laughed. "I'm not that bad, am I?"

The garage manager grinned. "No, not really."

Karen, one of Sabyl's reservationists, a twenty-six-year-old with hair dyed bright red, usually in a ponytail, brown lipstick and long, sculptured fingernails to match, walked in and greeted her. "Sabyl, here's the info you asked for about Vassette. Hey, George."

"Karen, you actually said a full sentence without dotting it with 'like.'"

She rolled her eyes. "Like, later." And left.

George leaned against the door. "These plane crashes. Pretty terrible. You think its terrorists?"

"Most likely. What else would it be?"

"What does Scott think?"

Dotty walked in. "She hasn't had a chance to talk to him yet. He's kind of busy, ya know."

Sabyl smiled. "I'll let you both know when I talk to him, okay?"

"Okay," George grunted. "Well, I'll be heading on back to the garage. Got a transfer at Dulles in about an hour."

"Oh? Who?"

"That fiddle player from Chicago who's going to do his thing at the Kennedy Center tomorrow night."

Dotty frowned. "Theodore Fleisher? He's hardly a fiddler, George. He's one of the greatest living violinists—"

"Aw, I know. I just don't like all that sawin' . . ."

"Sawing? You've got no class, George."

George looked at Sabyl and shrugged. "There she goes again. She's been like this ever since I won the football pool."

"I'm always like this." She handed a mug of freshly brewed coffee to Sabyl. "Rudy called and said he would be delayed getting to Starbucks. Here you go. Just the way you like it."

"Thanks, Dotty. That's very thoughtful of you."

George turned to head back to the garage. "See ya later."

Sabyl took a sip and sat the mug down. "What the heck is wrong with this thing?" she said, staring at the screen of her computer that looked like a TV screen with satellite reception during a storm.

"Want me to call somebody?" asked Dotty.

"Yeah, but I don't know who."

Jenny Wong, one of Sabyl's reservationists, a petite young lady whose father was a chauffeur for the Japanese embassy, walked in at that moment. "Don't know who what?"

"Don't know who to call to fix her computer."

Jenny brightened. "Derrick can fix it."

Sabyl looked up. "Oh, of course, Derrick. I met a professor yesterday who was singing his praises. Said he was a bit of a genius."

Jenny beamed. "He is."

"So he repairs computers too?"

"He will for you."

"He certainly did a good job on my website."

"Want to call him or should I?" asked Sabyl.

Jenny said, "No, I'll email him. He doesn't have a phone."

"Not even a cell?"

"Nope. Says he doesn't want to be bothered with it."

"Thought he was a high-tech guy," Dotty said.

"He's also very private."

"Whatever." Dotty shrugged and went back to her desk. Jenny headed for her computer.

Sabyl looked through her phone messages. After completing her calls, she walked into Frank's office. He was on the phone with one of the drivers. The volume was low on the wall-mounted TV across from Frank's desk. She stepped in the door and watched it for a moment to catch up on the latest news. A reporter stood in front of the site where a plane had crashed near Reading, Pennsylvania.

Dotty and Frank joined her in silence. They watched along with a shocked nation as pictures of what was left of an airplane burned, its wreckage strewn over a large field. Their eyes stared in horror at the gruesome scene. Scores of emergency vehicles were on site. A profusion of eye-shocking strobes served as a backdrop for interviews of eyewitness accounts from those who saw the plane fall from the sky.

A reporter held a microphone up to the mouth of a young man with a stocking cap pulled tightly over his ears. He stood hunched over with his hands in his pockets.

"Please tell us what you saw, sir."

"Yeah, it was surreal. I heard a loud explosion—it was like a big fireball in the sky. I knew right away it had to be a plane. And the next thing I knew—it was like a meteor shower fell in that field over there.

I ran inside and told my wife to call 911. The fire trucks came about ten minutes later. My brother and I walked over there to see if anybody, you know, might be alive. We didn't see anything but burning pieces of wreckage."

"And approximately what time was that, sir?"

"I don't know, about an hour ago, I guess."

"Thank you," the reporter turned to the camera. "Reporting live from Reading, Pennsylvania, this is Jay Van Horn with Fox News."

Frank bellowed, "This is nuts!"

"You got that right!" Dotty agreed heartily. "That's three planes in two days! When are they going to put a stop to this?"

Sabyl quickly looked away and went back into her office and looked at the pictures of her husband and son encased in small silver frames on the corner of her desk.

CHAPTER SIX

Tourists were everywhere—seasons didn't matter. Summer or winter they came, cameras in tow, eyes gazing at the sights. Traffic was heavy, as always. The work day was over for those with day jobs, and they were ready to head home or to their favorite bar for happy hour. Traffic patterns changed for rush hour, which was always confusing for tourists. Rock Creek Parkway was bumper to bumper. At that time of day, traffic ruled.

When Sabyl arrived at the garage entrance of her condo in Northwest D.C., she pulled out her magnetic key card and waved it over the scanner. The red and white striped arm went up and the garage door slowly lifted. She drove inside, and the heavy door came lumbering down behind her. Her tires squealed on the painted concrete floor and echoed through the massive garage as she headed down the first ramp, circled around and down another to the lower level and parked in her assigned parking place, number 720. The garage was as nondescript as any underground parking garage; a forest of gray concrete pillars, unpainted walls, and security cameras strategically placed and scanners at the thick metal doors.

She let Beau out, walked over to a heavy brown door, waved the key card over the security scan box, went inside and got on the elevator. It stopped on the seventh floor with a slight jolt. Sabyl stepped off and walked twenty feet to her left to the door of her condo. Upon entering the spacious, eclectically decorated living room, she dropped her keys on the glass coffee table, unleashed Beau, picked up the TV remote and turned on Fox News. Static crackled as she pulled her coat off and hung it up in the closet next to the front door and then sat down on the elegant cream-colored sofa, kicked her shoes off, leaned back and checked the voicemail on her cell phone. She sat up straight when she saw that Scott had called. She speed dialed her voicemail number. Beau lapped water noisily from his stainless steel bowl in the kitchen.

"Yeah, Sabyl, it's me. I'm sorry I won't be able to come by tonight, honey. Kind of busy with these bombings. I'll call you when I can. Love you, babe."

She sighed and sat back down on the sofa. Poor Scott. He must be exhausted. Looking up, she saw the words NEWS BULLETIN on the screen. She grabbed the remote and turned up the volume.

The news anchor reported somberly, "We just got a report that a plane departing out of JFK airport in New York has gone down in the Atlantic just off Long Island, near the area where Flight 800 crashed in 1996. We are withholding the flight number until their families have been notified.

Sabyl stood up, startling Beau. She yelled at the TV, "Another one? This is unbelievable!"

The anchor continued, "This is the fourth plane to go down within a two-day period. Sunday morning, Flight 819 exploded in midair over Kansas. It originated from Washington's Reagan National (DCA) heading for Denver, Colorado. All 380 passengers and crewmembers aboard that ill-fated plane perished. Another flight, number 356 also out of Reagan heading for Sacramento, went down just south of Kearney, Nebraska. All 420 passengers and crewmembers aboard died in that crash as well. Then this morning Flight

84 out of Washington National heading for New York crashed near Reading, Pennsylvania with 164 passengers and crewmembers aboard. And now another one, this time a transatlantic flight out of JFK.

We are told that due to dense fog, rescue efforts are impossible at this time. The tragedy is worsened still as so many of the victims of these plane crashes were on their way home or to a vacation destination for the holidays, many of them college students out of the D.C. area. Investigators suspect, but have not yet officially confirmed, that these are acts of terrorism, until they have an opportunity to examine the facts. The death toll so far has risen to 964, but with this latest plane going down in the Atlantic, it could increase significantly as transatlantic flights can carry over 800 passengers and crew, depending on the type of aircraft. We are not sure if this plane crash is in any way connected to the other three, but we will keep you posted as soon as we have more."

Sabyl shook her head in dismay. She started to get up to feed Beau when the reporter was interrupted by a breaking news report. The familiar seal of the President of the United States appeared on the screen. Byron William Anderson, dressed in a dark blue suit and pale blue tie, sat with his hands folded at his desk in the oval office, looking into the lens of the camera and into the eyes of America.

"Good evening," he said as pleasantly as he could. His face did not entirely hide the seething rage just under the surface. His words, though well-chosen and agonized over, seemed trivial and he knew it. What could possibly be said to assure the nation at a time like this?

"It is my sad and solemn duty to report to you that our nation is once again under attack. As you have heard reported, four airplanes have exploded in midair within the last forty-eight hours. It is feared that all souls aboard have been lost. The most intensive investigation since Nine/Eleven is underway. It is obvious that these are acts of terrorism. We will get to the bottom of these terrible acts, and I assure you those perpetrating them will be brought to swift justice. All our resources are committed to solving these heinous crimes. The National Transportation Safety Board has coordinated the resources of the federal government with those of local and state authorities and those of the airlines to begin appropriate procedures to meet the needs of the victims and their families. The First Lady and I and my administration are heartbroken for the families of those who have perished. Please know that our thoughts and prayers are with each person who has been personally impacted by these tragedies. Ladies and gentlemen, I am asking you once again to report anything suspicious to your local police, or you can call the number at the bottom of the screen. Again, if you see something, say something. Thank you and good night."

After his brief remarks, the camera faded to the news anchor who continued his report.

The president returned to the White House Situation Room to meet with his top advisors monitoring the investigations, while the rest of the world watched in stunned disbelief as the news continued its round-the-clock coverage of the bombings.

Sabyl watched the pre-taped video of those awaiting the arrival of their loved ones at the various airports, their faces contorted in grief as they received the dreadful news. Memories flooded back to the day she received that fateful knock at the door from a sympathetic police officer who, after being notified by the FAA, came to inform her that her husband, Gary, and eight-year-old son, Mike, had died when their single-engine Cessna went down in the Rocky Mountains near Leadville, Colorado after a three-day hunting trip in Montana. They were on their way to Albuquerque for an overnight visit with Gary's sister, Laura, and then planned to head back the next morning to Pittsburgh where Gary had a thriving accounting practice. The news was shattering. She knew exactly what those poor people on the screen were going through.

Her throat constricted and tears welled up in her eyes as she remembered her son's smile; how he enjoyed riding his bike, his love of baseball, his funny little laugh when he watched his favorite cartoons on Saturday mornings. She had been denied watching him reach his teen years—and by, now—manhood. She wondered, what would he be doing now? He'd be out of college...maybe working with his dad in the accounting office? And Gary. Memories of her husband washed over her with new sadness. His gentle touch, his handsome face, his easy-going smile, his deep faith, and constant encouragement. Oh, Gary...I know you and Mike are in Heaven with Jesus, but I miss you so much.

Sabyl closed her eyes and let the tears come once again. She was almost glad for the tears. For a while, she thought she had gone numb.

Finally, she took a deep breath and thought, I've got to stop this...I can't let myself get...upset. Grabbing a tissue out of her pocketbook, she wiped her tears and looked back at the screen. Seeing the grief-stricken faces of those on the screen; the raw, crushing pain ... she shook her head and thought, Gary and Mike's death was an accident. That was bad enough. Those poor people...their loved ones were murdered by some evil...She couldn't imagine how they would be able to work through this. God, please comfort them.

CHAPTER SEVEN

After his morning shower, as was his custom, he spent a half-hour in prayer, and then shaved and dressed for work. The students at AU knew he had been detained—it had almost cost him his job, a job he had worked hard to get, a position that suited his purpose for being in America. It had been a long hard road—one he and his mentors had planned carefully—for computers were the gateway to his dream, a dream that in essence was the purpose of his life.

The run-in that Abdul had had with the FBI had been a wakeup call for him. He had not personally felt the wrath of America towards people like himself, a Middle Easterner and a Muslim, until then. At first, he was frightened, and then fear turned into anger. He prayed that his anger would not turn into rage—for rage caused a man to lose control, and he could not risk that. He had too much to do.

He had few friends. The other Muslims he had met in America did not have the same zeal to serve as he did. Many of them had compromised themselves and had slid into the western lifestyle of materialism and immorality. Why couldn't they use the opportunity they had been given to do something for Allah? For their cause? For their homeland?

He shook off these thoughts and finished dressing. He had much more important things to think about. He must stay focused on the task at hand and hopefully stay under the radar of the FBI. He couldn't afford to be detained again.

~ ~ ~

Frank took off his headphones, unfolded his six-foot frame out of the chair and ambled over to Sabyl's office.

"Hi, Frank," she said without looking up. "How's Barb?"

His wife, Barbara, was pregnant with their first child at age forty. Frank was delighted but nervous about the prospects of complications that could happen for Barb and about being a father at his age of forty-five. "Fat and sassy. Craves donuts. She can't get enough of them. I should have bought stock in Krispy Kreme."

Dotty stepped in and interjected, "Whoa! You'd better tell her to take it easy on the sweets. It could lead to preeclampsia, you know."

"Pre what?" Frank demanded.

"Preeclampsia. It can lead to some pretty serious problems."

Frank shoved his hands in his pockets and looked over his glasses at her. "Like what?"

"Like high blood pressure, liver and kidney problems and difficulties during delivery, that's what. Just sayin'."

"She's right," Sabyl agreed. "We don't want to alarm you, but, well, I'm sure her doctor has discussed it with her, right?"

"Not that she's mentioned to me, but then she might not tell me. She knows I'm already concerned about her having a baby this late in life."

"Still, you'd better make sure," said Dotty.

"Okay, I'll tell her, but she's not going to like it."

Sabyl suggested that he Google it and print out the information. "Let her read it for herself. That way maybe she'll take it more seriously."

"Okay. I sure don't want her to have complications. By the way, she's pretty excited that you guys are giving her a baby shower. That's really nice."

"Glad to do it," Dotty beamed. "But it sure would be easier if we knew what she's having. She might get a lot of stuff that's yellow instead of pink or blue."

"I'd like to know too, but she doesn't want to know until it's born."

Sabyl nodded. "Well, that's her call. And she can always exchange them for a different color."

"Right."

"So what do we have on the books?"

Frank handed her some papers. "First you need to look at these." He gave her two emails that had come in that morning.

She looked at them and frowned deeply. "I was afraid of that. I'll deal with it before I go home. What else do we have?"

For the next half-hour, he briefed her on all that was going on.

Sabyl laid down her pen and stretched and yawned. "Sounds like we'll be pretty busy for the next few days."

"Yeah. Oh, and Audrey Aberholdt called. We've got eighteen limos booked for her party next month."

"Eighteen? That's three more than last year."

"Yeah. Guess she's not going to let that terrorist that messed up her party last year get the best of her."

"Good for her!"

"Oh, by the way, that Nigerian guy that used to drive for Vassette wants to come to work for you. He likes your style. His name is..." He extracted a small piece of paper from his shirt pocket. "...Ken A-min-u. Not sure about that pronunciation."

"Oh, yes, I remember him. He's always done a good job when we subcontracted Vassette. Seems conscientious. What did you tell him?"

"That I'd talk to you and if you're interested I'd call him."

"Okay, call him. See when he can come in."

"Will do." Frank stood up. "Hey, looks like we're doing that funeral of that family that died in that pile-up on the Beltway."

"Yes, the Patterson family. Such a tragedy."

"That's for sure. A whole family getting wiped out like that..."

Sabyl stood and picked up a file. "I've got to go over the accounts with Floyd. Be back in about a half hour."

Frank turned to go to his office. "Okay, boss."

Floyd Crabb, her accountant who looked amazingly like Clark Kent, Superman's alter ego, greeted her with a nod and continued with his phone conversation. His tie was loose and pulled to one side. His glasses perched on the end of his nose. He scribbled something down on a legal pad and pushed back from the desk, the wheels on his chair making the plastic floor mat crackle. She sat down across from his desk. He finished and hung up. "So, are you ready?"

"Let's do it."

All of her clients had running accounts, which they went over weekly, and were billed according to the drivers' log sheets. When Sabyl's company sent out a bill, she wanted an honest and fair amount for services rendered. She never padded her bills, and when one of her accountants had attempted it two years ago, he was promptly fired.

That particular year was a bad one for Sabyl. On top of being diagnosed with breast cancer, and Scott deserting her, her general manager, Jack Forsythe, tried to take over her company. When he heard the news that she had cancer, he came to the office late one night and made copies of all her accounts. He even had business cards made up and wrote letters to her clients that he would be the new CEO of the company. He told them that she was going to die. Frank came in from an AA meeting and caught him. Needless to say, Jack Forsythe was canned as well.

After Sabyl finished going over the accounts with Floyd, she went into her office and called Rebecca.

"Rebecca, how are you?"

"Oh, darling, I'm wonderful, and you?"

"I know this is late notice but are you busy tonight? I'd love to get together."

"Oh, honey I can't, I'm going to the Corcoran tonight with Paul Larson to hear a string quartet and then dinner."

Sabyl smiled. "Sounds heavenly."

"How about tomorrow night?"

Sabyl thought a minute. "Let me see…yes, that will work for me. I'll fix dinner."

"Great! Around eight?"

"Perfect."

"See you then."

Dotty buzzed her. "Mr. Isao Lee on line one."

"Thanks, Dotty." She picked up the phone, "Mr. Lee, it's good to hear from you. Did you have a nice flight?"

Isao Lee was President of WorldGlobe Bank and one of Sabyl's best clients. The Asian gentleman whispered in near perfect English, "Sabyl, I just thought I should let you know that Mr. Chan and I will be late getting into the terminal."

Sabyl thought his voice sounded uneasy. "Is everything okay?"

"Yes, we are at Dulles, but we are being delayed as two marshals just boarded our plane. It looks like they're arresting someone. This may take a while."

"Okay, thanks, Mr. Lee. I'll call the greeter and your driver and let them know you'll be down to baggage claim a little later. I've already texted you your driver's cell number. You can call him when you deplane."

"Wonderful. I'm looking forward to seeing you at the Grande Continental Hotel. You will be coordinating the transportation again this year, won't you?"

"Absolutely, sir. You're all set with your car and driver."

"Thank you so much."

Sabyl put the phone in its cradle and leaned back in her chair and thought, Maybe they're arresting the bomber.

Frank came into her office and sat down and pulled a piece of paper out of his jacket pocket. "Barb gave me a list of things to pick up for her upcoming trek to the hospital. She's got this idea that she might go into labor sooner than the due date of December 30th." The thought of it kept Frank's stomach in a perpetual knot.

Sabyl looked at the list and handed it back to him. "It's not very busy right now. This would be a good time to go pick up those things."

"Thanks, Sabe. I'll only be gone a couple of hours. I need to get a few things for Christmas too. Haven't had a chance to shop."

"Take your time, Frank. Karen can handle the phones."

"Okay. I'll go brief her as to what's going on, and I'll see you later."

Frank went back to his desk and buzzed Karen and asked her to come up front. He went over the dispatcher list for the day with her and then left.

Sabyl spoke with Lawrence, who was at Dulles waiting for Mr. Lee, and told him that he would be delayed and that she would text his number to Mr. Lee.

She then went into Frank's office. "Karen, thank you for covering for Frank. By the way, I would like for you to be my assistant for the WorldGlobe meetings at the Grande Continental Hotel on Monday and Tuesday."

Karen's eyes widened. "But I've never, like, done anything like that before. I wouldn't know what to do."

"I realize that. Don't worry, it's not that hard. I'll brief you before we go on sight. You're a smart girl. You'll catch on quickly."

"Okay…but…"

"You'll need to wear black slacks, a white blouse, and a black jacket. If you don't have anything like that, I'll loan you one of mine."

"I have the slacks and the blouse but not a nice enough jacket."

"Not a problem, we're about the same size. I have a couple of jackets that should work. I'll bring them in tomorrow, and you can try them on. Thankfully, the weather will be a little warmer so we shouldn't need overcoats."

"Okay. Wow! Thanks, Sabyl. I feel kind of, like, honored."

Sabyl laughed. "You may change your tune after it's over. We'll be on our feet pretty much all day."

"That's okay, I'll be sure to wear, like, comfortable shoes…uh, nice ones."

"Great. It's all set then." Sabyl looked at her watch. Four o'clock. Still time to deal with something she had been dreading all day. She told Karen to hold any calls for a few minutes.

Karen nodded and grimaced, wondering if Sabyl was going to deal with the two drivers that had caused some clients to be unhappy. The emails Frank showed her had come in almost simultaneously that morning from two of their best clients complaining that the drivers had not picked them up on time and had displayed a bad attitude; something Karen knew Sabyl would not tolerate.

She walked down to the garage to meet with them. Both drivers were drinking coffee and watching the news. They looked up when Sabyl entered the lounge area. Neither spoke. The only other driver present was George, who was busy cleaning his car.

She confronted them with the accusations. Neither responded well. One just shrugged his shoulders and stared at her, the other said the allegations were untrue.

"Then what is true?" Sabyl asked, gaining impatience.

The other driver kept watching TV.

She waited for an answer and continued. "These are some of my best clients, and they were gracious enough to let me know that they knew this behavior was not typical for my business and have agreed to continue to use my services but have asked that neither of you would be used to service them ever again."

They looked at her in defiance. Neither enjoyed working for a woman, and it showed.

"Well, since you're unwilling to even express any kind of interest in working for me, you may both consider yourselves unemployed!" She turned and walked back to her office.

They glared after her and said something in low tones to each other.

"You can leave your keys with me," George said as he smiled watching them gather up their belongings.

CHAPTER EIGHT

The Potomac Ballroom on the lower level of the Grande Continental Hotel was the nerve center for the WorldGlobe Bank meetings. Married to an American businessman from New York, Ling Morrison was the coordinator for the fifty-two VIP's who had flown in from all over the world to meet with various senators, representatives, executives and each other, in multiple meeting places all over Washington, D.C.

Ling's name in Chinese means clever; intelligent, and spiritual and she was all of those and more. She had the impossible job of directing and coordinating every move, making sure that each of the visiting bank execs kept their appointments and that their transportation was taken care of for each meeting. Sabyl and many other limousine companies had worked with her for several years and knew what she expected of them. Perfection!

Several limousines were parked in the large circle drive of the Grande Hotel. Some of the execs had his/her own car and driver assigned to them; others were driven in shared pool cars.

Sabyl and Karen stood just outside the massive iron and glass doors of the elegant hotel, each holding their clipboards with the lists of drivers and VIP's their company would be responsible for. As Ling would notify them of one of the VIP's approach, they would signal their driver to pull around to the front. It worked like clockwork. That is, until now.

As sometimes happened, some of the executives, upon completing their meetings, would ask the pool car driver to take them sightseeing in America's famous capital. The drivers were instructed to never argue with a client and must take them wherever they requested to go, which left the coordinators with one less pool car for the other execs to share.

Sabyl stood talking with Mr. Lee who had his own car and driver. He told her of the excitement that happened on the plane that the feds boarded and made an arrest. They had hoped the man they arrested might be the bomber, but quickly found out he was arrested for something unrelated to the bombings.

Karen got a call from Ling alerting her that Mr. Lewis from London was coming up the escalator and to have a pool car available to him the moment he came out of the doors. She walked over to Sabyl and whispered loudly, "Sabyl, Ling just called and said that Mr. Lewis from London is, like, coming up the escalator and needs a pool car. There aren't any pool cars!"

Sabyl smiled and nodded and said, "There'll be a car."

At that moment, a pool car pulled into the circle drive. Sabyl walked over and opened the door for the executive just as Mr. Lewis came out. He smiled, thanked her and got in, and they drove off.

Karen stood with her mouth open in amazement. "How did you know there'd be a car?"

"I just knew."

"But...how?"

"I've been doing this a long time, Karen. I dedicated my business to God when I first started my company and asked Him to take charge of it because apart from Him I can do nothing."

Karen stared in disbelief. "Wow! That's, like, so cool!"

Sabyl laughed. "Yes, it is. Very cool. He is faithful, and I've seen Him step in so many times to help me in time of need that…well, I knew there would be a car."

Karen looked at her wistfully and thought, I wish I had that kind of faith.

~ ~ ~

The floodlights that illuminated the memorials in the nation's capital were veiled and appeared anemic. Low hanging fog obscured the red blinking light atop the Washington Monument, reducing it to a feeble pink throb to warn any low flying aircraft crazy enough to be out in this soup, much less daring to disregard the rigid D.C. airspace restrictions.

In a building not far from the famous obelisk, Special Agent Scott Terhune stood next to his longtime friend and partner Lou Martz in the tactical command center of the newly formed Unified Agencies Task Force (UATF). As they walked into the central nerve center, Martz whistled softly, "How did they put this together so fast?"

"I guess the government can move pretty fast when they want to," Scott answered.

Technicians had worked feverishly throughout the last several days and nights to finish installing soundproofing and the latest state-of-the-art electronics, which included dozens of built-in monitors that took up one entire wall, racks of communications equipment, computers, monitors, and keyboards. It had just been repainted. The smell of latex enamel still hung in the air.

Upon their arrival, the new director, Ron Keefer, introduced the other agents to one another. They were handed security paraphernalia, code numbers for the keypads on certain doors, magnetic cards and ID's which were to be worn on their person at all times while in-house. A few knew each other, mostly by reputation only. Some shook hands; most nodded when introduced.

Scott thought, So much for pleasantries. He had never seen so many spooks in one room.

Keefer then gave them a tour of their new facility, showed them their private offices and introduced them to the techs and support staff who spent the next hour demonstrating some of the electronics they would be working with. They then settled around a large conference table in the center's tactical room. The agents had a laptop in front of them, each connected to their particular agencies and a file with a report. All were looking over their notes ready to compare their findings, which were sparse, to say the least.

"I'm certain you have questions, gentlemen and I'll take them now." Keefer gave the agents an opportunity to ask anything they wanted. As they did, he answered each one with his usual quiet demeanor and sat gazing at them steadily, anticipating the next question.

Scott found himself watching the other agents. Their faces were expressionless, their eyes locked on the screens that were split into four sections, one for each downed plane.

After the Q and A session, he said to them, "It is a privilege to work with the finest men and women from each agency. All of the agencies represented here are vital and have unique areas of investigative expertise. You each are bringing to this task force wisdom that is unique to your background, fieldwork, and experience. There are no walls or confines between agencies here. You will not keep any intelligence from one another or from me." Keefer steepled his fingers and leaned forward on his elbows. "We saw where it got us before Nine-Eleven. If information had been shared between agencies that were not looking to cover their own behinds, maybe Nine-Eleven would've been prevented.

You are all on the same pay level, which, by the way, is substantially more than you've been getting. There's no seniority here. We are one unit. Get used to thinking as a single unit and not an arm of your specific agency, although you will be in constant contact with your respective bureaus. They will answer to each of you and you to me and me to the president."

The president expects—no—demands full cooperation from each agency to feed you whatever information you need and then we process it together and make decisions and hopefully get solutions. If anyone here cannot agree to that, you need to let it be known now."

One of the CIA reps cleared his throat and asked, "What about electronic spying? Are we still going to have to dance around that?"

"Glad you asked. We have two federal judges who will be with us here in this center and will be available twenty-four/seven. They can give us an answer as fast as you can punch "enter" on your computer.

Keefer leaned back in his chair. "Terrorists are more sophisticated now than ever. They've learned how to encrypt communications so they can't be seen. They have their own Dark Web. If we can't see them, we don't know what they're saying; what they're plotting.

We've stopped a lot of attacks but we've known for a long time that we can't stop them all, and we certainly can't stop what we can't see. Yes, there have been attacks on a smaller scale, but we've apparently made the mistake of thinking they can no longer carry out attacks on a massive scale. But now here we are, four planes down and we're no closer to knowing how those bombs got on board than when they first started. Why? Because we're fighting a different kind of war. The ones who perpetrated the attacks on our top government leaders last year didn't fit the M.O. of the..." he used his fingers for quotation marks..." typical" terrorists we have dealt with in the past. Their tactics keep evolving to suit their evil endeavors. We can take nothing for granted. When they started using trucks to plow into innocent people out for a stroll in London, or on a bike ride in New York, we saw another tactic plus we have this insidious cyber war that keeps us blind and we've got to stop it, ladies and gentlemen. We've got to have our best minds break into their computers and not just sit and watch them break into ours."

He was talking Scott's language now. Beyond being on protective detail for eight years, his true expertise was in the ECSA. Having been under the auspices of the Department of the Treasury before the Secret Service agency was moved to the Department of Homeland Security in 2003, his work was with local law enforcement on computer crime. But with the attacks on the government officials last year, and with the greater need for protection, he was once again brought into various protective details. Once the threat was over, he returned to where he was needed the most.

After the widespread hacking fiasco into the top government agencies, he was needed more now than ever in his area of expertise. Not only did foreign agencies gain enough classified information to threaten the United States' security, but DHS was sure they were more than happy to sell the information they had obtained to Iran or any other enemy of the U.S.

Director Keefer stood up. "Any more questions?" Each agent looked at one another. A few shrugged, all sat silently. He nodded and said, "Good. Welcome aboard, ladies and gentlemen. Now let's get to work and get this thing solved. With any luck, we may get to be with our families for Christmas."

CHAPTER NINE

Dotty was beside herself with frustration. Her new floor was to be put in on Thursday, but the drainage people were dragging their feet. The insurance agent working with her refused to call another company, claiming the original company needed to "make it right." Dotty retorted, "How can they make it right when they don't even return our calls? It's supposed to rain Monday and if you guys want to pay for another floor going in, be my guest! I guess we can do this until the cows come home!" The insurance man said it would be dealt with and not to worry. She took two Tylenol and was in a snit the rest of the day.

Sabyl tried to make her feel better by offering to take her to lunch at her favorite place Chef Geoff's on New Mexico Avenue. She thanked her, but declined, saying, "Not today. I'm not in the mood. You've got enough on your mind; you don't need to hang out with somebody that looks like they've been baptized in pickle juice. I'll be okay as soon as this mess gets taken care of."

Frank, overhearing their conversation, hoped she didn't mean she would remain in her present state until the drainage company did her right. It might be a long haul. The thought of it gave him a stomachache.

"Okay," Sabyl smiled, "but if you change your mind, let me know."

Dotty put the disc in of the new software that she was learning and attacked it with a vengeance.

Frank buzzed Sabyl. "I've got Ken Aminu on the line. He said he'd like to come in now. That okay with you?"

"Yeah. Now's fine."

"He said he'd be here in two minutes. Said he's in a café up the street."

"Okay." She hung up and stared at Ken's last name and hoped she would pronounce it correctly when he came in.

A few minutes later, a young Nigerian man came through the front door, letting in a cold blast of air. Frank went out and greeted him and escorted him into Sabyl's office. Recognizing him immediately, Sabyl stood, smiled, and gave him a firm handshake and offered him a seat and sat back in her chair. She decided not to chance the last name. "So, Ken is it?"

"Yes, mum."

"Do you have a resume?"

"Yes, mum." He pulled an envelope out of his coat pocket and handed it to her across the desk. He sat back and folded his hands like a schoolboy in the principal's office.

Sabyl pulled her readers on. "So you want to drive for Martin Transportation. May I ask why?"

"Yes, mum. I have been in America for six years, and I have worked for several companies, but when I subbed for you, I found that you are different. You care about people. I feel that this is very important and I would like to work for such a company."

"That's very nice to hear. Are all your papers in order? Your 31-C?"

"Yes, mum. And I have a CDL and experience driving a bus. And I have my green card," he said proudly.

"That's good. Now, you understand that we won't be able to use you on certain jobs because you have to be an American citizen to get clearance. But we'll keep you busy."

"Thank you, mum."

"Well, Ken . . . um, is that your real name?"

He laughed, "My name is not one that is easily pronounced in your country."

Sabyl smiled, "Try me."

He shrugged. "Okay. My name is Kenechukwu Dumetochukwu Aminu-Ibo."

"Wow. That's …really beautiful. But you're right. Maybe we'd better stick with Ken for now."

He smiled and nodded.

She leaned forward on her elbows and looked at him intently. "Okay. If you're going to drive for me, there are a few basic things about me you need to understand. I take my clients' needs very seriously, whether they're a head of state or a pop star. This is a service. These days, people seem to have forgotten what it means to serve others. Most of my clients are extremely busy, important people. I respect the problems they have and the pressures they're under. They have a hundred other things to worry about. Once their transportation needs are in my hands, I don't want them to have to think about it. If I take them as a client, they become a part of my life—their lives are literally in my hands for a period of time. I take that very seriously, and I expect my drivers to do the same. We have a responsibility to get them where they want to go, not only comfortably, but safely. I want a chauffeur who will take his passengers' safety seriously. You've been driving for other companies, so you've probably noticed that sometimes clients' heads are in the clouds when they come to Washington. They've got dozens of things on their minds, and they'll often get out of the car in the middle of the street."

"Oh, yes, mum."

"I want you to look out for them. Make sure they get out on the right side of the car at the curb. And never pull up so close to the curb that they have to step out on it. That's very uncomfortable for them. Give them room to step out and step up."

Ken nodded in agreement.

"Also, when doing an airport transfer, we have a greeter there to meet clients at the security gate with a sign and escort them to baggage claim. We show them which exit door to walk out of, tell them to watch the second lane and the chauffeur will come around with lights on for identification. If they're a security risk, you'll take someone with you so that one person can remain with him or her at all times. For security sake, we do not put their names on the sign. We either put our company name on it or their company logo. Otherwise, someone else can come up to you and say, "Yeah, I'm So-'n-So," and you wind up with some character in your back seat whose getting a free ride, and our client is left at the airport with no transportation. The other drivers can fill you in on the various airports and where you're allowed to park."

Ken nodded vigorously.

"My name is on my business, Ken. My name is my business. If I say I'm going to do something, you can believe I'm going to do it. If I don't do what I say, my word means nothing. I want my clients to know they can count on me, but the only way that can happen is if I can count on you."

Ken sat grinning and nodding.

"So, you think you can handle all that?"

"Yes, mum. I believe I can."

"Good. I'll take you on, and if you do a good job, you'll be well paid and well taken care of. I not only care about my clients, I care very much about my employees."

"Thank you, mum."

"Have you been through the CTDC yet?"

He cocked his head to one side like a puppy. "No mum, what is that?"

"The Counter Terrorism Driving Course in Winchester, Virginia."

"No, mum."

"We'll send you over there as soon as we can get you in. Our drivers have already taken it. I'll take you down to the garage and introduce you to George, my garage manager, who's also a driver."

"Yes, mum."

"By the way. What does your name mean?"

"Kenechukwu means 'To Thank or Praise God.'"

"How lovely."

"Yes, mum. And Dumetochukwu means 'Join Me in Praising the Lord.'"

"And do you?"

"Oh, yes, mum. Every day."

Sabyl smiled, "You and Rudy will have a lot in common. And your last name?"

"Aminu means Reliable or Trustworthy. Ibo means that I am from Nigeria."

"I'm trusting you to live up to your name."

"Which one?" he smiled.

She laughed, "I hope all of them." She stood and walked around the desk.

He stood up and said, "You do not have to take me to the garage, mum. I can find my way. You are a very busy lady."

"Let me at least point you in the right direction." They walked to the front door. "Go out this door and turn left. Just follow the brick colonnade down towards the garage, and you'll probably find George and some of the drivers in the lounge area. I'll buzz him and tell him you're on your way down."

"Thank you, mum," he grinned. "Praise God!"

Sabyl chuckled, "Amen." She went back to her desk, sat down, and punched the garage number. "George, I'm sending a new driver down there. His name is Ken Aminu." She felt confident with his last name now and hoped one day to learn how to pronounce the other two. "Introduce him around, will you? Thanks."

Ken walked out the front door and Sabyl walked into Frank's office and asked him if Rudy was back yet.

"No, he's still at the Patterson family funeral."

Sabyl noticed the words BREAKING NEWS on the wall mounted TV in the corner of his office. "Frank, look!"

He quickly picked up the remote and turned up the volume. "Looks like another explosion."

"Maybe not. Maybe it's just a train wreck. I don't mean *just* a train wreck..."

He pulled his headset off, stood and thrust his hands in his pockets. "I know what you mean, but that's not just a train wreck. Look at that one car. There's nothing left of it. That's an explosion."

"Oh, no," she groaned.

It showed an aerial view of a demolished Amtrak train. The news anchor stated, *"The Miami-bound train originating from New York, wrecked about 45 minutes after it left Washington D.C.'s Union Station. There are several fatalities feared, and many passengers are seriously injured."*

Dotty joined them. "Not another one!"

A reporter on the scene spoke, *"Survivors said they heard a loud explosion and felt a tremendous jolt just before the cars began leaving the tracks. As you can see from our Skycam, several cars rolled down a 20-foot embankment. It is not yet determined if this is part of a pattern of several explosions that have taken place in the past 72 hours. We'll keep you updated as we learn more."*

Frank took his hands out of his pockets, sat back down at his desk and rubbed his face. "Here we go again."

CHAPTER TEN

The Situation Room at the White House was full of military strategists and half of the UATF agents with Director Ron Keefer sitting directly across from the President. Many questions had been asked, but few answers were available as to why the bombings were able to continue, how they were able to get on board airplanes undetected, how the bombings might be related and how much longer is this going to go on? Every scenario had been hashed out over and over again, but details didn't add up, and the president did not like it when two plus two didn't equal four.

They were getting hammered by the media, and the general public was getting impatient. The stock market was taking a hit, and the late-night comics were having a field day blaming the administration. Social media junkies were burning up the Twitter feeds and Facebook folk were unfriending people right and leftover comments that were considered to be offensive and/or racist. But then everything offensive was being called racist, ad nauseum, so the repetitive grievances were becoming increasingly annoying. But that didn't stop the onslaught of negative word wars being fought out in cyberspace.

One pastor said in a Sunday morning televised service that "If we could see the spiritual warfare being waged in the atmosphere, we would be on our knees perpetually."

Unfortunately, his remarks sparked even more controversy as most considered them offensive. His retort was, "Getting offended at every little thing is a sign of immaturity," which sparked another round of offenses.

Scott looked around the room at the haggard faces of some of the most intelligent and powerful men and women on the planet, all in much need of sleep but in more need of answers. Each agency had thousands of people working hard behind the scenes, each in their level of expertise, to bring answers, but so far to no avail.

The president spoke up, "It's like trying to work a jigsaw puzzle without the box lid. So many pieces and none of them fit and no clear picture to go by. In fact, no picture to go by at all! But ladies and gentlemen..." he rose and leaned forward on his arms, looking very much like a bull about to charge, "... we're going to get to the bottom of this and we're going to do it soon, is that clear?"

No one answered. But they got the message.

~ ~ ~

Sabyl looked over her readers at Rudy. "The funeral went smoothly for the Patterson family, don't you think?"

"Yes. So sad to see an entire family wiped out like that."

"Yes, it sure is. What do you have today?"

"I've got to run Stubby over to pick up that Mercedes Sprinter you had wrapped."

"Great! They sent me a text earlier this morning of what it looks like." She picked up her phone and brought up the text. "Look at this. I'm very pleased with it."

Rudy took the phone and let out a soft whistle. "Wow! That looks great, boss!" He handed the phone back to her.

"I'm very pleased with it. Wrapping a bus is a lot cheaper than painting one. Pretty amazing technology the way they can put just about any design on a vehicle like that; even big buses!"

"And it looks really sharp."

"It does. I love that if there's a scrape on one of the fenders or a door, instead of having to have it repainted, they can just replace the wrap on that one panel."

"That could save a lot of money. Are you going to have the vans and mini-buses done too?"

"I will for the commuters but not on all. Our clients don't like advertising on the vehicles, especially when they're used as a security van."

"Right."

"So did you meet Ken?"

"Yes. He seems very nice."

She took her glasses off. "I thought you'd like him."

Frank stepped into her office and fell heavily into one of the leather chairs across from her desk and sighed loudly.

Rudy stood and said, "I've got to take Stubby over to get our Sprinter."

"Okay, Rudy. See you later." Sabyl looked at her head dispatcher through worried eyes. "What's wrong, Frank? You seem nervous lately."

Frank shook his head slightly. "Aw, just trying to get used to becoming a father at my age."

Sabyl smiled sympathetically. "Forty-five's not so old."

"I'll be sixty-five when he's twenty."

"He? So you know you're having a boy?"

"No, but Barb doesn't want to know until it's born. I just don't like calling it an it."

"I know what you mean, Frank," Sabyl smiled. "But you could be having a little girl, you know."

"Yeah, I know, and that's fine. I'm not trying to be sexist or anything."

Sabyl laughed, "I know it, you big lug. Just teasing you. You look like you could use a laugh."

"Just kind of concerned for Barb. This is our one and only chance to have a baby, and it's got to go right. Her body clock is ticking and…"

"It will go fine, Frank. Don't worry. We're all praying for her. And for you."

"Thanks, Sabe. Oh, by the way, guess who called earlier?"

"Who?"

"That Pollack guy . . ."

Sabyl rolled her eyes. "Oh, great."

"Yeah. He blew his stack when he found you weren't in yet."

"Why?"

"Aw, you know how he is. Wants everybody to bow and scrape—thinks he's the only person on the planet. And that you're the only one who can take care of his business."

"He'll get over it," Sabyl said wryly. "So what does he want?"

"Wants to be taken to Flaming Leaf Country Club. Guess he's going to take advantage of this nice weather we're having."

"Can't blame him for that."

Frank shifted and crossed his long legs. "Do you think we'll be getting calls for funerals regarding these bombing victims? I mean three of the planes were out of D.C."

"It's a possibility but way too early to tell. I hope to God there won't be any more bombings. This is too creepy."

"Sure is." Frank heaved himself up. "Later." He sauntered back to his office.

Karen walked in. "Guess what?"

"What," Sabyl replied without looking up.

"Jenny's got a new boyfriend."

"Yes, I know."

"He's a senior at AU," she continued as though Sabyl knew nothing about it. "Majoring in Computer Science. A real geek. Jenny and I met him at Starbucks. You know how, like, crowded it can be, sometimes. He was standing with his Latte, and we felt sorry for him, so we invited him to, like, sit with us."

"That was nice of you," Sabyl said, leaning back in her chair.

"Yeah, he's one of those, you know, like, serious types— a real nerd."

Sabyl smiled, "And that's good?"

"Yeah. He and Jenny hit it, like, right off. He's the quiet type. Perfect for Jenny. A steady diet of that would drive me, like, nuts."

"He built my website."

"Hey, that right! I forgot about that."

Just then, Dotty buzzed Sabyl's phone. "Scott on line two."

Karen grinned, "I'll talk to you later."

"Okay, dear. See ya." She punched line two. "Scott! I didn't think I'd hear from you for days. How are you? You must be exhausted."

The voice on the other end sounded strained. "Yeah, a little. Not much time for sleep. Just wanted to hear your voice."

"Awww, that's so sweet."

"So are you doing okay?"

"Yes, busy as always. I miss you."

"I miss you too, babe. Gotta go. Love you, bye."

Sabyl placed the phone back in the cradle. He sounds so tired. Please strengthen him, Lord. She buzzed Dotty and pulled out her phone and looked at her calendar.

Dotty answered, "You rang?"

"Hi, Dotty. How about the 23rd for our office party?"

"That should be okay," Dotty answered. "I'll get back to you if I see any problems."

Sabyl entered it into her phone just as it chirped again.

"Yes, Dotty."

"Okay, the 23rd will work."

"Good. Did you ever hear from the drainage people?"

"Nope. Not a word."

"That is so wrong."

The unmistakable hulk of Alfred Pollack was coming up the driveway toward the door. Dotty rolled her eyes and sighed, "Oh, no, not that loud-mouth boor from Miami. Get your boxing gloves on. That guy Pollack is here."

Sabyl made a face as though she just got a migraine. "Oh, great. That's all I need. Thanks, honey." She hung up, stood, took a deep breath, and stepped out of her office to greet him. She offered her hand. "Hello, Mr. Pollack. How are you?"

He ignored her hand and said, "Well, I see you're still taking up space in the business world. I guess you know it's because of you females that the employment rate is so high. You push men out of their jobs when you women ought to be home pushing a mop and tending to your brats like you were created to do."

Frank and Dotty peered around the corner and watched as Sabyl shifted her weight, folded her arms and cocked her head to one side as she often did when she was annoyed. "I assume you are here because you want to hire a car?"

"Well, of course, that's what I'm here for. Do you think I'm here to admire you?"

Sabyl raised one eyebrow. "Sir, if you want to hire a car and driver, that's fine. We're here to accommodate you, but I don't have to listen…"

"Aw, just get me a damn car. My tee-off time is at ten."

"What is your destination?"

"Flaming Leaf Country Club, where else?"

"Of course. I'll take care of this personally."

"It's about time," he muttered. "Stand here yakking all day…"

Sabyl excused herself and headed for the garage. George was wiping down one of the cars. Sabyl smiled and waved at him and then spoke to one of the drivers. Within a few minutes, she returned to the office and escorted the client to the front circle drive. A long, shiny stretch pulled up. Sabyl opened the door for him. He glared at her, heaved his golf bag inside and promptly got in the back seat and sat smugly with his beloved Ping golf clubs at his side. Sabyl closed the door, waved and smiled as they pulled out and drove away.

Dotty and Frank smiled knowingly at one another.

~ ~ ~

The driver stopped at the front gate of the famous Flaming Leaf Golf Club, got out and opened his door.

"What do you think you're doing?" Pollock said, his paunchy face turning crimson.

Marty took off her chauffeur's hat, letting her dark curls fall down to her shoulders and replied, "Sorry, sir, women aren't allowed inside Flaming Leaf. You'll have to get out and walk the rest of the way."

His eyes bulged with rage. He screamed some of his favorite expletives. "It's more than a half mile to the clubhouse!"

"I wouldn't know, sir."

He cursed her again, dragged his clubs out of the car and began the long, winding trek to the clubhouse, snorting and cussing all the way. "You'll hear from me about this!" he screamed.

"I'm sure we will, sir," a calm Marty replied with a smile. She slammed the back door, got back in and drove away.

But they never did hear from again, nor did they ever collect from that particular fare. He, however, received a letter from Martin Transportation that his account was closed.

~ ~ ~

Sabyl's doorbell rang. Beau barked loudly until the door opened and he saw it was a friend and not a foe.

"Bec, I'm so glad you came." They hugged like old friends do.

"Here, let me take your coat. Sit down and get comfortable. I'll just hang this up."

Rebecca walked into the living room over to Sabyl's Christmas tree. "Thanks, dear. How have you been?"

"Busy but good. I made a quick dinner. Caesar salad with grilled salmon topped with zucchini relish and my pineapple-cheese casserole."

"Sounds perfect!'

Sabyl had set the small table next to the large double window that overlooked the courtyard seven stories down. Lights twinkled in the shrubbery and along the tall iron fence that encased the grounds down below.

"Your Christmas tree is stunning! Oh, and the one in the lobby downstairs is dazzling!"

"Thanks, dear! Yes, they do a good job of decorating every year." She beckoned for her to take a seat at the table.

They chatted and ate leisurely and when they finished they each took their plates into the kitchen, rinsed them and put them in the dishwasher. They dried off their hands and headed into the living room.

Rebecca looked at Sabyl and asked, "Are you alright? You look like something is on your mind."

Sabyl smiled. "You know me too well."

"What is it, honey?"

"Just had a rough day."

"Every day for you is rough. You're in one of the toughest businesses there is. Is it getting to you?"

"I try not to stress out."

"Well, with your business and all these bombings, no wonder you're stressed!'

Sabyl leaned back on the sofa. "Yeah, it's awful seeing the pictures of those families getting the news of their loved ones…so many young people…it's just so sad."

Rebecca took her hand, "Oh, honey, no one knows that better than you."

"But I can't dwell on that. It's too painful, and I'm trying to avoid TV as much as I can, but it's almost impossible, and I need to know what's going on. But I do enjoy my work and my clients. The problems that come with it just goes with the territory, and I've learned to pretty much cope with those…but here lately…I mean it reminds me so much of last year."

"How well I know. It's like that…but different. It seems these terrorist acts are so well coordinated and no one seems to be able to stop them. The way things are going, you couldn't catch me getting on a plane!"

"I'm flying to New York on the 20th."

Rebecca sat up and leaned toward Sabyl. "Oh, dear, do you have to? I mean, can't you get out of it?"

"I could, but I can't let these crazy people dictate my life."

"I understand, but…"

"So just pray for me…"

"I will, honey. By the way, I'm enjoying my Bible I bought last year. I'm learning so much!"

"Oh, Bec, that's wonderful!"

"I still don't understand everything about, you know, what it all means, but I'm trying."

"Well, there is a scripture, I think in Matthew, that says, 'Seek and you shall find.' You are seeking, and so you will find. And the wonderful part is, it doesn't say you might find. It says you will find."

"But I'm not even sure what I'm looking for."

Sabyl smiled knowingly. "You'll know it when you find it."

"I do have one question, though. How can I be sure Christianity is right for me? I mean aren't there many paths to heaven?"

Sabyl leaned forward. "Bec, if that's the case, the cross was a waste of time. Jesus could have come and set up motivational seminars on which path to take. But He had to die, didn't He?"

"But, why?"

"Because there has to be a sacrifice for sin and Jesus was and is the final Lamb...the Lamb of God who takes away the sin of the world."

"I...I'll have to think about that."

"Yes, think about it and pray about it because that is part of the seeking process."

"Okay, I will. Thank you, Sabyl. You're such a wise, good friend."

Sabyl reached over and hugged her. "You're welcome. Now, how about some dessert?"

CHAPTER ELEVEN

Washington was not always a user-friendly town in terms of parking. Most towns have parking areas laid out for their patrons to park their cars, get out and walk into their store of choice, i.e. strip malls, shopping centers and the all-time favorite, Wal-Mart. Not so in D.C. Parking was a nightmare. And if you were fortunate enough to find a space, if it was at a meter or on the street, your car fell victim to the relentless meter maid whom you were certain had it on her agenda to target you for a ticket.

Limousines were a particular problem. The seasoned drivers knew secret places to park until some other driver found out about it. Trying to find a place to park, plus being within eye view of his or her client's return was sometimes impossible. A cop might tell the driver to park down the block—yet he cannot leave his vehicle to watch for his or her client. However, for some events, the drivers were allowed to park along the street nearest the venue, but even then, they could become the target of a moody Metro Policeman.

Some of the cops were friendly and sympathetic to the limo drivers' plights and others seemed to get a rush out of harassing them and handing out tickets like candy.

The smell of scorched coffee permeated the air in the drivers' lounge area. Half empty coffee mugs, with the Martin Transportation Group logo on them, and a full ashtray, littered the small table where George, Maurice and Stubby sat listening to Ricko complain about getting yet another ticket.

Maurice stood and picked up his mug to take it to the sink. "Just take it to Frank, Ricko. He'll take care of it for you. Hey, aren't you going to Columbia to see your family for Christmas?"

Ricko brightened. "Yes! It's been almost six years since I have seen them." He stood and pulled on his chauffer's coat. "I have to head to Reagan for a transfer." He tugged at his sleeves and said, "Why does that airport have so many names? It's confusing!"

"Yeah," George chuckled. "Some say, 'Take me to Reagan, some call it National, still others call it Reagan National."

"And some call it Washington National," chimed in Maurice.

"How come it's got so many names?" Ricko asked.

George leaned back in his chair and folded his arms over his chest. "Well, it was formerly known as *Washington National*. Then they changed the name to *Ronald Reagan Washington National Airport* in 1998. But many people, especially D.C. Democrats, still can't bring themselves to call it that. So they just call it National."

"Okay, well, I call it Reagan and that's where I'm heading. See you later."

"See ya, Ricko." Headlight appeared on the garage wall. "Hey, here comes Rudy!"

Rudy carefully nosed his limo into the garage, parked in his place, got out and walked over to George and Stubby.

"Hey Rudy! How's it going?"

He sat down heavily, took his hat off and rubbed his head.

George cocked his head to one side and said, "You look rough, Rudy. What's the matter? These bombings getting to you?"

The Egyptian-born man looked up and frowned. "Maybe."

"Can't say as I blame you, man," said Maurice. "After what you and your boy went through last year, you've got a right to be nervous."

"It's not the same, of course. These attacks are not as..."

"Up close and personal?"

"Yes. Something like that."

"Sabyl's probably feeling the same way."

"We're all nervous," said Stubby. "These terrorists are attacking our country again and it's enough to make you..."

Rudy's cell phone buzzed. He flipped it open. "This is Rudy." He walked over to the door to get maximum amount of bars on his phone and talked quietly.

Burt Hastings walked in. "What's the latest? You been watchin' the news?"

"Naw. Kind of tired of hearing it," answered George. "Makes my stomach hurt."

"You and my wife both."

"Hey Burt. Where's your car?"

"I parked it out in the circle drive. Gotta leave again in a couple a minutes." He walked past him. "Gotta use the john." He headed for the restroom and closed the door.

Rudy closed his phone and returned to the kitchen area shaking his head and frowning.

"What's the matter, Rudy?" George asked.

"My son, David. He wants to know if I'm all right. He's worried about his mother and me." He sat down and leaned back. "He's the one who went through that nightmare last year."

Stubby nodded. "Yeah. Poor kid went through a lot. But so did you. Driving those maniacs around, not knowing…"

Rudy put his hat back on. "And yet my son was more concerned about his mother and me than he was about himself. He knew his mother would be worried with all that's going on."

"He's a fine boy," offered Stubby.

George asked, "How's he doing in school?"

Rudy brightened. "He's doing well. His second year of medical school is difficult, but he's studying hard and making good marks."

Sabyl walked in out of breath. "Turn on the TV, guys. This is getting bad."

George grabbed the remote and hit the power button. The 55" inch screen came to life.

"It is reported that another explosion has occurred in a private jet that may have been owned by the department store magnate, Rufus Merriweather."

George leaned forward. "Merriweather? Isn't he one of our clients?"

Sabyl nodded solemnly.

The news anchor continued, *"Investigators are trying to determine if it is related to the previous explosions that began Sunday that have rocked the nation."*

"I just drove him last week," Rudy said. "I picked him up at Dulles and took him to the Mayflower Hotel."

"Doesn't he have a daughter who goes to school here?"

Sabyl put her finger up to her lips. "Shhh, listen."

"The well-known businessman has not been heard from since he and his two daughters, both students at Georgetown University in Washington, D.C., flew out of Dulles this afternoon. It is reported that they were heading for a ski trip in Vermont for the Christmas break."

Burt came out of the restroom and asked what was going on. They filled him in and continued their comments.

Sabyl folded her arms and said, "I know this isn't the same as last year, but I want you guys to be aware of anything unusual—pay attention to conversations—report anything strange."

"We'll keep an eye out, Sabyl."

Burt pointed a crooked finger at her. "Yeah. You be careful too, boss."

George asked, "Hey. Aren't you supposed to fly somewhere soon?"

"Yes. To New York on the 20th."

"I don't like it, boss," Rudy said.

"Me neither," said Stubby. "Can't you cancel?"

"That's a few days from now. I'm sure they'll have this figured out by then. Besides, we can't be held hostage by these nut case terrorists. We go on with our lives as always...or they win."

George took a deep breath. "She's right."

Stubby folded his beefy arms. "I still don't have to like it."

~ ~ ~

Sabyl nearly ran to the door when the doorbell rang. Beau barked in protest at the sound and settled down when the door opened and he saw Scott.

The weary agent stepped inside and quickly pulled her into his arms.

She reached over and closed the door as his lips rushed to hers. He kissed her eyes, her cheeks, her forehead and back to her lips, all the while saying between kisses, "I've—missed—you—so—much!"

She just smiled with each kiss and finally was able to say, "I've missed you too."

He pulled back and looked at her. "You look beautiful, as always."

"And you look exhausted," she said as she reached up to touch his cold cheek.

He took her hand and kissed her palm. "I'm okay." His face grew more serious. "I guess you've heard there's been another bombing."

"I saw it on TV. Rufus Merriweather. Scott, he was one of my clients!"

"Oh, honey, I didn't know."

"This is all so horrible!"

He sighed deeply. "Yeah." He took her hands. "Look, I don't know when I'll be able to... as long as this is going on, I'll be..."

She put her fingers on his lips. "I know, honey, I know."

He looked at her large hazel eyes. "I'll call you as soon as I can. Oh, and I have a gift for you."

She held up her hands. "No. This will be over soon. And then we'll have our Christmas together. Until then, I'll pray for you every day and pray you'll catch the bad guys."

Her voice was so tender it caused him to wonder if his heart could take it. He looked at her sadly. "I have to go. I love you."

"I love you too," she said, pressing her cheek to his. "Be careful," she whispered.

She closed the door and leaned against it and whispered, "Lord, please keep him safe."

CHAPTER TWELVE

Cars were parked curbside for two solid blocks on the shaded street in Bethesda, Maryland, some displaying their driver's apparent inelegance of parallel parking.

The modest yet well-ordered two-story brick home was filled with lively women from various walks of life who had come together to celebrate, equip and adorn the yet-to-be-born child of their friends, Frank and Barbara Lauriette. Among them were a few of Barbara's cousins, some of her college friends and co-workers, and Burt's wife, Phyllis and George's wife, Betty.

The sunlit living room, decorated in colonial style, was arrayed with yellow and white balloons, crepe paper streamers and large bows of pale yellow tulle tied around the lampshades. On one side of the room was a playpen filled with gifts of assorted sizes and shapes.

Barbara's mother, Helen, drove up from Lorton, Virginia the night before to help decorate; bringing her carefully packed plates, tablecloths and silver trays for the hors-d'oeuvres she had spent the morning preparing. The dining room table was covered with a white lace tablecloth laden with Helen's inherited crystal plates, flowered napkins, and a silver three-tiered server loaded with cupcakes topped with booties made of icing. A punch bowl, another of Helen's collection, was filled with a pale yellow punch with orange slices floating on top and frothy lemon sorbet mixed in. The centerpiece was a large watermelon carved in the shape of a baby carriage filled with melon balls. Plates of hors-d'oeuvres and party favors of little paper diapers folded and pinned and filled with candy were on doily-lined silver trays. And of course, the obligatory white sheet cake with tiny pacifiers decorating each cut square.

After Helen offered a short blessing for the food, Dotty took her place ladling the punch while Sabyl brought in another tray of goodies. The ladies gathered up their napkins and silverware, filled their plates and returned to the chairs they had claimed in the living room before someone else grabbed them. Balancing their plates on their knees, the ladies chatted amiably and managed to avoid bringing up the subjects of politics or the bombings. They were pleasantly encased in a comfortable bubble of denial where they somehow felt safe, even if only for an afternoon.

Barbara was dressed in a loose turquoise top with black pants and shoes. Her dark, smooth skin glowed with excitement as she sat in one of the two Queen Ann chairs at the end of the living room in front of the fireplace. She had wanted to have a cozy fire but knew it would get too hot in the small room with so many people. Dotty, already fanning herself, had asserted earlier how quickly all these ninety-eight-point-sixes could heat up a room.

One of Barbara's old college roommates named Tiffany Lange from Atlanta, a petite, wide-eyed blond dressed to the hilt spoke up, "Barb, didn't you know its bad luck for a pregnant woman to sit in a Queen Anne chair?"

Thinking she was joking, everyone laughed.

Dotty, standing in the back, holding her plate in one hand and her cup of punch in the other asked, "Okay, what's the punch line?"

"I'm not joking," she said with a frown. "My Aunt Bessie May from Tifton, Georgia told me so. She told me that during her marriage, Queen Anne's, that is, that she had seventeen pregnancies; twelve were miscarriages or stillbirths, and four of the children died in infancy."

Some of the women gasped; most just looked at her uneasily.

Barbara raised an eyebrow and replied. "Tiffany, thank you for your, uh, concern, but I'm not superstitious."

Undeterred, Tiffany continued, "The one child who did survive past infancy, Prince William, Duke of Gloucester, was ill most of his life and died at the age of eleven."

Helen put her plate down and said, "Young woman, you aren't serious!"

Tiffany cocked her head to one side and stared at her.

Barbara leaned forward. "Mama, please. It's okay."

"It is not okay," Helen continued, "Why would you bring up something like that at a baby shower? We're here to celebrate this gift of God, and you bring that devil talk in here?"

Dotty spoke up. "Yeah! That's the pigs!"

Tiffany sat her cup and plate down and stood up. "Well, don't say I didn't warn you!" She grabbed her coat and stormed out.

The women were stunned. Betty said, "What in the world was that all about?"

"I've nev'ah heard of such nonsense," Phyllis said in her South Carolina drawl.

Barbara apologized to the ladies. "I'm sorry, you'll have to overlook Tiffany. She's a bit...eccentric."

"Weird's a better word," offered Dotty.

"Please don't let this ruin our time together here."

Sabyl reached over and took her hand. "We won't, honey."

Helen stood up like a soldier going to war and announced, "It's time to pray!" Some of the women hesitantly bowed their heads; others were so startled they just sat looking at Barbara with wide eyes.

Helen began, "Father, we ask that You take away this fear that was spoken in this house. You have not given us a spirit of fear, but of love and power and a sound mind. We ask You to remove any negative thoughts that may linger and that only Your joy and peace will remain. Your Son became a curse for us, and we will not entertain any silly curses that this woman has spoken. And we pray that You will open her eyes to this deception and help her to see the truth. Thank You, Lord, that we can receive Your peace right now, as You are the Prince of Peace. In Jesus name, Amen."

Everyone mumbled, "Amen."

Dotty quickly spoke up. "Who needs a refill on their punch?"

"I do," said Sabyl as she held up her cup.

Another woman smiled and said, "Me too, thank you."

The ladies, feeling a sense of relief, resumed their chatter.

Sabyl, sitting in the other Queen Anne, said, "One day soon, you'll be holding your little one in your lap."

Barbara smiled and placed her plate on the small table between them. "I know. I can't wait." Looking down at her large belly she sighed, "I'll be glad to get my lap back."

After everyone was finished with their plates, Helen and some of the other guests helped take up the dishes and take them to the kitchen. When they returned to the living room, Barbara announced that they were going to play a couple of games and then she would open her gifts. The games brought much laughter, something that was badly needed by all, and then it was time to open the gifts.

Pretty cards with happy sayings and warm wishes were read aloud. Dotty handed Sabyl a large plastic trash bag for the wrapping paper, which had begun to pile up while the bows were saved in a smaller plastic bag. Oohhs and aahhs resounded with the exhibiting of each gift. Loads of white and yellow baby clothes, blankets, and booties, stacked up; bottles, diapers and clever things some of the older ladies had never seen nor used were placed on display on the large coffee table in the middle of the room.

When the shower was over, there were thanks, hugs and goodbyes and promises of prayers for a healthy baby and a safe delivery. Soon the cars pulled away from the tree-lined curb one-by-one, and a worn-out Barbara sat back down and smiled gratefully. Their baby would lack for nothing—that was for sure.

Dotty and Sabyl helped Helen with the dishes while Barbara called Frank at the office. He was glad to escape that "girlie thing" and was enjoying watching the game with the drivers in their lounge. Careful not to mention the incident with Tiffany, she chattered happily about how well it went and all the gifts their friends had blessed them with. Frank smiled and nodded and said he would be home in about an hour.

She hung up and put her head back and smiled and prayed a small prayer of thanks for her loving, generous friends and for her husband. She was most grateful to have Frank back. For the first twenty years of their marriage he had been an alcoholic; one of the kind ones, not abusive, but half the time she didn't know where he was and the money he spent on booze took its toll on their finances. The anguish that his addiction brought nearly destroyed their marriage. She smiled and closed her eyes and thanked God again for His mercy. Frank was sober and had been for four years now. His mother-in-law, Helen, had faithfully prayed for him and was overjoyed with his transformation.

At that moment the three emerged from the kitchen and sat down to relax for a few minutes.

Barbara's face turned crimson, and she began to breathe heavily. She grabbed her head and closed her eyes in pain.

Helen jumped up and ran to her. "Honey, what is it?"

"Mama, my head hurts…"

"Look how swollen her hands and feet are!" Dotty yelled. "We've got to get her to the hospital!"

"No, no, I'll be fine," Barbara protested.

"No way, girlfriend," Dotty said. "This is preeclampsia, I know. I've been there, done that!"

Helen, a retired nurse, checked her pulse. "Oh, Lord, it's pounding like a drum! Honey, where is that new wrist blood pressure monitor I bought you?"

"It's in the top drawer of the vanity in my bedroom."

"I'll get it," offered Dotty. She hurried out of the room.

Barbara grabbed her upper left abdomen and cried out in pain.

Dotty handed the BP monitor to Helen. She placed it on her daughter's wrist and pushed the power button. It sprang to life, and within seconds the large digital numbers appeared. "Oh, Lord! It's 153 over 92!"

Sabyl quickly called 911 while Helen helped her daughter over to the sofa to lie down, grabbed some pillows and propped her feet up. She got a damp cloth and wiped Barbara's face with it and prayed, "Lord, please help my baby. Don't let anything happen to her or my grandbaby." She opened her eyes and hollered, "Devil, you better back off! You got no place in this house!"

Sabyl called Frank. Dotty stood on the front porch and watched for the ambulance.

CHAPTER THIRTEEN

Several UATF agents, wearing lanyards with their creds attached, sat around the Strategy Room conference table with their laptops opened in front of them, each keeping in constant communication with their respective agencies. Some were emailing orders to their officials; others were watching the progress of specific investigative activities. Images flickered across the multiple monitors on the walls. The remaining ones were either at the crash sites or in other locations putting maximum pressure on their agencies to gather more intelligence about the bombings.

Although the usual antagonism among the diverse agencies had begun to evolve into good-natured banter, there was still tension among a few of them, mostly because of old rivalries of the past. They were careful not to express them in front of the other agents and certainly not in the presence of the director.

Keefer sat down, rolled up his sleeves and pulled a handkerchief out of his pocket, took off his glasses and began cleaning them.

Scott and Martz sat down and drew up their chairs.

Keefer rubbed the back of his neck and began his opening remarks. "Good morning, ladies and gentlemen. Despite the massive effort to investigate so many bombings, we still need some very definitive answers." He looked at a thick-shouldered man sitting at the other end of the table. "What has NTSB found out so far, Jim?"

He was addressing Jim Snow, investigator-in-charge of recovering the aircraft fragments and putting together a fast-track analysis of what caused the bombings. The former Navy SEAL known as "The Snow Man" leaned forward and cleared his throat. "Concerning flight 819 that went down over Kansas, from what we can ascertain so far, the bomb exploded in the forward part of the aircraft."

"Forward part? Like where?"

"Looks like the First Class section."

"Go on."

"Could be a couple of things. There's a First Aid box where there's medical equipment."

"Are these replaced regularly?"

"Yeah. The flight attendants have the responsibility to inspect their sections, and they check to see if the medical equipment has been compromised."

"How?"

"They look to see if the seals have been broken."

"And, obviously, if they had been, that would have been reported, and that flight would not have taken off. Correct?"

"Correct."

"Okay, what else?"

"The caterers. They get their serving carts from catering services."

"Do the flight attendants check those out as well?"

"Yes, sir. Nothing seemed out of the ordinary."

"What else?"

"That's about it. The captain, first officer and flight engineer all have to order separate meals from the crew schedule. They can't all eat the same thing. In case someone has tampered with the food."

"Well, somebody's tampered with something—or else we've got another device aboard that we're just not seeing. Thank you, Jim."

He turned to the massive screen on which the other NTSB agent, Mark Riley, appeared on the screen with a tiny microphone attached to his lapel.

"Okay, Mark, what have you got?"

Agent Riley cleared his throat and began, "Flight 4105, the one that crashed in the Atlantic, radar data indicated that it experienced an in-flight breakup. Pieces of the aircraft were strewn over a wide area of the ocean. The breakup was caused by an explosion near the center of the aircraft, somewhere in the vicinity of the right wing, which was the first piece to separate from the plane. It was recovered in the westernmost edge of the wreckage grid, referred to as the "Red Zone." Further east, the fuselage was next in the breakup sequence located in what we've labeled the "Yellow Zone." The pieces that are being pulled out of the easternmost part of the wreckage area are labeled the "Green Zone." All these fragments are tagged with a red, yellow or green tag to help us put together a better scenario as they are found. However, since we are fast-tracking this investigation, I will give you my first impressions: Truth is sir, we got lucky. The first vessel on the scene of the wreckage site, a fishing boat out of Nova Scotia, recovered some pieces that are pretty telling. They seem to indicate that a bomb, rather than a missile was used to bring flight 4105 down."

Keefer leaned forward. "How can you tell?"

"Because of certain distinctive localized damage signatures that tell the story, such as pitting, sooting in certain areas, cratering, hot gas washing and petaling; others by how they broke apart, which way the metal bent, stuff like that. A missile can cause these types of damage, but a bomb was most likely detonated inside the plane because of localized, severe fragmentation of the seats. Another reason we do not believe a missile was used is that a SAM can only reach an altitude of 1,200 to 1,500 feet, depending on the type. All the flights that have been brought down were above that altitude."

"Anything else?"

"No, sir. We hope to recover a black box from at least one of the wreckage sites within a day or two. This will tell us if the plane was overtaken by individuals on board the plane or not."

"What about Flight 84 and Rufus Merriweather's private jet?"

"We're still gathering information on those two. So far, nothing to report except they both look like they were destroyed by an inside bomb."

"So one bomb exploded in the forward part of the plane and another in the midsection." Keefer rubbed the back of his neck. "Thanks, Mark."

"Thank you, sir."

Keefer then turned to the representative from the FBI. "What have you got, Gordon?"

Gordon Marsh, a twenty-year veteran of the FBI leaned back and began. "We've been tracking a lot of chatter by ISIS and others, but it seems to be generated by the aftermath of these explosions. It seems the communications among those who would be very excited about such a massive attack knew nothing about it. This does not fit the usual pattern, so we're beginning to think the plan was either unknown to them or they've learned to keep a lid on it."

The agents around the table looked at one another with new interest.

Keefer frowned deeply. "So what you're saying is it may be a new menace within our borders?"

"One that does not communicate with the usual supporters of terrorist enemies of our country."

"So we're not looking for the usual al-Qaeda or ISIS type?"

"It's hard to say. Al-Qaeda usually likes to make a big splash, so the pattern is not unusual for them. Of course, due to all we've learned from their past behavior, al Qaeda may be changing their modes of operation to keep us guessing. They seem to be very pragmatic—learn and adapt as they go, as we've seen them do in Iraq and Afghanistan." He continued his investigative assessment, and Director Keefer then turned to the agents from NSA. "Boyd, Hank, do you have something?"

Boyd Bradford leaned forward and addressed the Task Force. "I have video from Dulles that I thought was interesting." He pressed a button on a pad in front of him and pointed to one of the large screens on the east wall of the Strategy Room. "These bombings have come during the time of winter break at most universities, so you can see there are a large number of students boarding the plane."

The agents watched intently as he continued. "As you can see, person after person went through the screening area, most are carrying some sort of carry-on luggage—mostly backpacks, and different types of cases for laptops, notebooks, pocketbooks, and various parcels, which is not unusual. What is disturbing, as you can also see, the screeners often look away or are chatting with someone. Unfortunately, when there has been a relatively long period of time without incident, security tends to, well, let's say, not be at full alert. These videos were from before the first explosion."

Keefer frowned. "Which means screeners are not as wary and scrutinizing as when a known threat is looming."

Bradford nodded. "Right. We've all heard the reports of lack of security at the airports. Much of the problem is not a lack of security personnel on site, but a lack of top-notch people who remain focused and enough sophisticated screening devices to alert for explosive materials. That's disturbing enough, but here is video of screeners after the fact." The images showed very little change in the behavior of some of the screeners.

Keefer scowled, "My God! What is it going to take to make these people understand the seriousness of these catastrophes?!"

"I know, sir," Bradford continued. "I'm in no way excusing their behavior but those folks are under a great deal of pressure and the turnover for those jobs is unbelievable."

"Then we need to start putting better-trained people in there. This is unacceptable, Boyd!"

"We're working on it, sir. Funding is a problem..."

"Well, it won't be for long." Keefer ordered his aide to get the president on the phone.

"Yes, sir!" He quickly left the room.

Agent Bradford removed his glasses and continued. "There were no bomb-sniffing dogs on site at most of the airports—mostly because of the dogs' work regime. Some bomb-sniffing dogs can only work at thirty-minute intervals; others two to three hours at a time. It's impossible to supply an airport with enough dogs to be on the job twenty-four/seven."

Keefer rubbed his eyes with his fingers. "Okay. Hank, what did you guys come up with?"

NSA veteran Hank Childers took over. "There were no suspicious people on board any of the first three flights; there were some Middle Easterners on the domestic flights, and as far as we can tell through the flight manifest, there were four on the Trans Globe flight, but they all check out."

"Great. So we're back to square one." Keefer thanked them and went on to other areas of the investigation. After the meeting, the agents made quick calls to their respective agencies for the latest update. So far, at least for the time being, all agencies were cooperating.

Keefer's aid brought him a secure phone and announced, "The President, sir."

CHAPTER FOURTEEN

Balloons with the words "Get Well Soon" and smiley faces swayed and gently bumped against the ceiling. Barbara slept peacefully. Frank held his wife's hand and gently rubbed her arm. Sabyl sat next to him watching the pulsating beat of Barbara's heart on the monitor as it quietly beeped in the background. Two IV's dripped, one in each arm; fluids for hydration and to lower her blood pressure and the other for magnesium sulfate to prevent seizures. Blood tests for creatinine levels to determine kidney function were done earlier along with several other tests. On her belly were two electrodes with a transducer to monitor the baby's heart rate. The doctor had prescribed a sedative and instructed the nurses to monitor her blood pressure closely.

Helen sat caddy-cornered across the room praying silently and keeping an eye on the pulse oximeter.

Sabyl patted Frank on the arm. "She's going to be okay."

"I know," Frank replied hopefully.

A nurse in a light blue smock came in to check on her patient.

"Do we need to move?" Frank asked as he started to get up.

"No, you're fine," she said. "I just want to get her temperature real quick." She used an ear thermometer, carefully placing it in Barbara's ear.

Helen, watching closely, said, "They didn't have those gadgets when I was a nurse. We had to wake up the patients and stick it in their mouths."

The young woman smiled. "You were a nurse?"

"For thirty years."

"That's great," she replied as she looked at the reading on the thermometer. She seemed satisfied and left.

Sabyl stood up and said, "Frank, I need to get to the office. She bent down and kissed the top of his head. "I'm praying for Barbara."

"Thanks, Sabe. I'm, uh, counting on yours and Helen's prayers."

"And don't worry about work. We've got you covered."

"Thanks, boss."

Sabyl walked over to Helen, reached down and hugged her. "See you soon, dear." She turned and slipped out the door and headed for the elevator, glad to be leaving. She'd had enough of hospitals for a lifetime with two bouts of breast cancer. She walked to her car, got in and closed the door, fastened her seatbelt, said a quick prayer and drove to the office.

~ ~ ~

Sitting at his desk, Karen was talking through Frank's headset while trying to adjust it to fit her much smaller head. She started up his computer and pulled out the notes Dotty had handed her when she arrived. She typed in the new information and hit "Enter."

Dotty buzzed Jenny and asked her to come to her office.

Jenny unhooked her headset and walked around the corner into Dotty's office.

"Oh, good, there you are. Did you say your new boyfriend is a computer whiz?"

"Yes. He can do anything on a computer."

"But can he fix them?"

"Absolutely. He's a genius."

"He gave me his business card a while back when he did Sabyl's website." Dotty held up his card and squinted through her glasses. "I don't see a phone number."

"Oh, no. He doesn't take phone calls. Just emails."

"That's weird. How does he call you?"

"He doesn't. He emails me."

"He asks you out through an email?"

Jenny laughed. "I know it sounds weird, but it works out okay."

"Does he have a cell phone?"

"If he does, I've never seen it."

"Okay, well Sabyl's computer is messed up, and she really needs it fixed fast. Do you think he would come in right away and take a look at it?"

"Oh, I'm sure he will. Do you want me to email him?"

"Yes, if you don't mind. I'm sure he would open yours a lot faster than mine."

"Okay, I'll do it now. I'll let you know when I hear back from him."

"Okay. Hope it's soon. If not . . ."

"Oh, he always answers right away."

Dotty slapped the top of her desk in approval. "Good! Talk to you later."

Jenny settled herself behind her computer and clicked on her email icon and clacked out a message on the keyboard to her boyfriend.

DERRICK. BOSS NEEDS HER 'PUTER FIXED ASAP. CAN DO? LEMME KNOW. CHIO. JW.

A few minutes later. Sabyl came in. "Good morning, dear," she said brightly.

"Good morning, boss. Want some coffee?"

"That would be great, thanks."

Sabyl put her pocketbook down and pulled her gloves off. "I just visited Barbara in the hospital. She's doing better, but they're keeping her another day or two until they're sure it's okay for her to go home."

Dotty lowered her voice. "I don't want to sound negative but what if she doesn't get...you know...better?"

"Then they'll most likely induce labor. They said it's the safest thing to do. But if her blood pressure remains too high, they'll do a C-Section."

"Wow. I hope it doesn't come to that."

"Yeah, me too."

Dotty helped her with her coat and said, "Hey, can you believe that Tiffany person yesterday? How weird was that? That was just the pigs the way she..."

Sabyl put her hand up. "Let's not go there. I'm sure she meant well, but she's obviously got some unusual, uh, views."

"You're right. I just hope Barbara doesn't think that nonsense about the Queen Anne chair is for real."

"Don't worry, she doesn't. Like she said, she's not at all superstitious. And Helen took care of it with her prayer."

Dotty smiled. "That she did. She's quite a prayer warrior. She reminds me of that gal that played Clara in the movie War Room."

Sabyl laughed, "You know, I thought the same thing." She picked up her pocketbook and turned to go into her office. "So what's going on around here?"

"Hang on. Let me get your coffee." She hurried to the coffee bar in the foyer and returned with a steaming mug and set it down on Sabyl's desk.

"Thanks, honey."

"You're welcome. Hey, Jenny's boyfriend will probably be coming to look at your computer. Not sure just when, but hopefully within the next day or two."

"Good. Hope he can fix it. I'm kind of lost without it."

"You can always use mine."

"I know, but, you know how it is, I need my own..."

"I know." Dotty lowered her voice. "By the way, Dr. Solomon's office called. Said you need to make an appointment."

Sabyl looked startled.

"Just for a checkup," she said quickly.

"Oh, yes. Okay," Sabyl said, looking relieved.

"Gotta keep up with those checkups, boss. The good Lord has brought you this far . . ."

"I know, and I'm grateful. I truly am."

"I know you are. So am I."

"He's brought us both through a lot, hasn't He, Dotty?"

"You bet He has. Especially last year. 'Hope we don't ever see another year like that again!"

"Yeah, me too."

The glass front door opened and Conrad, Sabyl's pet sitter, emerged with Beau.

"We're in here," Dotty bellowed.

He stepped into Sabyl's office. "Hey Sabyl, Dotty."

"Hi, Conrad," Sabyl smiled as she sat down behind her desk.

The slender young man was a Howard Law School dropout making good money as a "Critter Sitter." He had a thin face, a well-groomed goatee, impish blue eyes and long blond hair pulled back in a ponytail. He unleashed Beau. Without hesitation, he looked up at Dotty and headed straight for her desk, knowing a treat was waiting.

Dotty laughed and said, "I guess I'd better follow him. He knows on which side his bread is buttered."

"How did he do at the groomers?" Sabyl asked as she picked up her purse and searched for her checkbook.

"Fine. He's always good but always glad to leave."

Sabyl put on her readers and quickly wrote a check out to Conrad and handed it to him.

He took it, folded it and put it in his wallet. "Thanks, Sabyl. Hey, what does Scott think of all these bombings?"

Sabyl looked over her readers and smiled.

"Uh, I guess he couldn't tell you if he knew, right?"

"Right."

"Got it." He stuffed his wallet in his pocket. "Thanks again, Sabyl."

"Thanks, Conrad. Oh, by the way, we're having a Christmas party here on the 23rd. We'd love to have you come."

"I'd like to, but I'll be at my girlfriend's house in Chevy Chase. She's throwing a bash with some of her college friends." He winked and said, "If it gets too rowdy, I might show up over here."

Sabyl chuckled, "Okay, great. If I don't see you before, have a blessed Christmas."

Dotty walked in and said, "And don't forget what Christmas is all about, dude. It's not Santa, ya know. It's Jesus."

He smiled sheepishly and replied. "Yeah, I know. I never did buy into the Santa thing."

She put a hand on her hip and said, "Well, have you bought into the Jesus thing?"

"Uh, sure. Look, I gotta go." He quickly went out the door and got into his yellow PT Cruiser and drove off.

Sabyl grinned. "You're getting pretty bold in your old age."

"Yeah, well, somebody's got to talk about it. This world's going to hell in a handbasket."

~ ~ ~

It was not a little-known fact that Abdul Arib had one of the best computer minds on campus, as did Derrick and Kyle. Ted Hickson, Professor of Computer Science, had taught all of them at American University. As young minds do, each had gone further, especially Derrick, whose genius was incomparable. There was nothing he couldn't hack into; no program was impenetrable for him. The program he had worked on for two years was his ticket to wealth, to financial freedom and a bright future. Only one problem. Someone had stolen it. Even the backup disc was erased and rendered useless. Only one person could have done it—or was there more than one? Kyle? No, he was good, but he wasn't that

106

good. Abdul? No way. He didn't even know about it. That left Professor Hickson.

Derrick stood and walked around his apartment with his hands in his pockets. His anger had been replaced with the firm satisfaction that his plan would work out perfectly. There was no doubt about it. He sighed deeply as though he had let go of a heavy burden.

He went over to the small refrigerator and took out a bottle of water and sat back down and stared at the clippings on the corkboard over his desk. He had read every story, every scenario, and every commentator. He read them over and over again. He knew them by heart. He turned the ideas that were stored in the corridors of his mind over and over. It was like he was bleeding the life out of the scenario that he believed was the perfect crime. It was the strategy that he himself was devising, and it was coming along nicely.

CHAPTER FIFTEEN

The laptops around the conference table whirred softly while fingers flitted across the keyboards. Constant reports from around the world, transmitted through satellite feeds, flickered across the expansive screens on the wall. Several agents who were working in the field presented their reports via satellite phone.

Director Keefer stood and announced, "Ladies and gentlemen, we have some good news to report for a change. Our NTSB agents have reported that the black boxes from two of the downed planes have been found and have just been analyzed."

Images of UATF's two NTSB agents appeared on the giant screens. They were on site at the warehouse where fragments of Trans Globe Flight 4105 that went down in the Atlantic were being analyzed.

All the agents around the table paused what they were doing to watch and listen.

Keefer spoke. "Okay, Jim, we're all ears. Tell us what you found out from the black boxes."

Jim Snow answered, "Thank you, sir. We have retrieved the ones from Flight 84 that went down north of Reading, PA, and Flight 819 that crashed in Kansas. We've listened closely to the tapes along with the crash experts. From what we can ascertain, the pilots had no anxiety in their voices—nothing that would indicate anything out of the ordinary."

Keefer answered, "So, the pending threats were unknown to the crew members?"

"Looks like it, yes, sir," said Snow.

"Did the recordings give an indication as to their altitude?"

Snow's partner Mark Riley spoke up. "They usually give the announcement that the captain has turned off the seat belt sign when they reach 10,000 feet. Any time before then is considered crucial time—the pilots are talking to the tower—the flight engineer is doing his thing; the flight attendants can't even talk to them during that time unless there's an emergency."

"So had the announcement been given that the seat belt had been turned off?"

"Yes, sir."

"How much time after that did the explosion on Flight 84 occur?"

"About ten minutes after."

"And the one that went down over Kansas?"

"It had been in the air for almost two and a half hours."

Keefer took a deep breath and let it out slowly. "Okay, so on one of these flights, we can assume that the bombs were either set for a certain altitude or—or what? Help me out, guys."

"Or maybe the X-ray, as they went through security, set off a timer," Scott interjected.

"That's a possibility. But how are these bombs getting through security?"

FBI agent Fred Causewell, sitting at the other end of the table spoke up. "Good question. They've got bomb-sniffing dogs out there now. Hopefully, that'll stop any future bombings. On airplanes, at least."

Keefer looked back to the image of Jim Snow. "Where are the bombs exploding? In the restroom—the galley or from an assigned seat?"

"It's too soon to tell about the last two. They're still picking up the pieces and bringing them to the reconstruction sites to put them back together."

Keefer snorted, "That could take months. We need answers now."

"I'll talk to NTSB again. Maybe they can tell something by some of the pieces before they put the puzzle together."

"We'd better hope we've seen the last explosion."

"Yeah. Let's hope," offered Martz.

"And pray," said Scott.

~ ~ ~

Jenny Wong came into Sabyl's office, said a quick hello, and put another pile of messages on Sabyl's desk. She smiled at Sabyl, who was frowning in an obvious response to the person with whom she was talking, waved, and went back to her computer.

Sabyl's face flushed when the Italian ambassador asked if she would ride out to Dulles to meet his son's plane. He knew that the young Giovanni was more than fond of her. They had met at a party at the American Embassy in Italy when Sabyl had lived there. He was handsome, charming and interesting. That evening at the party, he would not let Sabyl out of his sight. He was apparently enamored by the long-stemmed American beauty. Giovanni had called her the next day and asked if she would allow him to call on her. Sabyl wasn't ready for a relationship, knowing that she was vulnerable after such a short time after Gary's death. Plus, she knew the reputation of some European men. Marital fidelity was not their strong suit. She gently turned him down. Unaccustomed to being denied the pleasures of his presence, he set out to win her over—an exercise in futility. A year later Sabyl was gone—back to the U.S. to start her new life and her new company.

"Mr. Ambassador, I appreciate your thinking of me, but I'm afraid I will be working."

He replied, "I have not told you the time of his flight yet."

"Most overseas flights arrive at Dulles in the morning after an all-night flight. I really can't."

110

"He will be most disappointed. May he call you sometime during his visit?"

Sabyl was taken off guard. "Uh, I'm afraid my soon-to-be fiancé wouldn't approve."

"Your fiancé?"

"Yes."

The ambassador was silent for a moment. His voice went flat. "I'll tell Giovanni. I'm sure he will understand."

"Thank you, Mr. Ambassador. Again, thank you for calling."

They hung up. Sabyl sat back in her chair and sighed. She hoped he wouldn't call again. Perhaps his mind would be on more important things since the bombings.

She felt a twinge of guilt since Scott had not yet officially proposed to her, but she had a feeling that would come soon.

Dotty tapped on her door. "Come in."

"Here's the schedule you asked for. You look like you've just fought a battle."

"I have. But I think I won."

"Derrick will be here to look at your computer this afternoon."

"Good! Hope it's not anything serious."

"He's good. Jenny says he can fix anything."

"Well, he certainly did a good job on my website. I'm afraid I won't be here when he comes. I've got an appointment..."

"I know—your checkup. It'll be fine. I mean, it's been a year since you had breast cancer."

"Let's hope it continues to..."

"It will—I know it will."

Dotty plunked the mail on Sabyl's desk.

"We're getting calls for funerals."

"It was bound to happen after all these bombings."

"Yeah, the drivers are going to be busy. We may need to sub some limos again."

"Okay, bring me the info. Since I can't get into my computer, you'll have to print it out for me."

"Will do. Hey, did I tell you they're putting my new floor in Thursday?"

"This Thursday? Wow, that was fast. For D.C., that is."

"Yeah, I'm tickled pink. It's gonna stink like anything for a couple of days, though. You know...that glue they use."

"Why don't you come stay at my place? You can have the guest bedroom."

"Nah, I'll tough it out. But thanks for the offer. I'll just close off my bedroom door and open a window if I have to."

"So what about the drainage situation? They've got to fix that before there's another big rain."

"They said they'd be out tomorrow. The insurance guy really got on their case."

Sabyl had a gut feeling they were jerking her around. "Hope they get with it."

Dotty went back to her office muttering, "They'd better get it fixed. I'm not going through this again."

~ ~ ~

Professor Hickson drove up in his new Mercedes Cabriolet and parked in front of the Computer Science Building. He unfastened his seatbelt and looked up and saw Derrick standing at the entrance of the Tech Center.

Hickson's conscience kicked in a little, but not enough to keep him from enjoying his newfound wealth and to be able to lavish Eva with everything she desired.

The day Derrick told him about his software idea, Hickson asked if he could study it and kept the thumb drive, headed for his lab, inserted it and marveled at the genius of his young former student. Hickson then downloaded the software into his own computer, destroyed Derrick's, hacked into Derrick's computer and destroyed all files connected to the software and then headed for the patent office. Now Mar-Tech, the largest computer software company in the world, has bought it and the professor was set for life.

He opened the car door and got out, arranged his suit jacket and closed the door. He looked directly at Derrick and waved and headed for the Computer Science Building, smiling.

~ ~ ~

"Sorry, I'm late. NTSB faxed this over about an hour ago," Scott said as he handed out copies to Martz and Keefer and the other agents.

Keefer leaned forward and said, "What have you got?"

Scott sat down next to Martz. "Naturally, since all this has been happening during Christmas break, there were a lot of students on board."

"Yeah, so."

"Students from AU, UDC, Howard, GW and George Mason. All D.C. area schools. There were students from all of those universities on some of the flights, but there was only one university that had at least one student on all the flights."

"Who?"

"American University."

"So you're saying that there were students from other universities, of course, but in every instance, there was an AU student?"

"No wonder so many of the planes originated from D.C. All but one."

"You mean the one that blew up after taking off from New York? It had originated at D.C. as well."

"Yeah, I know. It was a layover. I'm talking about Rufus Merriweather's plane."

"We're not sure that one is related to the others."

"But he had two daughters who attended school here."

"Yes, but both went to Georgetown."

"Like I said, all but one."

"It's still worth checking out," said one of the agents from NSA.

"Yeah, it might be a connection; it might be a coincidence."

"Okay, so this tells us what? That someone has it in for AU?"

"Maybe a student at a rival school? The Eagles butchered the last three teams . . ."

"Maybe a student that has it in for his own classmates?"

"Pretty farfetched, but we don't have anything else to go on. We've only assumed so far that it's terrorists who are doing it."

"Here's something else to consider. AU has a substantial Jewish enrollment and even a curriculum on Jewish studies."

"So these could be hate crimes?"

"It's one more thing to think about."

Keefer said, "We'll try all leads. That's three of 'em. Go."

The agents stood, grabbed their overcoats and headed out the door.

~ ~ ~

Derrick parked his VW in front and walked into Martin Transportation.

Dotty looked up from her computer and saw him. "May I help you?"

"I'm here to look at a computer," he said.

"Oh, yes! You must be Jenny's friend."

"I'm Derrick," he said simply. Dotty got up with a grunt. "I'm Dotty Stevens, Sabyl's secretary." She led him into Sabyl's office. "It's this one."

"Any idea what the problem is?" he said, as he took his backpack off and laid it on the floor.

"She said it won't let her get into her files or get online..."

He turned it on and stared at the screen.

Dotty crossed her arms. "It turns on, but it won't let her..."

"Okay, I'll see what I can do."

114

"Thanks. I'll be right in there if you need me."

He ignored her and began typing something on the keyboard.

Frank came out of the accountant's office and saw a man sitting at Sabyl's desk. "What the..."

Before he could say anything further, Dotty said, "Whoa, Frank, it's okay! He's fixing Sabyl's computer."

Frank looked at him warily. "Okay," he said, still eyeing him. He turned and walked into Dotty's office. "What do we know about this guy?" he asked in a low tone. "There's some pretty sensitive information in there."

"He's Jenny's boyfriend. A real geek, as she calls him. Says he's a genius—says he can fix anything."

"Oh, yeah. He's the one who did our website."

"Right."

"I was just wondering, what about your floor?"

The drainage people are coming Tuesday."

"About time."

"Told Better Business about the last floor company too. They said they've had a lot of complaints. My insurance company won't be using them anymore."

"Great."

"Yeah. Just pray we don't have a deluge between now and then."

Just then, Sabyl drove up and parked in her private parking space. Derrick turned and looked out of the large tinted office window and watched as she let Beau out and put his leash on him. So that's Sabyl Martin, he thought.

He continued clacking on the keyboard. White letters appeared across a black screen.

Sabyl opened the door, and Beau went in and headed for Dotty's office, hoping for his usual treat she kept in her drawer. Sabyl stopped in her doorway, "Oh, you must be Derrick."

He stood and stretched his hand across the desk. "Derrick Blake," and sat back down.

"How does it look?"

"Not good. I'll have to take it with me."

"Oh, no," she groaned.

"I can probably have it back to you by tomorrow morning."

"Okay," she said, resigned.

"In the meantime, I'll leave this with you. You can at least check your email," he said, as he pulled a laptop out of his case. "I might even be able to download some files for you—tell me which ones are the most important—that you need today, and I'll see what I can do."

"Oh, that would be great. Thanks."

He sat down again, took a wire out of his bag, and attached it to the laptop and then to Sabyl's computer.

"The General File, if possible. That will get me set for today at least."

He clacked on the keyboard and Sabyl could hear it whirring.

"I'm no computer whiz, but it seems that if you can download the file onto another computer, that you'd be able to open it on mine…"

"Doesn't work that way," he said without looking up. He stood and picked up the computer and took it to his car.

CHAPTER SIXTEEN

Dotty left her house after letting in the men who were there to put in the new parquet tiles. She gave them instructions to be sure to call her when they were finished. "Don't leave until I come home and take a look at what you've done. I want to make sure it's right."

They agreed and got to work. Dotty got in her car and smiled to herself. That boss guy is pretty cute, she thought. She drove to the office, exasperated at the fact the drainage people never showed or returned her calls. She had a bad feeling in her gut about them and called her insurance company. They said they'd take care of it.

Upon arriving at the office, she went into Frank's office and turned on the TV and punched in the numbers for the Weather Channel. Rain was not expected until Monday. She breathed a sigh of relief.

~ ~ ~

His dark eyes squinted at the monitor. Frustrated at the shortness of time he had, he fumbled with the keys, making mistake after mistake.

Finally, he stood up and ran his fingers through his hair. Perhaps a short break would clear his head. He knew every trick in the book. Hacking into someone's email account wasn't usually a big deal, but Abdul had protected his cyberspace well.

After a drink of water and a splash of cold water on his face, he returned to his computer and resumed his task. Clattering on the keyboard, he was finally able to break in. "There it is," he said aloud in the quietness of his room. "I'm in." Not only was he hoping to find something interesting that would be of use to him, he realized that he just might have struck pay dirt.

~ ~ ~

The floodlights shining on the castle at the Smithsonian caused a red glow that made it look like a fairyland.

Five of Sabyl's limousines lined the block. The drivers stood around talking, swapping stories and keeping an eye on the massive clouds that were rolling in. All the drivers had large, black umbrellas they would use, if necessary, when their clients came out. They chatted about their wives and kids, the playoffs, the weather, and what they were going to get their kids for Christmas. But mostly, they talked about the bombings.

Tiny lights had been carefully hung on the edges of each umbrella over the festive tables in the courtyard in case some of the more warmly dressed attendees wished to sit outside, but the threatening weather caused all to stay in to enjoy the music. The stewards watched warily as the wind picked up and decided to close the umbrellas and tie them down.

Inside a string quartet played as the guests mingled. Attending the event were several dignitaries that had Secret Service protection. Their black Suburbans with U.S. government plates were parked across the street from Sabyl's limos. Their occupants waited patiently while their protectees enjoyed themselves at the event. Other Secret Service agents wore tuxedoes and blended in with the guests.

Rudy sat in his car and listened to the latest taped sermon that his father had sent him. He was concerned about his seventy-two-year-old father. A minister for more than forty years in Egypt, he was still preaching in Al-Kosheh. Rudy knew his father had been threatened several times, but he would not cease preaching the Gospel, even if it cost him his life.

"None of us are without sin," his father continued in his sermon. "Even the religious leaders of Jesus' day were puffed up with pride, a sin particularly grievous to our Lord. His word clearly tells us, 'God resists the proud, but gives grace to the humble.' I don't know about you, brothers and sisters, but I don't need God resisting me. I've got enough problems. I want Him on my side."

Rudy smiled. Father has not lost his sense of humor, he thought. The tape ended, and Rudy ejected it from the small cassette player he had bought on eBay and placed it in the small plastic case. He then turned on his car radio. The news station was reporting about the bombings. Rudy turned up the volume and listened carefully.

"...Investigators are unsure if the recent chatter is related to the bombings of airplanes, Amtrak and a private airplane owned by department store magnate, Rufus Merriweather. Investigators are trying to find out what caused the explosions and why no one is claiming responsibility for them. We will continue to keep you updated as news comes in to us. Stay tuned for more information on WMAL 630 AM, Washington's news station."

Rudy sighed deeply and bowed his head and prayed.

~ ~ ~

Dotty sat in one of her dining room chairs and kept her eyes glued to the bottom of the door like a cat watching a mouse hole. She had her weather radio by her side listening to the taped message repeating the same thing over and over.

"This is the National Oceanic and Atmospheric Administration. A band of showers stretching from Hagerstown, Maryland to Springfield, Virginia is passing through. The greatest concentration of rain is in the Washington, D.C. area. Stay tuned to NOAA Weather Radio with updates every fifteen minutes."

Her face knotted up. "Great. That's just great. I thought they said it wasn't supposed to rain until Monday."

Her phone rang. It was the boss that had just installed her new floors. "Dotty, this is Dan Johnson with Johnson Flooring and Tile. Are you watching the weather?"

"Of course, I am. And praying like crazy that it doesn't flood again. I shouldn't have let you guys lay my floors until after the drainage people did what they were supposed to do."

"I understand."

"But I just got tired of looking at that mess."

"Of course. I understand."

Dotty smiled as she remembered his kind face.

"I just wanted you to know that if you have any problems, we'll make it right. We're not going to leave you with a mess again."

"Are you serious? Are you for real? Service like that doesn't happen in D.C.!"

"Well, it does with my company."

"Well, that makes me feel a little better, but I still don't want to go through it again. Those drainage people have never gotten back with me, and here it is threatening rain again."

"I could come over and put some sandbags around your back door if you like. Would that help?"

"Uh, sure, if you've got some handy."

"We keep them around in case of emergencies. This seems to be a potentially heavy rain heading our way."

"Come on, then. And thank you for your kindness."

"See you in a few minutes."

Dotty hung up and smiled. "He's so nice. And cute! Woo-hoo!"

She rushed to her bathroom mirror and put on fresh makeup and fixed her hair.

~ ~ ~

A cold rain streaked down the window. Thunder skipped across the sky, an unusual sound in December. Derrick stared out the window of his tiny apartment on Macomb Avenue, paid for by his aging mother. The money would run out when she died, he knew.

He would have been set for life if…

He walked over to his desk and sat down at his computer. A smirk played about his mouth as he considered his plot. He was not aware of the time when he was at his computer. It sucked him into another world where he could travel anywhere, ask any questions, get amazing answers and learn whatever he needed—even how to murder someone. The possibilities were endless.

A knock came at his door. Derrick closed his laptop and stood up and stared at the door. He never had visitors and he didn't want any now. He walked slowly over to the door and looked through the peephole. It was Kyle.

He knocked again.

"What do you want?" Derrick yelled through the door.

"It's me, Kyle. I gotta talk to you."

"Not a good time, man."

"C'mon, man, I really need…"

Derrick opened the door an inch. "I said not a good time."

Kyle looked through the opening at the eye staring back at him. "I've got to talk to you."

"What's your problem, dude?"

"Something's up. Something big. And I've got to talk to somebody about it."

"Something big? Like what?"

"The bombings. I think I know who's doing them."

"You're crazy, man."

"No! I swear! I gotta talk to you—to somebody!"

Derrick sighed. "Go downstairs and wait in the lobby. I've got a lady friend in here," he lied. "I'll send her away. Then you can come up."

"Okay, thanks, man."

"Yeah." He closed the door.

Kyle turned and headed for the elevator.

Derrick quickly pulled the corkboard above his computer off the wall and shoved it under his bed.

Kyle got off the elevator, walked across the lobby and sat down on a chair by a large potted palm tree. The desk clerk ignored him and continued reading the paper.

He hoped it wasn't Jenny that was with him. She's a nice girl, he thought. I wonder what she sees in him. At first, he thought it was pretty cool that his boss was dating his sister's best friend, but Derrick's behavior had changed so much—he had become almost morbid lately. He wasn't sure he liked Jenny being around him anymore.

Fifteen minutes passed. A young woman stepped off the elevator and went out the front door. Maybe that was his lady friend, Kyle thought. She doesn't seem his type. In fact, nobody seems his type. Wonder if Jenny knows about this?

A buzzer rang at the front desk. The man looked at Kyle and said, "Mr. Blake said you can go up now."

Kyle thanked him and got on the elevator and pushed the button for the fifth floor. It slowly rose and stopped with a jolt, and the marked-up doors opened. He stepped out into the dimly lit hallway and walked to Derrick's apartment.

Derrick opened the door and stood aside. "You picked a heck of a time to come calling."

"Sorry, man, but this is important."

Derrick gestured for Kyle to sit. He flopped down on the sofa. Derrick sat across from him in an overstuffed leather chair.

"Nice place."

"Thanks. Now make it snappy. My girl is coming back in half an hour."

"Thought you were dating Jenny," Kyle said wryly.

"Okay, so you caught me. Jenny and I aren't engaged or anything, so what's the big deal?"

"She likes you a lot."

"And I like her, but I'm not really into…"

"Okay, so…"

"What do you want, dude?"

"I think I know who's doing the bombings."

Derrick stared at him, crossed his legs at the ankle and spread his hands across the rounded arms of the chair. "Is that so? Who?"

"Abdul."

"Abdul?" Derrick threw his head back and laughed loudly.

"What's so funny?"

"Abdul couldn't find his rear end with both hands, much less put a bomb together."

"He's gotta be the one—I'm sure he's a sleeper."

"Why? Because he's Middle Eastern?"

"Because he was detained at the first of the year and he hasn't gotten over it. He's got it in for the school and some of the students who avoid him now and for the government."

"And how did he get the bombs aboard the planes?"

"I don't know. He probably has helpers. You know, operatives."

"You're crazy."

"Am I?"

"So what do you plan to do with this revelation?"

"I don't know. That's why I came to you. You're close to Abdul."

"Nobody's close to Abdul. He's a loner."

"All the more reason to suspect him."

"I'm a loner too. Do you suspect me?"

"No, of course not—"

"And what if you're wrong?"

"Doesn't it strike you as being pretty amazing that on every one of those crashes there was an AU student?"

"There were a lot of students aboard those flights from lots of different schools. It's Christmas vacation. Everybody travels—"

"But..."

Derrick picked up a newspaper and threw it on the coffee table in front of Kyle. "What about this?"

The headlines read: CHAIN STORE MAGNANT'S PLANE BOMBED

"No AU student involved there."

Kyle picked it up and read the first paragraph:

Washington Post: The founder and CEO of Bassinger's Department Stores was killed when his Gulfstream V exploded in midair last evening, investigators say. His wife and two daughters, both students at Georgetown University, also died in the blast.

He put the paper back down and pulled some papers out of his pocket and unfolded them. "What about these?" He handed them to Derrick.

"What's this?" he said, taking them.

"I hacked into Abdul's computer—into his email. Read some of those and tell me he isn't the bomber."

Derrick leaned forward in his chair and read. After reading a few of the printed out emails, he folded them back up and handed them to Kyle. "This doesn't make him out to be anything except a disgruntled Middle Easterner who's homesick for his family."

"You don't think his words are a little strong?"

"He might be mad about being detained, but he's worked through it."

"How do you know? He's not exactly going to tell you he's..."

"Give it up, dude."

"How come you've been in such a rotten mood lately? I can't even have a discussion with you anymore without you biting my head off. I asked you about your program that you were so excited about and you...what's up with that?"

Derrick looked away for a few moments, then back at Kyle. "Look, dude, it's been stolen, okay?"

"Stolen? By who?"

Derrick's eyes grew cold. "Hickson."

"Professor Hickson? Are you serious?"

Derrick squinted his eyes into slits. "I'm dead serious."

"Geez, man. Have you reported it? To the dean?"

Derrick laughed cynically. "Yeah."

"So what happened?"

"Nothing. The professor has friends."

"What about the law?"

"I can't prove anything. He took my data, hacked into my computer and took all the files pertaining to it."

"You don't have it backed up anywhere else?"

"Yeah, parts of it, but he got into my files and changed all the dates on it to make it look like he came up with it first and then by the time I called the cops, he had already put it in the hands of Mar-Tech."

"Mar-Tech? Geez, they're the biggest..."

"Tell me about it."

"How much is the program worth?"

"Millions."

"But surely..."

"Time's up, pal. My girlfriend will be back any minute."

"So what should I do about Abdul?"

"Nothing. Unless you want to make a complete fool of yourself."

Kyle stood slowly and stared at Derrick. "I still say..."

"Save it, man. Leave the gumshoeing to the NTSB."

"Okay. Thanks, man. Sorry if I screwed up your date."

"No problem. Go and have a nice Christmas drink. It'll make you feel better."

"Sure. Thanks."

Derrick opened the door. Kyle just stood there.

"Go, dude."

Kyle stepped out into the hall and heard the door close behind him.

Derrick exhaled, went back to the bedroom, pulled out the corkboard and hung it back on the wall and sat down at his computer.

CHAPTER SEVENTEEN

Rudy pulled up to the curb in front of the two-story brick house in northwest D.C. He saw a distinguished looking man kiss a blond woman goodbye and watched him walk out toward the limousine.

Rudy quickly got out and took the man's luggage, an overnighter, and placed it in the trunk. The man stepped in and laid his briefcase beside him and fastened his seat belt.

Rudy settled in behind the steering wheel and headed toward Reagan National airport.

After crossing the Fourteenth Street Bridge and onto the George Washington Parkway, Rudy saw nothing but a sea of brake lights.

His passenger looked at his watch, sat forward and pleaded, "Please tell me this traffic will break up soon."

"It is hard to say, sir," Rudy answered with a note of sympathy in his voice.

Ted shoved back against the seat and threw his hands up. "Oh, this is just great. Just great!"

The traffic was at a standstill for ten minutes.

Rudy watched his passenger in the rearview mirror.

Ted was cursing under his breath and fidgety. He leaned forward and looked ahead several times as though it would get the traffic moving. Finally, he decided to do a little work. He opened his laptop and turned it on.

~ ~ ~

"Frank, you're staring at me like something is coming out of my nose."

He frowned. "Not your nose. Your eyes look like two holes burned in a blanket. Were you up all night?"

"Yeah, babysitting my dining room floor."

"Oh, hey, how'd that go?"

"Fine! The worst of the rain stayed to the north, around Sabyl's neighborhood." She wasn't about to tell him about Dan Johnson coming over to help. She'd never hear the end of it.

"So what's going on with your drainage thing? That guy ever call you?" He hoped he hadn't pushed a button that would put her back in a snit.

"Nope. And here it is raining."

"Well, it's supposed to stop around noon and clear up and then it might rain again tonight." He quickly added, "But maybe it won't flood your floor again."

"I've decided I'm not going to worry about it. If the insurance company wants to keep putting new floors in for me, fine. Of course, then they'll probably raise my premiums. I'll probably turn into an addict from sniffing that glue they use to put down those tiles. You guys can come visit me in the detox center." She got up from her desk with a grunt. "Well, I'm off to the Eastern Shore to pick up Mary for the holidays." Dotty snatched her coat off the coat rack and stopped by Sabyl's office. "I'm outa here, boss."

Sabyl looked up and smiled. "Have a good trip, dear."

"Will do. Just hope I can keep my eyes open."

Sabyl stood up and walked around to the front of her desk. "Wait a minute. Your eyes do look tired."

"Yeah, I just told Frank, I was up watching my floor all night."

"Dotty, I can't have you driving clear over to the Eastern Shore when you've had no sleep. I'm sending you over in a limo."

"Are you serious?"

Sabyl picked up the phone and buzzed Frank. "Frank, do we have any drivers who aren't busy? Ken? Okay, great. Send him around with a car, will you?"

"Sabyl! I can't..."

"Nonsense. It'll be one of your Christmas presents." She hugged her shoulder. "Now go."

"Well, I do feel pretty dysfunctional. Hey! You just put the fun in dysfunction!" She smiled and whispered, "You're the best."

"So are you, dear. Now go get my girl." Dotty went out and climbed into an extended sedan, and Ken closed the door and got in the driver's seat, slipped it in gear and drove off, happy to have something to do. Dotty sat back in the luxurious seat and smiled at the driver. "Wow! This thing is as big as an aircraft carrier!"

Ken smiled back at her in the rearview mirror. "Yes, mum."

~ ~ ~

The quietness of the afternoon was a rare treat for Sabyl. She regarded it as a gift and treated it as such. She was determined to make the best of it—to catch up on some emails and paperwork and to finish up in time to leave early enough to do some Christmas shopping. She couldn't wait to see Mary. She always loved coming to D.C. for a visit. Sabyl had some special plans for her "favorite girl" and couldn't wait to take her to their special place, a luxury spa in downtown Washington.

Sabyl was trying to get her ducks in a row so she could leave to go to her country place in Pennsylvania for the weekend. Her home in Fairview was maintained by a couple, Jerry and Kate, who had worked for her for years and had become good friends. They lovingly kept the house immaculate and her yard perfectly groomed. Sabyl rarely enjoyed Christmas parties, but Jerry and Kate's was always fun with Jerry's sense of humor keeping everyone laughing. She could use a good laugh, and she definitely needed some good downtime.

Her cell phone chirped. "Hi, babe."

"Scott! How are you?"

"I'm fine. Look, I may not be able to make it to your office party. You know how pressed we are."

Sabyl's heart sank. "Oh, of course, I understand," she said, unable to hide the disappointment in her voice.

"I'm so sorry, babe, but…"

"That's okay, I know you can't help it. Is everything going okay? I mean…"

"Can't talk about it, but yeah."

"Are you getting any sleep at all?"

"Not much, but I'm not the only one."

"I'm praying for you, sweetheart."

"I know. I can feel your prayers. I miss you, angel face."

"I miss you, too."

"Look, I gotta go. I'll call you when I can."

"Scott, I'm going to Pennsylvania for the weekend. You have my phone number up there."

"And you have mine, for emergencies only, of course."

"Of course."

"Love you, babe."

They hung up. Sabyl sat there for a few moments and then sighed and opened the laptop Derrick had left for her.

~ ~ ~

Barbara's doctor walked in with a huge smile on his face. "Well, young lady, I think you can go home. You've responded well to treatment, and I'm pleased with the latest lab reports, so it looks like you can be home by this afternoon."

"Oh, how wonderful! Thank you, doctor!"

"Praise the Lord!" Helen said, lifting both her hands toward heaven.

The doctor turned to her and smiled, "Amen!" He turned back to Barbara. "Is your husband around or do you need to call him?"

"No, he's here, but he stepped out for a few minutes. He'll be so happy to hear this!"

"Well, the nurse will be in shortly with some papers for you to sign. Keep an eye on your blood pressure and no more donuts!"

Helen spoke up. "Don't worry, doctor. I'll make sure she's a good girl."

Barbara smiled. "I have my own private nurse, doctor."

"So I've heard." He turned to Helen. "I'll bet you thought your nursing days were over. I'm counting on you to take care of my patient."

Helen smiled. "Don't you worry. I've been looking after her for a very long time."

"Great!" He turned back to Barbara. "The nurse will be in shortly. If you have any questions at all, just ask her, and I hope to see you back here in a couple of weeks from now when you're full term. If I don't see you before then, have a happy holiday."

"Merry Christmas," Helen retorted. "It's all about Christ. It's not about the holidays!"

The doctor smiled and said, "Yes. Have a good one." He turned and left.

Helen mumbled, "What's the matter with these people? Can't say, 'Merry Christmas.'"

"I know, Mama."

A few minutes later Frank walked in with a Styrofoam cup of coffee in one hand and a magazine in the other.

Barbara told him what the doctor had said. He put down his coffee and magazine and leaned over and kissed his wife on the top of her head. "Thank God," he said. "We can go home."

~ ~ ~

Karen was sitting at Frank's desk taking calls and checking his computer to see if there were any repeat clients. Satisfied that everything was okay, she started working on log sheets. On the first ring, she answered the phone and sat frozen, staring wide-eyed at Sabyl's office door. With trembling hands, she took down the information that was being given to her and croaked a weak, "Thank you," and hung up. She walked slowly to her bosses' office and knocked gently.

"Come in." Sabyl looked up. Seeing the strange look on Karen's face, she asked, "What?"

Karen couldn't get the words out. "That was…was…"

Sabyl stood up. "What!"

"Rudy's car, like, like…blew up!"

Sabyl fought for air. "What do you mean, blew up? Where is he?" She grabbed the piece of paper out of Karen's hand and read a phone number.

"It was the police… they gave me that number…"

Sabyl sat back down and quickly punched in the number.

A voice answered, "City Morgue."

~ ~ ~

The atmosphere in the small apartment was dark and damp. The dusty blinds were mostly closed, letting in little light as the overcast sky remained over the capital city. One dimly lit lamp was on a table by the sofa and another on his desk. The TV was set on CNN but the sound was muted. The icemaker clattered in the refrigerator. Muffled voices of his next-door neighbors could be heard through the wall. An ambulance siren howled on the street below as it passed his building. Squeaky brakes on a utility truck joined the traffic sounds.

He opened his laptop and turned it on. It whirred and clicked gently as it came to life. The familiar desktop appeared on the screen. He clicked on an icon and opened his email. He sat back in his chair and took a sip of lukewarm coffee. When his emails appeared, he scanned the inbox. An email from his mother. He started to open it but decided he would read it later. Right now, he had business to tend to.

The cursor blinked steadily beside a name on a list. He began to shake each time he sent the email entitled, "AN URGENT MESSAGE FROM YOUR PROFESSOR." Strangely enough, his hands were completely steady when putting the bombs together.

~ ~ ~

When Sabyl heard the voice answer, 'City Morgue,' she slammed down the phone and looked at Karen. "There must be some mistake. That was the City Morgue!" Karen was speechless. Sabyl quickly ran past her into Frank's office, snatched up the remote on the corner of his desk and punched the 'On' button. The wall-mounted television screen came to life on the Fox News Channel. An aerial view of a charred limousine with smoke billowing out of it slapped her in the face. "No! No, that can't be Rudy's car. How would they know it was Rudy's car?" she asked the television.

Karen stood in the doorway. "Sabyl, you want me to call somebody? Frank? Dotty? Scott?"

"No. I just need a minute to get my thoughts together." She sat down at Frank's desk, quickly grabbed his mouse and clicked on the Ground Transportation Program (GTP) icon to see who Rudy was driving and his destination. "Ted Hickson!" she said out loud. "To Reagan National. Oh, God! The explosion happened on that route! Oh, God, Karen!"

Karen stared at her, feeling helpless. She then said, "I know! Call the police and find out why they think it was, like, Rudy's car!"

"Yes! Good idea!" She quickly dialed the number for the Metro Police. "Let me speak with Max Hawks! Please! It's an emergency!"

The voice on the other end told her the chief was not in. "Never mind! I have his cell number." She turned to Karen. "Quick! Go get my cell phone out of my pocketbook!"

"Right!"

In the meantime, Sabyl clicked on the GPS icon. Rudy's car did not show up at all on the radar screen. Tears welled up in her eyes. She whispered, "God, please let Rudy be okay."

Karen grabbed Sabyl's pocketbook and took it to her. "I don't want to go through your purse."

Sabyl took it, pulled her cell phone out and scrolled down to her friend, the Chief of Police's cell number and, with trembling hands, punched 'Call.'

A gruff voice answered.

"Max! It's Sabyl! They called my office and told me the car that exploded was Rudy's car! I'm looking at the pictures on TV. There's nothing left of it! How could they possibly know it was his car?"

Max Hawks could hear the near panic in her voice. "Did my office call you?"

"Yes," she sobbed. "They gave me the number for the City Morgue!"

"God, I'm sorry, Sabyl. Have you called them yet?"

"Yes. No. I…I hung up. I thought it was a mistake. It is a mistake, isn't it, Max? I know it!"

"Sabyl, I just arrived on the scene. I was on my way back from Baltimore when I got the call. Hold on a minute."

Sabyl stared at the black, mangled carcass of the limousine, the tires still burning.

"Sabyl, are you there?"

"Yes!"

"The license plate was blown off. It's intact. It's registered under the name of Ramose Abana. Is that Rudy's real name?"

"Oh, God."

"Did he have a passenger in the car?"

"Yes! He was taking a man to National."

"Who, Sabyl? What man?"

"Ted Hickson, a professor at American University."

"Rudy was, uh, is a big man, but it's hard to tell, you know…" His voice trailed off. "Wait a minute, I'm getting something. Hold on."

She grabbed a tissue and blew her nose. She had to control her thinking.

"Yes. The ambulance has already taken the remains to the morgue. Sabyl, I have to go. I'll call you if I find out anything. I'm…I'm truly…sorry."

"Thanks," she said weakly. She stood slowly and went back to her desk and dialed the number to the City Morgue.

"Hello?" The voice continued. "Hello?"

"I, uh, was given this phone number by the police. I'm calling about Ramose Abana. Is he...I mean...he's not there, is he?" She could feel her heart thumping, sure the person on the end of the line could hear it too.

"I'm sorry, ma'am, the name again?"

"Ramose Abana! I know he's not there. He can't be!"

"When would he have been brought in, ma'am?"

Sabyl's face flushed. "There was a car explosion. It's...it's on the news. Please, can't you tell me something?"

"We're not sure of the identity of the person that was brought in yet, ma'am."

"Person? There was only one person?"

"Yes, ma'am. There was only one person in the car."

"Was it the driver? Or the passenger?"

"I have no way of knowing that, ma'am."

Through the long window, Sabyl saw a taxi pull up onto the brick circle drive. Rudy got out and walked toward the front door. She dropped the phone and ran out of her office and threw her arms around him. "Rudy! You're...you're..."

"Alive! Yes! Praise God!"

"What...how...?"

"Traffic was backed up really bad. My passenger was anxious about possibly missing his flight. I got out to see what was holding things up. I heard the explosion. My passenger...my car..." He shook his head woefully.

"Oh, Rudy, how horrible! But thank God you're safe!"

They walked arm-in-arm toward the door. Karen opened the door and squealed like a ten-year-old at a birthday party. "Rudy! You're not, like, dead!"

"No, I'm not," Rudy grinned.

"Sabyl, your cell phone rang, I answered it," she said, handing it to her. "Hope you don't, like, mind."

Sabyl smiled and took it from her. "No, I don't mind." She put the phone to her ear. "Sabyl Martin."

The voice was Max Hawks. "Sabyl, good news. Rudy's alive. He was in shock for several minutes before he could talk to one of my officers, but he's..."

"I know, Max! He's here!"

CHAPTER EIGHTEEN

"Another bomb and we've got nothing! This time a limousine! What the heck is going on?" Keefer rubbed the back of his neck in frustration.

"And another American University connection. Hickson was a professor at AU."

"None of it adds up," Martz said. He turned to Scott. "Wasn't that one of Sabyl's limos, Scott?"

"Yes, it was. One of Sabyl's favorite and most faithful drivers, Rudy, escaped being killed because of a traffic jam. He got out to see what the holdup was and..." He pushed back from the table and stood up. "What's the common denominator here? I mean besides the AU link, which doesn't completely add up."

"I don't know," Keefer answered, "but we're going to find out. I want a report from the forensic investigators who have been working on the remains of the limo. I want to know what the cause of the explosion was and I want it pronto."

"Yes, sir." They grabbed their coats and exited the building.

~ ~ ~

Secretary of Homeland Security John Killian left a meeting with the President and was now at the Capitol building working his way through the corridors of the House of Representatives to meet with the House Intelligence Committee. His broad shoulders and thick chest still conveyed his Marine Corps years.

The news media began gathering like early arrivals at a yard sale. Several reporters stuck microphones in his face. One asked if the various agencies were working together. "I assure you, we are in sync," he said through his teeth, and then disappeared behind Congressman Allen Teleman's office door. A very large, very serious Secret Service agent stood between them and the door. The press got the hint and headed down the corridor looking for another victim.

Representative Teleman, Congressman from Iowa, worked alongside Senator Tucker Shelton, Chairman of the Taskforce to Combat Domestic and International Terrorism (TCDIT). Shelton, known as "The Warlord of Capitol Hill," was in no mood for political posturing. He knew that would not come from Secretary Killian, but there were some congressmen in the room that loved to politicize everything. He knew he would have to keep his temper on a short leash.

He unbuttoned his suit jacket and sat down. An aide brought in coffee and bottled water and quickly left the room.

Teleman cleared his voice. "Alright, John, where are we in this mess?"

The beleaguered Secretary loosened his tie and began filling them in on the new task force, how well they were working together and how he hoped to have some answers soon.

One of the committee members spoke up. "In other words, you have nothing to report except what we already know, is that right?"

"We are waiting for reports from the NTSB. They're working as quickly as they can to piece together something that will take us to some solid answers."

Shelton spoke. "What about you, John? How was your meeting with the president?"

"He wants answers, and he wants them yesterday."

"Don't we all," chimed in Senator Lyle Betts from North Carolina. "So what are we supposed to do? Sit around like a bunch of jacklegs waitin' for the next plane to blow up? I'm getting' hammered by my constituents back home wantin' answers!"

"We all are," answered Killian, "but we can't give answers we don't have."

"Yet," Teleman injected. "The answers will come, Lyle."

"Well, we'd danged better get some soon. Or I just might have to bring your behind up before a committee."

"Is that a threat, Betts?"

Teleman stood up "Gentlemen! We don't need to fight among ourselves. That's the last thing we need. We're here to work together!"

Senator Betts folded his arms tightly across his chest and said, "When we have somethin' to work with!"

Killian said, "Look, we're all on edge. But we've got the best of the best working on this thing."

Betts sputtered, "Yeah, the best of the best. Ha!"

Shelton could feel his temper rising. His face turned crimson and his blood pressure felt like it would take his head off. He stood up and announced, "This is a waste of time. I've got work to do. And I suggest you do the same." With that, he left. His protector fell in step with him as they headed toward the exit.

~ ~ ~

The grandfather clock downstairs chimed four gentle bongs in agreement with the red numbers on the digital clock on the bedside table. Barbara turned on her right side and pulled the cover over her arm and realized she had been awakened by strange pains in her lower abdomen. She tried to go back to sleep. The central heat came on. Frank's snoring was not as bad as it used to be when he drank. She was grateful for that.

There it was again. Could it be labor? No. Surely it wouldn't feel like this. Her mother had told her that labor felt like bad menstrual cramps. These were just little twinges. There was another one. She wondered, Should I wake Frank? No. Poor guy is already nervous; no point in worrying him needlessly if it turns out to be nothing. She fluffed her pillow and looked at the red digital numbers on the clock and took a deep breath. Maybe I'd better time them just in case.

~ ~ ~

As Sabyl drove to the office earlier, before heading out of town, she peered up at the sky that looked like it had come straight out of a Thomas Moran painting. But she could see where several aircraft in early morning flights had marked up the sky like a child marks up a wall. The dawning sun cast a pink and yellow glaze on the Capitol dome. "Our beautiful Capitol," she half whispered to herself. Would the terrorists try another Nine/Eleven-type scenario?

Terrorists like Al Qaeda were usually determined to finish what they started. It was a well-known consensus that Flight 93 that went down in Pennsylvania was meant for the White House or the Capitol Building. But the hijackers were unable to carry out their abomination because of the heroic acts of those brave passengers. What kind of havoc would that have caused, she wondered? Tom Clancy had written about just such a scenario—only in his story, all of Congress, the Joint Chiefs, the Supreme Court Justices, the Vice President, and the President were assembled together for the

President's State of the Union address. A disgruntled Japanese pilot flew his plane into the building, killing all but Clancy's hero of several of his books, Jack Ryan, who was detained for some reason in the tunnel that takes them into the House chamber. She couldn't remember what detained him; only that he was the only one left alive.

She was sure that Scott and all government agents knew of that scenario and shuddered. The F-16's that were now in place patrolling the D.C. skies made her feel somewhat better. Still, if all the big wigs were gathered together in one place—all politely sitting listening to the president's State of the Union address, who would the control tower call for permission to shoot down an incoming plane that breached D.C's airspace? As slowly as the U.S. government worked, by the time it went through the proper channels, it would be too late. She assumed the feds had it all worked out...or at least she hoped so. But who would make that decision? The Attorney General? Wasn't he usually at those addresses? Secretary of State? Defense? Weren't all of the President's cabinet members seated in that room? Then who? She remembered that a designated survivor would be sworn to secrecy and taken to some safe place. Would he or she be the one to make that call? She would ask Scott the next time she saw him. She sighed and wondered when that would be.

Since September 11, 2001, a few congressional leaders, representing both parties, have also been chosen to stay at home and watch the SOTU on TV...just in case.

Sabyl pulled into the circle drive at her office and went inside to grab some paperwork she wanted to take with her. She walked down to the garage, found it empty, headed back to her car and left for Pennsylvania.

Beau as he looked out the window at the passing cars. Sabyl finally began to relax as she thought of spending a quiet weekend in her country home in Fairview in the house where she was born. Well, quiet except for the party tonight. I wonder what I should wear.

A wet leaf that was caught in the wiper blade fluttered against the windshield like a tiny orange bat wing trying to escape the jaws of the rubber and metal monster. She was enjoying listening to her favorite tenor, Andrea Bocelli when the Bluetooth connection to her cell phone interrupted the music and announced an incoming call.

"Hey, Karen, what's up?"

"Guess what! Frank's at the hospital with Barbara. She, like, went into labor last night."

"Oh, wow, that's wonderful! Thanks for letting me know."

"Okay, I'll call you as soon as I, like, hear anything else."

"Great. Thanks, dear."

The call ended and she wished she had asked what hospital they had gone to. I'll ask her when she calls back. Maybe I should turn around and go back. No, I'll wait and see what happens. It might be a false alarm.

As soon as she turned onto the Pennsylvania Turnpike, she got another call.

"Frank! Karen told me Barbara went into labor."

"It's a girl!"

"What? Already? Oh, Frank, that's wonderful! When?"

"About a half hour ago."

"Is everybody okay?"

"Yes, everybody is okay. Sabyl, she's beautiful."

"I can't wait to see her. I'm on my way to Pennsylvania, but I can turn around and come back. Which hospital?"

"No, you go on. You can see her when you get back on Monday. She'll be home by then."

"Well, okay, I'll see her as soon as I get back."

"Great!"

"Congratulations! You're a daddy! I'm so happy for you!"

"Do you want me to come in today?"

"No, of course not. You stay there with Barbara and take as much time as you need. Karen can look after things."

"Okay, thanks, Sabyl."

"What did you name your little daughter?"

He lowered his voice. "We named her after you."

Tears came to her eyes. "Oh, Frank, are you serious? You named her after me?" She grabbed a tissue out of her pocketbook. "I don't know what to say! That's so dear!"

"Yep. We named her Sabyl Lynn. You mean a lot to us, Sabe. I mean, all you've done for me…you've bailed me out so many times…"

"Well, you're worth it, Frank. You'd have done the same for me." She could hear him blow his nose. "Thanks for letting me know. I'll see you soon. God bless you. Give my love to Barbara."

Just then another call interrupted Bocelli. It was Scott. "Babe, have you left town yet?"

"Yes. I'm on 270 heading for Pennsylvania. Why?"

"I need to interview Rudy. Martz and I are coming by your office. Do you think he's there?"

"Oh, blast. I'll miss seeing you! Not sure if he's there or not. If not, I know he'll be happy to come to you if need be. Here's his cell number."

"I have it."

She wished she hadn't been in such a hurry to leave town. "Oh, honey, I'm so sorry I'm going to miss seeing you."

"Yeah, me too. Guess we'll just have to wait a little longer…until we get this thing to come to an end…"

"I hope it's soon."

"So do I. When you get to Pennsylvania, will you stay in tonight?"

"No, I'm going to a Christmas party at the home of Jerry and Kate, you know, the couple that takes care of my place when I'm out of town."

"Oh, sure. I remember them. I hope you have a good time. Will you be late?"

"Probably not. I should be home by 8:30 or 9:00."

"Okay. Keep your doors locked and stay safe, okay?"

"Okay. You sound worried. Is everything alright?"

"Yes, I'm sure it is. Just want you to be okay." He couldn't help but think of what happened to her last year.

"I'll be fine. I hope you're getting some rest."

"Not much, but I'm okay. I need to go. Love you, babe."

~ ~ ~

Rudy was glad it was Scott that was sent to interview him. He had already been questioned by the police and was ready and willing to help the authorities get to the bottom of these acts of terror as soon as possible.

Scott looked sympathetically at Rudy, knowing the strain of losing his client, his car and his peace of mind with an act of terrorism hitting so close to him once again. He remembered the look of fear on Rudy's face last year when the terrorists had kidnapped his son. And now the same type of evil was knocking at his door once again.

Scott shook Rudy's hand and said, "It's good to see you again, my friend."

"You as well, Mr. Scott. Too bad it has to be under these circumstances."

"Yes, I agree. Where can we talk?"

"We can go into Sabyl's office." He opened the door and turned on the light, and the two sat in the overstuffed chairs across from her desk.

Her scent was still in the room. "Rudy, tell me everything you can about that day."

Rudy took a deep breath and leaned forward, both elbows on his knees. "I'm afraid there's not much to tell," he began. "I picked up Professor Hickson at his home at precisely 8 a.m. and began making my way towards Reagan National."

"What was Professor Hickson's demeanor? Do you remember? Was he relaxed? Was he friendly? Did he seem nervous…anything like that?"

"He seemed perfectly fine until the traffic slowed to a stop. After not moving for about ten minutes, he began to get fidgety and demanded that I get out of the car and go and investigate what the problem was. I wanted to argue with him and tell him that it would do no good, but Sabyl won't allow us to argue with the clients, so I got out and did as I was told."

"Thank God. It saved your life. What was the last thing you remember before leaving Hickson?"

"I can't remember anything else. All I remember is, I walked about forty yards up the road and saw that there was nothing I could see that would explain the reason for the traffic jam, so I headed back toward my car and all of a sudden, BOOM!"

"Did you realize immediately that it was your car?"

"No. I couldn't see anything but smoke and fire. The cars beside mine and in front of it were also on fire. The occupants were getting out of their vehicles fast. One lady's coat sleeve was on fire and another driver jumped out of his car and helped put the fire out, and by then, there was so much confusion that it took me several minutes to realize that it was my car that had exploded."

"What did you do then, Rudy?"

"I...I'm not sure. I was so shocked and dazed that I couldn't think. It was like a bad dream. I think I yelled at some people, asking if they saw a man get out of my car. Nobody seemed to know. How could this have happened, Mr. Scott? Why are all these terrible bombings happening? Are they targeting us again? Why my car? Why would anyone want to harm Professor Hickson?"

"I don't know yet, Rudy. But we're going to find out."

Suddenly it occurred to Scott that maybe the terrorists were after Rudy again. If that's the case, they would be after Sabyl as well. But all the bombings...it just didn't add up.

CHAPTER NINETEEN

The rarified atmosphere of Washington, D.C. had changed in some ways, but despite the unnerving terrorist activities that dominated the news and were at the center of everyone's thoughts and conversations, life went on as usual. In stark contrast to the ever-present news helicopters, flags at half-mast and protesters braving the cold to demonstrate, the nation's capital was still starting to look a lot like Christmas.

Wreaths hung on street lamps, Salvation Army's bell ringers were out in full force, and shoppers scurried from one store to the next, hunting the best bargains. Certain embassies were decorated with Christmas lights and greenery draped over their gates. The city hosts 176 foreign embassies as well as many international organizations, trade unions, lobbying groups, and professional associations. It was easy to see which nations believed in the celebration of Christ's birth and which ones did not, simply by the display or absence of wreaths and garlands on their embassy doors.

Hoping that the past inconsistencies of airport security had vastly improved, nervous passengers still boarded planes, realizing that life must go on, hoping theirs would go on, and that they would arrive safely at their destinations. They would not be denied their freedoms. Terrorism had hit home. Again.

It had only been a year since the assassinations of three of America's top government leaders had the nation's capital on lockdown. And now the bombings were, once again, bringing to mind that this sort of thing just isn't supposed to happen here in the Land of the Free.

Powerful institutions of democracy were placing enormous pressure on, not only the investigative agencies, to get to the bottom of the bombings, but on governments around the world to hand over any and all information they may have regarding their intelligence gathering. Some would comply, some would not, leaving more questions and distrust in the minds of the investigators and some politicians, all of which gave fresh fodder to the media, whose stories were fed from national and international networks around the world.

Avid soap opera viewers wearied of having to miss another one of their episodes as breaking news of the bombings trumped their programs.

Weary of the world's tragedies being reported continually, Frank muted the wall-mounted TV he had been watching in the small hospital room, keeping the volume low while his wife slept. She had come through childbirth just fine, but the doctor said he wanted to keep an eye on her blood pressure for the next few days. Frank was grateful she would be able to go home tomorrow and they promised to monitor her BP there.

He gazed down at his baby daughter lying on his lap, her tiny body wrapped in a white blanket. She had long delicate fingers and a full head of hair. The nurses had even put a little pink bow in it. Her tiny features exhibited his strong chin and her mother's nose and dimples, rendering a beautiful portrait of the oneness of their love. He had never seen anything so beautiful in his life.

Barbara snored softly in much needed sleep after giving birth and being relieved of the perfect little burden she had been carrying for almost nine months.

Frank looked up at the television. It was muted, but the pictures screamed loud and clear that terrorism was once again the center of attention at a time when most people would be thinking of finishing their shopping or looking for new recipes to try out on their families as they anticipated their arrivals for Christmas.

He had heard about Rudy's car. They had talked on the phone a couple of times. It unnerved him to the core. He couldn't help but wonder what the world would be like when little Sabyl Lynn grew up. The thought of it brought an ache to his heart like nothing he had ever known. The burden of responsibility of keeping her safe weighed heavily on him. He took his eyes away from the TV and back to his infant. *God, if you're real, you're going to have to help me. I don't think I can do this by myself.*

He remembered seeing a Bible in the drawer of her bedside table. Careful not to disturb little Sabyl Lynn, he reached over and opened the drawer and drew out the soft covered Bible placed there by the Gideons. He opened it and began to read. It fell open to Ephesians 2:8 *"For by grace are ye saved through faith; and that not of yourselves: it is the gift of God."*

He felt a warmth in his chest like a throbbing, glowing ember. He bowed his head and whispered, "Lord, I have not paid much attention to You. In fact, I've pretty much shut You out of my life and I'm sorry for that. Please forgive me for all I've done wrong. I need this grace I just read about and I wonder if You have some extra for me. I don't deserve it but I sure could use Your help. I believe in Your Son and I need Him in my life. Please help me to live a better life and help me to be a good dad. Amen."

A new kind of love washed through his body. He never felt so clean in his life. He sat quietly for a few minutes and let the tears come. "Oh, God, why did I wait so long? Thank You...thank You."

His mother-in-law, Helen, had been listening at the door. She walked in and quietly said, "Praise the Lord. I've been praying for this day for years." She bent down and hugged him tightly, wiped his tears with her thumb and said, "Welcome to the family of God, son."

~ ~ ~

Sabyl plugged in the Christmas tree lights that Jerry and Kate had put up for her as she stretched her long legs and wiggled her toes in front of the crackling fireplace, glad to be out of the cramped, albeit fashionably hot boots she had worn to Jerry and Kate's Christmas party. The evening had been fun. Kate had gone all out in decorating their small home and had clearly put a lot of time in creating various kinds of hors d'oeuvres, which Jerry jokingly called "horse's ovaries." Their gift to her was a warm cozy throw, which she pulled over her legs. As she sipped her tea and looked around the beautiful room she had added on, a kaleidoscope of good and bad memories of her country home tumbled through her mind. She was born in this house but her childhood had been filled with abuse and sadness. Yet, after her mother died and Sabyl was left with dealing with the house and all of her mother's things, she decided to keep the house and bring the TLC it never got. It was her way of erasing the old and bad memories and saturating it with new and good ones.

The tiny tree lights twinkled and glowed, throwing shards of refracted light against the walls. She stared at the fire, mesmerized by its dance that was accompanied by a quiet sizzle and an intermittent pop. The clock on the mantle quietly ticked, moving the hands closer to her bedtime.

The phone rang, startling her. She picked it up and answered, "This is Sabyl...hello," she frowned. "Hello." Unfazed, she hung up. *Probably a telemarketer,* she surmised. *Although it's a bit late for even them to be calling.* She stood up. "Come on Beau, let's go upstairs and get ready for bed."

He wagged his tail amiably and followed her up the wooden steps, his nails clicking all the way. He walked over to his doggie bed fell into it and yawned heartily.

It was a pleasure to get out of her clothes and to put on her knit pajamas.

The phone rang again. She sat down on the side of the bed and picked it up. "Hello. Hello." She could tell that someone was on the other end of the line, but they did not speak. "Hello!" Frowning, she hung up.

Beau was instantly on his feet. He sat in front of her, his head tilted, wondering why she seemed disturbed. She patted his head. "It's okay, boy."

After washing her face and brushing her teeth, she put her robe on and went back downstairs to turn out the lights. The phone rang again. *What if Scott's trying to call me but he keeps getting a bad signal or something?* "Hello."

No one spoke.

"Scott?"

Nothing.

The phone was replaced in its cradle. A creepy feeling crawled along her nerves. Tired and wanting to get some rest, she decided to turn the ringers off all her phones. She turned off the ones in the kitchen and her office, and headed back upstairs, turned off the lights, took off her robe and climbed into bed and pulled up the coverlet. Beau lay down and sighed heavily, glad to be going to bed.

Before she could get her pillow adjusted, the phone rang. She stared at it. It rang again. She snatched it up. "Hello!"

"Hi babe."

"Scott! I'm so glad to hear your voice."

"What's the matter? Are you alright?"

"Of course. Why wouldn't I be?"

"Just checking. You sounded alarmed."

"Did you try to call a little while ago?"

"No."

"Oh. Well, I'm so glad you called when you did. I was about to turn the ringer off my phone."

"Why?"

"The phone's been ringing and every time I answer, no one says anything."

"You have caller ID, don't you?"

"I just never had it put in up here in the country."

"After that episode last year with the terrorist, I'd think you'd..."

"Please don't fuss at me, Scott."

"I just want you to be safe, that's all."

She sighed, "I know. I'm sorry. I'm just tired."

"So how often has the phone rang?"

"About every three or four minutes."

"Call me if it keeps happening, okay?"

"It's not going to keep happening, because I'm turning my ringer off. I've got to get some sleep."

He didn't like the sound of it but not wanting to scare her, he said, "Okay. Maybe it's somebody who keeps getting the wrong number."

"Yeah, probably."

"How'd the party go?"

"It was nice—just a little neighborhood thing."

"They love you up there for getting rid of the Oswald brothers."

She laughed. "Yeah. They'd put a statue of me in the Courthouse Square if I'd let them."

Scott laughed, "Not a bad idea."

"That would scare away any would-be criminals, for sure."

He chuckled...and then got quiet. "I miss you."

"Miss you too," she said, meaning it. "Anything new?"

"Yeah, we might have a lead. Nothing I can discuss, but..."

"I understand."

"Did you see the news tonight?"

"No, I've been out all evening. What?"

"Another explosion."

"Oh, no! A plane?"

"No, looks like this one happened at a condo in Aspen. Pretty strange. Not even sure it's tied in with the others, but we'll find out soon."

"That's weird. It wasn't just some accident?"

"No, the FBI has already found evidence that it was a bomb."

"Whose place was it?"

"A family rented it for skiing. A lawyer and his wife and kids. All were killed."

"Oh, Scott, how awful! Young kids?"

"A teenager and her older brother from Ohio. That's all we know so far. When are you coming back to D.C.?"

"Monday. Just needed a little down time. The office has been so hectic."

"I miss you, babe."

"I miss you too."

"Gotta go."

"Scott"

"Yeah, hon?"

"Be careful."

"Always."

"Love you."

"You too, angel face. 'Night."
"Night." She hung up the phone.
Scott sat staring at his phone.

CHAPTER TWENTY

His thin fingers deftly scrolled down the contents of Sabyl's files. There. That's what he was looking for; her scheduled flight to New York on the 20th. He quickly wrote down the Flight number and itinerary. This is perfect, he thought. Just another bombing like all the rest. This is going to be easy.

He took a sip of water from a plastic bottle, screwed the lid back on and sat it down. The cheap plastic popped and snapped in protest of having been disturbed.

He got up and grabbed a frozen pizza out of the refrigerator, put it on a paper plate and nuked it for a minute and a half.

CNN droned in the background. Pictures of the latest bombing at the condo in Aspen covered the screen. His chest swelled with satisfaction at his expertise.

He got up, walked over to the remote, picked it up and changed the channel just in time for a Fox News Alert. The anchor announced that President Anderson was pushing hard for Congress to pass a bill for funding for the Transportation Security Administration (TSA) to hire more and better-trained airport security screeners.

A cold sneer of contempt snaked across his mouth as he whispered, "A lot of good that will do. They'll never figure it out."

The news report then changed. The somber face of the news anchor spoke softly. "We now go to the state capitol of California in Sacramento where the flag-draped casket of Senator Martin Lyles, lies in state. Senator Lyles, one of the earlier victims of the bombings, was on his way home for the Holidays when Flight 356 out of Reagan National Airport in Washington, D.C. went down in Nebraska. His body will lie in state in the Capitol rotunda until Friday.

As you can see, mourners are quietly filing by to pay their respects..."

The microwave beeped in the background. He walked back into the kitchen, took the hot slice of pizza out and took it over to his computer desk. He sat down, took a couple of bites, wiped his hands on a paper towel and then began to deftly hack into the computer of another passenger he had been watching and sat back smiling at how well everything was falling into place. He finished his pizza, closed the laptop and turned off his desk lamp. His work was done for the night.

~ ~ ~

The phone rang again. Sabyl stared at it. Did she dare answer it? It rang and rang...and rang.

Beau got up and came to her bedside and looked at her, cocking his head from side to side as if to say, "Why don't you answer it?" It kept ringing. She decided to pick it up and then immediately dropped it back on its cradle and turned the ringer off.

Beau climbed into his bed and flopped down with a big yawn.

Sabyl pulled the covers up, picked up the remote and changed the channel to Fox News. There was the story. It showed a helicopter view of a structure that had been blown to bits. Snow was falling, and the pure white against the charred black mess was a stark contrast.

She stacked two pillows behind her and laid back and watched it for a few minutes. Her eyes warily slid over to the phone as if it had betrayed her and wondered if someone was still trying to call her.

She turned off the TV and settled down under the covers. Just before she turned out the light, she heard a noise downstairs. Beau didn't bark, so she felt it must be her imagination. There it was again. She sat up and listened hard.

Seeing the disturbed look on her face, Beau stood up and growled. Sabyl threw the covers back and grabbed her robe. Beau went into the hall and stood at the top of the stairs and waited for Sabyl.

She put on her slippers and slowly headed down the stairs. Beau went ahead of her, growling and whining.

Sabyl turned the lights on in the dining room and heard a noise in her office. "Who's there?!"

Beau barked and ran into the office and stood, waiting for Sabyl. Looking around the corner, she slowly stepped inside. She looked behind the curtains, behind the couch and stepped over to the closet. Beau sniffed under the closet door and looked up at Sabyl. Her heart was pounding. She opened it. Nothing.

Then turning around, she saw it. A fax. Releasing a sigh, she said, "That was the noise, Beau. It was my new fax machine."

Hearing the normal tone of her voice and the calm look on her face, Beau relaxed as well.

Since faxes often came to her at odd hours, she thought little of it. Probably one of the drivers needing some instructions. She picked up the fax and read: THE NEXT BOMB IS FOR YOU.

~ ~ ~

Layla smiled at her handsome son and then up at her husband as they left the church and headed for their car. Rudy was unusually quiet, and Layla noticed that David was too. As soon as they got settled in their car, seatbelts fastened and the decision made where they were going to have lunch, Layla spoke up. "Why are you two so quiet? This is the Lord's day. We are to rejoice and be glad in it."

Rudy grunted as he stopped at a stoplight. He knew that David was thinking the same thing he was. The terrorist bombings had unnerved them. They had been the center of an attack just a year ago, and they were feeling on edge that their country was under attack once again.

David saw the concerned look on his mother's face and patted her shoulder.

She looked up at him. "It's the bombings, isn't it?"

David shrugged. "They have everyone on edge."

"But what if they're back? What if they come looking for you and Rudy again?"

"Those men were all either killed or jailed, mom."

"Not the ones who sent them," she quickly responded.

Rudy was startled by her answer but knew he must reassure her. "Stop worrying, Layla, these bombings are not targeting anyone in particular like those others were. It is not the same thing at all."

"Then why are you two so quiet?"

They looked at one another, and Rudy looked at the road as he drove. Neither said anything more.

~ ~ ~

After attending church, Sabyl packed hurriedly and headed back to D.C. It had been good to feel peace after last night's ordeal, even if only for an hour. Fear had never been a part of her life, yet she felt it creeping into her mind. The sermon that morning seemed to be a special love note straight to her from Heaven. The pastor couldn't have known what she had been through. The scripture for his homily was based on II Timothy 1:7: "For God has not given us a spirit of fear, but of power and of love and of a sound mind." How comforting it was.

At the familiar Breezewood exit, she merged off the Pennsylvania Turnpike onto I-70 East. Still thinking about the sermon, she smiled as she remembered the wise old sage adding: "Fear is believing something is going to happen that hasn't happened yet. Faith is believing something is going to happen that hasn't happened yet. Which one are you putting your energy into?"

"Not fear!" she said aloud with gusto, causing Beau's head to pop up and look at her quizzically.

She put in a CD of Andrea Bocelli and fast forwarded it to her favorite song, The Prayer by David Foster and Carole Bayer Sager. Singing along with it in perfect Italian, tears formed in Sabyl's eyes as she sang "Donaci la fede così saremo sicuri."

"Give us faith so we'll be safe."

She concluded the song with a quiet "Amen."

It was now a little under two and a half hours to D.C. Still on edge and having had very little sleep, she had decided to come home a day early, knowing that the Sunday traffic would be light. The last thing she wanted to do was fight traffic. Bocelli's voice continued to calm her. And apparently Beau as well. He began snoring in the back of her Murano.

Sabyl hadn't been able to get through to Scott all morning. She knew he had to keep his private cell phone off while working and would use it only for emergencies. After stopping for gas, she tried his cell once more. She got his voice mail again. I'll just wait till I get home to try again.

The fax she received the night before was in her briefcase. Was the threat a prank? Who would send her such a thing? How did they get her number? And why would they threaten her with a bomb? Should she have called the police? The whole thing reminded her of the sixteen days of terror she and her nation had gone through just a year before. The thought of it unsettled her. *Please, Lord. I can't go through this again.* Then she reminded herself once again. No fear!

Her Bluetooth announced she had a call; she punched a button on her steering wheel to answer it.

"Sabyl, thank you so much for the beautiful flowers."

"Oh, Barbara, you are so welcome. How are you feeling dear?"

"I'm fine, and little Sabyl Lynn is sleeping in her daddy's arms."

"Barb, I can't believe you named her after me. I feel so honored! I can't wait to see her!"

"We can't wait for you to meet her. Are you driving? I hear road noise."

"Yes, I decided to come home a day early. I want to stop by the hospital and see you and the baby."

"Oh, Sabyl, you don't have to do that. I'm going home tomorrow...but...that would be so nice."

"I can't wait another day. I'll see you a little later this afternoon."

"That will be great, and I know Frank will be pleased."

Listening to his wife's end of the conversation, Frank smiled and nodded.

Barbara added, "He's so proud of her and can't wait to show her off."

"I know he'll be a great dad."

Frank sighed and thought, I sure hope so.

CHAPTER TWENTY-ONE

Riders of "Crotch Rockets," or super sport bikes, are four more times likely to die in an accident than other types of motorcycles for one reason and one reason only: speed; so said the insurance companies. With the ability to reach speeds up to 190 miles per hour, those who bought them no doubt had a need for speed but would often wind up as road kill.

The driver of the one racing along the open road didn't know that, and if he did, he didn't care.

The men who were ready to turn something even faster over to him watched as the dust erupted behind the silhouetted sport bike.

He slowed his *Ducati* down to 100, to 80 and then 60 then 40 and finally pulled up to the decrepit abandoned hanger in the middle of the desert in New Mexico. He got off the machine and walked over to the waiting technicians who had been there all night putting the last touches on the *Lear 85* that stood inside the cavernous hangar like a weapon ready to be launched.

He looked up at it and smiled. Then he turned and walked toward the door.

"Where are you going, Colonel Farage?"

He stopped, turned around and said, "I'm going to check the runway. This place is old and crumbling. I don't want to take the chance of wrecking it before I even get the plane off the ground."

"We had the runway patched up as best we could. There is no time to do anything more to it. You will just have to trust us."

"I trust no one. We have a couple more days before I have to fly it to Chicago. I will take a look." He walked away, stepped out of the hangar and got back on his motorcycle. He slowly drove the length of the runway, took note of some areas that were particularly rough, but decided he could manage to miss those before lifting off.

He headed back to the hangar and did a thorough check of the *Lear*. "This will do very nicely," he smiled. "Very nicely indeed."

~ ~ ~

Monday traffic was the usual tangle of cars trying to maneuver the streets of D.C. Sabyl pulled into her parking spot, turned off the engine and got out. Beau wagged his tail happily as he waited for her to open the back door of the Murano. She let him out and they went inside.

Dotty greeted her solemnly. "Are you okay?"

"Yes, thanks, honey. Sorry to alarm you when I called you this morning. I shouldn't have told you about the fax."

"Of course you should have! What are friends for?" She frowned, "So who do you suppose sent...?"

"I have no idea."

"Plumb spooky, if you ask me. That's just the pigs."

"I know. Hey, I stopped by the hospital to see Barbara and the baby yesterday. She's so beautiful! And so tiny!" She smiled as she pulled her gloves off. "I got to hold her."

"I can't wait to see her. How's Frank holding up?"

"Quite well. He's so proud of her."

Dotty smiled. "I heard they named her after you."

"They did. I'm just so honored! They asked me if I would be her Godmother."

"That's awesome!"

Beau looked up at Dotty and wagged his tail.

Sabyl laughed, "There's that look."

"Yep. He wants his treat." She turned to go to her desk drawer for Beau's tidbit. "Hey, Karen's doing a great job filling in for Frank." She gave Beau his treat. He walked away and headed for his bed beside Sabyl's desk. "Oh, by the way, Jenny called and said she isn't feeling well and won't be coming in."

Sabyl pulled off her coat. "Really? Wow! She's never sick."

Dotty took her coat from her and hung it up. "I know. Her voice sounded kind of…I don't know, funny."

"Funny? How?"

"I'm not sure. Strained might be a better word."

"Maybe she had a fight with her boyfriend."

"Yeah, maybe."

"Well, I've got a ton of work to do. I'm expecting a call from Scott. Put him through immediately, will you?" She sat down at her desk and looked through her phone messages then pulled a file out of the credenza behind her, and turned back. Karen tapped on her door.

"Hey, Sabyl. You have a good weekend?"

"It was okay. How about you?"

She shrugged. "Same old, same old."

"Who all's on Christmas vacation?"

"Just Ricko. He flew down to Columbia to be with his family. Hasn't been to see them in, like, five or six years."

A knock came at Sabyl's door. "Come in."

Jenny stood there, her face ashen.

"Jenny, what's wrong? I thought you were…"

"May I talk to you?"

"Of course, dear. Come in and sit down."

Karen whispered, "Uh, I'll, like, just go." She slipped out quickly and closed the door.

Jenny sank in a chair across from Sabyl's desk.

Sabyl leaned forward, her arms on her desk. "What's wrong, dear?"

Jenny closed her eyes and shook her head. "It's probably nothing, but…I'm scared, Sabyl."

"Scared? Of what? Has someone threatened to hurt you?"

"No, I…" She pulled a tissue out of her pocket. "I saw something that kind of frightened me."

"What is it, Jenny?"

"Last night I was in Derrick's apartment. He had a lot of work to do so I watched TV. I went to use the restroom and took my earring out. It was hurting my ear. I washed my hands and came out and dropped my earring on the floor. It just disappeared. I got down on my hands and knees and looked all over—then I bent down to look under the bed. I saw what looked like a piece of newspaper sticking out. I pulled on it to see what it was and it was attached to something. Out of curiosity, I pulled it out. There was this large cork board full of clippings—all of them about the D.C. Snipers."

Sabyl frowned deeply. "You mean those guys that went around shooting people back in, what, 2002? What are their names…Malvo and…"

"Yes."

"That's pretty weird."

"Yeah. I pushed it back under there. It gave me a weird feeling. I couldn't wait to get out of there."

"Did he see you looking at them?"

"No. I faked a headache and left. Sabyl, I don't know what it means, but I'm scared."

"Derrick is a rather unusual young man. I always chalked it up to his being, you know, so quiet. But I see no reason to be scared."

"That's not all. I talked to Kyle…"

"Who's Kyle?"

"He works for Derrick at the Tech Center at AU. He told me that Derrick despised Professor Hickson."

"Hickson? The one that was just…killed?"

"Yes. Kyle said that Derrick had something against him and said something like, 'He'll get his.'"

"Why would he say that?"

"Hickson hacked into Derrick's computer and stole some computer software he'd been working on that would have set Derrick up for life and Hickson sold it to Mar-Tech and was going to make a ton of money off it."

Sabyl sat back. "Has Derrick called the police?"

"I don't know. I just know what I saw and it seems strange to me."

"Yes, it does."

She shook her head and looked down. "I don't know what to think anymore."

"When will you see Derrick again?"

"We don't have any plans…"

Sabyl stood and said, "Maybe you should let things chill."

"Don't worry, I am. But he's going to wonder why I'm not…"

"Just tell him you need some space."

She smiled weakly. "Okay, thanks, Sabyl." She stood and said, "Well, I'd better get to work."

"Try not to worry, okay?"

"Okay." She left Sabyl's office and headed for her cubicle.

Sabyl sat back down and stared at the door. *The D.C. Snipers? Why would anyone keep all those clippings?*

A knock came at the door. "Come in."

Rudy walked in smiling. "Here's your *Starbucks*, boss." He carefully sat it down on her desk.

"Thank you, Rudy. Can you sit down for a few minutes or do you have to go?"

"No, I have a few minutes." The big man sat down where Jenny had sat.

"What do you remember about the D.C. Snipers?"

"The D.C. Snipers?" He rubbed his chin. "Well, there was a lot of chaos—a lot of traffic snarls because the police kept stopping white vans. I sat in traffic for an hour after I picked up a client from National...made him miss an important meeting. He was really upset."

"What else do you remember?"

Rudy looked puzzled. "Why, boss?"

"No reason, I just thought I had read something about that John Mohammed guy's ex-wife. That she was living in the area and he had planned to kill her and make it look like she was just another victim."

"Oh, yes. I remember reading that in the newspapers. Some of the drivers said it would have been the perfect crime if they hadn't been caught."

Sabyl nodded thoughtfully.

"Why, boss?"

"Nothing. Just curious. By the way, are you and Layla coming to the Christmas party?"

"We'll be there, boss."

"Good! I always look forward to seeing Layla. Will David be coming home for the holidays?"

"Yes. He's already here."

"I hope he'll come to the party."

"I'll ask him. I know he would love to see you."

"I'd love to see him too. How is he doing in med school?"

"It took him a little while to get back into the swing of things after...you know, that ordeal last year, but he is okay."

"Good."

Rudy stood up and looked at his watch. "I must go. George is taking me to pick up my new car."

"Already?"

"I would have had it sooner, but I asked for a cassette tape player to be installed so I can listen to my father's sermons."

"That's great, Rudy. See you later."

Sabyl sat back and wondered about what Jenny had told her. She didn't remember her saying she had found her earring. "Oh, my goodness," she whispered.

Her cell phone chirped. It was Scott.

"Hey, babe. Sorry you haven't been able to get in touch with me. Are you okay?"

She sat up straight. "Scott. I have to see you."

"What's wrong, sweetheart?"

"After I talked with you last night, I got a fax."

"From whom?"

"I don't know."

"What does it say?"

"THE NEXT BOMB IS FOR YOU."

There was stunned silence at the other end. Then he managed to say, "Do you have it with you?"

"Yes."

"Where are you?"

"I'm at my office."

"Bring it to me. Come out like you're going to my old office."

"Old office?"

"Yeah, I'll explain later." When you're close, call my cell and I'll direct you to my new office."

"But I can never get you."

"I'm leaving my cell on."

"It's okay to get a personal call?"

"This is no longer personal. It has now become business."

CHAPTER TWENTY-TWO

Sabyl walked into Scott's office and put her briefcase on his desk. He kissed her cheek then pointed to a chrome and leather chair. "Have a seat there and I'll be right back."

"Okay," she said and sat down.

Scott walked into Ron Keefer's office. He was on the phone. He looked up at Scott.

"She's here."

"I'll get back with you," he said into the phone. "Thanks." He hung up, stood, and pulled on his suit jacket and followed Scott into his office.

"Hello, Sabyl," he said as he extended his hand.

"Hi, Ron."

"Looks like we keep meeting under extraordinary circumstances."

She smiled sheepishly. "I really am trying to stay out of trouble."

Nobody laughed.

Keefer sat in a chair beside her and Scott on the other side. "Show it to me."

She pulled the briefcase off the edge of Scott's desk and put it on her lap and opened it. "Here," she said, handing the fax to him.

He looked at the paper carefully. "It was sent from an all-night print shop on M Street in Georgetown at 11:13 PM last night. Interesting that they sent it to your home in Pennsylvania."

She sighed. "Yes, I thought so too. What do you make of it?"

Keefer took his glasses off. "Not sure yet, but we'll check it out."

"Maybe it's some sicko playing a prank on me. After all, everyone knows about...you know, last year. Maybe they're just trying to..."

"We have to take it seriously, honey." Scott leaned forward and took both of her hands in his. "Sabyl, I don't want to alarm you, but I don't want you to go to Pennsylvania again until we get to the bottom of this."

"Alright," she said reluctantly.

"Promise me?"

"I promise."

"So you'll be here in D.C., and we can contact you at any time?" Keefer asked.

"Yes. Well, no, not exactly. I'm flying to New York to attend a Christmas dinner with one of my clients tomorrow."

"Flying?" Recalling Flight 84 that flew that same route, Scott frowned deeply. "Do you think that's wise?"

"I'm not going to let some nutcase rule my life and put me in fear. That's what they want. Besides, I'll be fine."

Scott stood, thrust his hands in his pockets and looked at the floor and then looked at her. "Okay, babe."

"You going alone?" Keefer asked.

"Yes."

"Who else knows you're going?"

"Dotty, Frank, John, Rudy..." She thought a minute, "And, of course, Jenny. She made the plane reservation for me."

Keefer frowned, "I know who Rudy is. Who are Dotty, Frank, John, and Jenny?"

"Frank is my day dispatcher, John is my night dispatcher, Dotty is my secretary, and Jenny is one of my reservationists."

"When will you be back from New York?" Scott asked.

"Tomorrow night. I'm just going up and back the same day."

"I want your flight itinerary," Scott said.

Keefer asked, "What kind of cell phone do you have?" She told him. "Okay. Follow me into my office, will you?"

"Uh, sure." She stood and the three of them went into Keefer's office. He sat down behind his desk and opened a drawer and pulled something out. "I want you to take this." He handed her a phone like she'd never seen before. "You should be able to get through to either Scott or me if you need us. But if, for some reason, you can't get through, leave a 911-text message, and we'll get back to you as quickly as possible."

Scott gave her a few simple instructions about the phone.

"Okay, I think I can handle it." She put it in her pocketbook.

He took her hand. "Promise you'll be careful."

"I promise."

Keefer stood up. "Scott, you and Martz go over to that all-night print shop and ask some questions. See if there's a security camera that may have videoed whoever sent that fax."

"We're on it." He turned to Sabyl. "Are you going home or to the office?"

"To the office. I'll have Dotty fax you my flight itinerary."

"Okay, babe. I'll call you later."

Sabyl walked toward the door. She stopped and turned. "There's something else I need to tell you."

"What's that?" Keefer asked.

She told them about what Jenny had told her that Kyle had said about Derrick. "He hated Professor Hickson for stealing his program."

Scott and Keefer looked at one another. "Okay. We'll check it out."

She left. Keefer picked up the fax and handed it to Scott.

He took it and reached for his jacket. "I'll buzz Lou and we'll head over to the print shop."

"I've changed my mind. I'll get someone else to go to the print shop. I need you and Lou to go over to AU and dig around there. See if you can find this Kyle guy."

"Okay." He pulled his overcoat on and shook his head. "I don't like the idea of Sabyl flying right now..."

Ron looked over his glasses. "Can't say that I blame you."

~ ~ ~

Scott and Martz parked their car and walked around the American University campus. It was virtually empty. "Everybody's gone for the holidays," Scott said as they walked toward a building that looked like it might be occupied. A light was on in one of the windows on the first floor. "Can you see if anyone is in there? I'll try these doors."

Looking through the window, Martz could see a dark-haired young man dressed in jeans and a sweatshirt sitting at a desk, slumped over as though asleep.

Scott turned from the doors. "They're locked."

"There's someone in there," Martz said, pointing at the window. "Looks like he's asleep."

The two agents knocked on the window, stirring the young man. He sat up, looked toward the window and stared at them.

The agents motioned to him to open the door. The man stood motionless. Scott showed his badge. The man slowly moved toward the door and opened it.

The agents showed their I.D.s. "Like to ask you some questions if we may."

The young man turned and ran away. Scott and Martz pulled their weapons and went inside. The corridors were dark. They yelled at the young man, "We're not going to harm you. We just want to ask you some questions."

No answer. They held their weapons with both hands and carefully moved down the corridor pointing their guns at the corners. Scott took one of his hands off the gun and felt along the wall. Finally, he felt the flat, smooth surface of a switch plate. He flipped the switches on, lighting part of the corridor. They saw a shadow move about halfway down the hall. They moved swiftly toward it. "You have no reason to run unless you're hiding something!" Scott yelled. "Running makes you look a lot more suspicious than you were two minutes ago. Now, why don't you just step out here in the light and let us ask you some questions?"

There was a long pause then he answered, "I'm coming out! Don't shoot me!" Kyle stepped out of the recessed doorway and stood with his hands up.

"Get on the floor!" Martz commanded. Kyle knelt down, and then fell prostrate on the cold floor. "Put your hands behind your head!" He did so.

Scott frisked him and saw that he was clean. "Okay, get up."

Kyle pushed himself up and stood looking down at the floor and shook his head.

"What's your name?"

"Kyle Sloan."

"Why did you run?" Scott asked.

"I got scared. I was afraid you thought I did it."

Martz eyed him carefully, "Did what?"

"Hacked into the professor's computer."

"Hickson?"

"Hickson? No! Warner! I wanted to see my grades!"

"That's not why we're here. We'd like for you to come downtown with us and maybe you can lead us to someone who can give us some answers."

"Answers about what?"

"We'll talk when we get there. Oh, and bring your laptop with you."

Kyle looked wide-eyed and fumbled for words, "It's— not mine. It belongs to the school."

"Bring it anyway."

CHAPTER TWENTY-THREE

Lawrence decorated his limo with greenery and bows just for this occasion. Soft Christmas music played through the stereo system. The heater warmed the well-appointed cabin. He sat behind the steering wheel, waiting.

When he saw Sabyl, Dotty and Mary come out of the salon on 19th Street, he got out and opened the door for them. They got in the waiting sedan, chattering away gleefully like three teenagers. Lawrence closed the door ceremoniously and got in the driver's seat. "Where to, ladies?"

Sabyl answered, "To the Four Seasons for lunch, Lawrence."

"We're on our way."

Mary laughed and leaned against Sabyl and looked up at her with her huge blue eyes. "Thank you for my pretty toes, Sabyl," she said in her husky voice, which was characteristic of her debility.

Sabyl hugged her and said, "You're more than welcome, Mary. I love getting prettied up, don't you?"

"Yes," she said, grinning.

Dotty smiled contentedly as the famous government buildings slipped past the tinted windows, her newly manicured hands folded in her lap. "Sabyl, thank you for the mani/pedis. You always make it so special when Mary comes to visit."

"You know how much I love her," she answered as she gave Mary's shoulder a little squeeze.

"You're not going to be too tired to fly to New York this evening?"

"No. I'm fine. Now you stop worrying, you little mother hen. If I get tired, I'll catch a little snooze on the plane."

"I don't like the thoughts of you flying with all these planes..." she lowered her voice as though to keep Mary from hearing..." you know..."

"I'll be fine."

"Here we are, ladies." The luxurious car pulled up to the curb in front of the Four Seasons on Pennsylvania Avenue. Lawrence got out and opened the door for them with a flourish. Mary stepped out and looked around wide-eyed, waiting for her mom to emerge.

"Thank you, Lawrence," Dotty grunted as she took his hand and stood up and straightened her coat.

"My pleasure." He turned to help Sabyl when his radio beeped. "Hey, John. Yeah, she's here, hold on."

Sabyl stepped out of the sedan.

"It's John. He said he tried to call your cell phone."

"I turned it off in the salon. Couldn't very well answer it with wet nails," she smiled. She took the phone from him. "Hey, John. What's up?"

"Scott called looking for you. Said it's urgent."

Sabyl's brow furrowed. "Thanks, I will." She closed the phone and handed it back to Lawrence. "Dotty, you and Mary go on inside. The reservations are in my name."

"Is everything alright?"

"Yes, I'll just be a minute. Go ahead."

"Okay, will do."

The doorman opened the heavy glass and metal doors for them, and the two walked in.

"You want me to wait or park?" asked Lawrence.

"Hold on," she said as she turned her cell on. "Let me see what Scott wants."

Lawrence stepped away for a smoke and to give Sabyl privacy.

She saw a message from Scott with a 911 code. She hit "Send," and he answered immediately.

"Sabyl! Where are you?"

"At the Four Seasons. What's wrong?"

"I want you to change your flight."

"I…I don't know if I can. I'm leaving in just a few hours."

"The airlines are hurting for business right now with all the bombings. I'm sure they'll accommodate you. If not, let me know. I'll get you a flight."

"Okay."

"Do it yourself, okay? Not through your reservationist."

"I'll call my travel agent right now and get her to change it. How is the investigation coming along?"

"We're still looking for that common denominator."

"What do you mean common denominator?"

"The bombings. Some on planes, one on a train, a limo and a cabin in Aspen. The only common denominator we have is that in nearly every instance, AU students were on board the planes and aboard the Amtrak."

"And Professor Hickson. He was a professor at AU."

"Exactly. That one really doesn't make sense. Yet, if an AU student is doing this…"

"Or someone who has it in for AU…"

"Right."

"But with Christmas break, it seems that…"

"I know. Students are going in every direction in every mode of transportation. We don't know any of this for sure. It could be some nut case like the Unabomber or Timothy McVeigh. Someone trying to make a statement. It could even be somebody whose luggage got lost and he's ticked off at the airlines. Or maybe even somebody who wants one person dead, but wants it to look as though that person was just another victim."

Sabyl's eyes widened. "Like the D.C. Snipers?"

"Yeah. Like that."

"Oh, Scott..."

"What, honey?"

She told him about what Jenny saw. "It's probably nothing, but I thought I should mention it."

She could hear him tell Keefer to get a warrant. "Sabyl, keep your cell phone on, okay? Don't ever turn it off."

"Okay, Scott. Did I hear you say you're getting a warrant for Derrick Blake?"

"We've got nothing else at this point."

"But why would he threaten me? The fax, I mean."

"This Jenny you just spoke of. She's also a reservationist, right? She made your plane reservation?"

"Yes."

"Maybe she told this Derrick character about your flight."

Sabyl was stunned at the thought. "Surely you don't think...Oh, and Scott, Derrick has my computer."

"What? Why?"

She explained how Jenny set him up to fix her computer.

"How long has he had it?"

"A couple of days."

"I'm going to change your flight for you. Don't tell anyone in your office about it."

"But what about the flight I already have?"

"We're not going to cancel it. You'll just be a no-show."

"You don't suspect anyone in my office, do you?"

"Not at this point. Just want to keep you safe. I'll send you your new flight itinerary to the phone we gave you."

"Okay."

She could hear him let out a sigh of relief. "Okay, honey. I've got to go. Have a safe trip and call me when you get back tonight, okay?"

"I will."

~ ~ ~

Kyle sat silently in the chair across from Scott and Martz. Keefer came in. "So who do we have here?"

"Kyle Sloan," said Martz. "Works in the Tech Center bookstore on campus at AU."

Keefer extended his hand. "Hello, Kyle."

Kyle shook his hand without looking up.

Martz continued, "He says we should talk to someone by the name of Derrick Blake. That he might be the one who killed Professor Hickson. We're arranging a warrant as we speak."

Keefer sat down next to Scott. "Why do you say that, Kyle?"

"When I heard that Professor Hickson was killed, I got to thinking…" He started sobbing.

"Okay, Kyle, just calm down. What's Derrick Blake got to do with it?"

"Derrick hated him."

"Why?"

"He stole his program."

"What kind of program?"

"Not sure. He was pretty tight-lipped about it. But he would have been set for life. He said it was worth millions."

"So he thinks Hickson stole it. How does he know?"

"He said he was the only one that was smart enough to hack into his computer and get it all out. He even changed the dates to make it look like he came up with it before

180

Derrick did. Made it look like Derrick tried to steal it from him."

"Did he ever threaten Hickson?"

"Not to his face. But I heard him say once, 'He'll get his.'"

"Did you ask him what he meant?"

"No. Derrick's not one you want to rile."

"Is he violent?"

"Not that I've ever seen. He's just—I don't know—intimidating."

"So you think he's doing the bombings?"

"No! I mean—I don't know. All I know is he hated Hickson."

"What else do you know?"

"I saw some clippings."

Scott and Martz looked at one another knowingly. "Newspaper clippings?"

"Yeah. He was interested in the D.C. Snipers. Too interested. Kept every clipping—I mean he had dozens of them pinned to some sort of bulletin board on his wall over his computer. I saw them when I came up to talk to him. He opened the door a crack and I saw them. He told me he had a girl in there and to come back in a few minutes. When I came back, the clippings were gone. Like he took them down and hid them or something."

"Go on."

"He said the D.C. Snipers could have pulled off the perfect murder. He said that Mohammed guy wanted to kill his ex-wife and make it look like she was just another one of the victims of the shootings."

"Go on," Keefer said.

"Derrick even sort of acted like he was mad at them for not pulling it off. Said they could have if they hadn't gotten greedy and started asking for money; that they got bloodthirsty or something—that they got caught up in the killings and failed to do what they set out to do."

"Yeah? So are you saying that these bombings are to make it look like terrorists, but he was really trying to kill Hickson?"

Kyle rubbed his forehead. "I don't know, man. Maybe. I just thought I should tell somebody."

"Is that all you saw?"

"Yes, sir."

"Do you think he's responsible for all the bombings?"

Kyle leaned back in the chair. "I don't know. I thought it might be Abdul."

"Who's Abdul?"

"He's the Instructural Tech Coordinator. I told Derrick I thought he might be the one."

"The one perpetrating the bombings?"

"Yes, sir."

"Why did you think that?"

Kyle told him why he suspected him. He reluctantly told him he hacked into Abdul's computer and retrieved several emails.

"Do you still have the emails?"

"No, I threw them away after I talked with Derrick."

"Assuming he's the bomber, how do you think he's getting these bombs aboard the planes?"

Kyle sighed heavily. "No idea."

"Where is he now?"

"I'm not sure."

"Did he leave town for the winter break?"

"I don't know."

"What about Derrick?"

"No, he said he's staying here."

"Okay, is that it?"

"I guess so.

CHAPTER TWENTY-FOUR

The passengers were quiet and subdued, their faces showing traces of anxiety, knowing that several planes had blown up within the past week. To board a plane now was not so much an act of bravery as it was a roll of the dice—or was it a bit like playing a massive game of Russian roulette? No, the odds were much greater here. With one bullet in the chamber of six, the odds were much more likely for one to be killed—but with nearly 100,000 flights per day and only five planes having been blown up, they no doubt had done the math and decided to roll the dice.

And it was the holidays; one of the busiest times of the year for air travel. Sabyl had noted that the tearful goodbyes at the curb were probably edged with fear. And who wouldn't be fearful? Being blown out of the sky was not high on anyone's bucket list.

A Belgian Malanois, a small, shorthaired canine, moved from person to person at the German command of its handler. "Nächsten!"

Foreign languages and hand signals were used in the event an unauthorized person might attempt to interfere in the performance of the dogs. The trained canines worked swiftly and obediently as they moved along the line of passengers waiting to board Flight 449. One man looked extremely nervous with the dogs nearby. Sabyl assumed he was anxious about the potentiality of a bomb. She couldn't know he was fearful that one of the dogs would detect the small pouch of pot in his pants pocket.

The uniformed officer's attention was suddenly averted to a Middle Eastern man who refused to undergo a search. "Durchsuchung!"

Sabyl watched as the dogs were released to inspect the man who was taken aside and questioned. The line she was in moved forward steadily. Those with laptops were asked to take them out of their cases and turn them on.

Sabyl took off her shoes, placed her large clump of keys in the bowl that was provided and laid her purse in the plastic tub and moved it toward the conveyer belt. She walked through the security gate, relieved that it didn't go off. She picked up her shoes and put them on, snatched up her keys and purse and headed for her gate.

The TV monitors at the airport boarding areas repeated news about the bombings over and over again, an unnerving reminder to those who were just minutes from boarding a plane, not that the thought was ever far from their minds.

After another thirty-five minutes, finally aboard the 737, Sabyl fastened her seatbelt and leaned her head back in the wide first-class seat and watched the other passengers as they entered the cabin. What are these people thinking about? The bombings? Their children's future in such a volatile society? Or maybe just what they're going to do for dinner.

Their faces were somber, having been through a thorough search, a grim reminder that a bomb might be aboard their flight. Prior to their boarding, flight attendants checked their respective sections and would examine the First Aid and medical equipment to make sure they had not been tampered with and that the seals had not been broken. Bomb-sniffing dogs were brought onboard.

Sabyl felt trapped and wished she was in the aisle seat. In fact, she wished she could be anywhere but here.

Looking out the window, she watched the luggage carts moving about like toy trains, driven by young men in puffy jackets with their employer's logo on the back. She appreciated how enormous the airline industry was. How can they even stay in business, she wondered? Especially after the latest bombings. Her thoughts were interrupted by the voice of the head flight attendant explaining there would be a slight delay. Big surprise. I'm amazed they're flying at all. She looked at her watch and hoped the delay wouldn't make her late.

The annual dinner party thrown by her client, John Thomas Cantrell, was something she attended each year and usually looked forward to, but this year she dreaded it. She was in no mood for chitchat or for the elderly CEO of Destry Oil to once again try to fix her up with his good-looking but narcissistic son, Alfred.

Her thoughts turned to Scott and how glad she was that he was back in her life after a painful break up three years ago. She thought about the simple solitaire engagement ring he had given her. After they broke up, she was tempted to throw it into the Potomac, but she decided to take the high ground and mailed it back to him. She almost wished she had it back. It would at least be a support to help rebuff Alfred's sloppy advances

I wonder if Scott kept it.

~ ~ ~

Martz and Scott sat in the cold car in front of Derrick's apartment building waiting. One had gone up, and the other took the elevator in case he somehow knew they were coming. Since he did not answer the door, they went back to the car and waited for the warrant they had requested and discussed the possibility whether Derrick Blake was the one doing the bombings. It was the only lead they had of any significance, but it was still maddeningly uncertain.

Scott's radio beeped. "Terhune."

Keefer spoke. "Anything?"

"Not yet."

"Okay, continue the stakeout. Maybe he'll show up."

Scott asked, "Anything on Abdul?"

"Nope. Not home. Hope he didn't skip town."

"Right."

"Out."

Scott stared at the front door of the apartment building on Macomb Avenue. "Blake's a pretty intense guy."

"Yeah. Kyle says he's a genius."

"So was Hitler, they say."

"Could still be a terrorist cell," Martz reminded him.

"Whether it's a domestic guy or an Al Qaeda type, he's still a terrorist."

"Yeah. It's amazing how one person in a world full of people can wreak such havoc."

"And some people want us to have civil discourse with them," Scott said.

Martz shifted his weight in the passenger seat. "Civil discourse is not in a terrorist's genes. They know one thing and one thing only. Fear. They'll never understand why freedom is better than bondage."

"Bondage is all they know," Scott said, as he cracked his knuckles. "A man doesn't know he's captive when he's born into captivity." He sighed with frustration.

"Yeah. There's an old saying, 'The problem with deception is you don't know you're deceived.'"

Scott's trained eyes continued to scan the area. "Whoever's doing this—I mean just think about the thought

186

and planning that's gone into this. Like a well-choreographed dance."

Martz's jaw tightened. "Yeah. A dance of death."

Derrick Blake seemed like the logical perpetrator. Was he the architect of these bombings? Or were others involved—and if so, who?

"Blake must really have hated this Hickson character," Scott said as he sipped his cold coffee. "Hickson was his mentor. He trusted him—looked up to him. So, for Hickson to betray him like that must have felt like a Judas kiss."

"Most likely."

"I mean, the closer the relationship, the higher degree of betrayal. You can't really betray a stranger. Guess that's why the betrayal of a spouse is the worst kind. How close can you get?"

"Yeah." Martz thought about that awhile.

The two agents studied the apartment, each working through their own thoughts. Finally, Scott broke the silence. "Did you ever work a jigsaw puzzle that had pieces missing?"

"Sure."

"You know what's worse than that?"

"What?"

"Having pieces of a puzzle in the mix that don't belong." Just then, Scott got a message on his radio. "Got it," he said. He turned to Martz. "We got our warrant."

"I'll call forensics."

"If this is our guy, there's no way there won't be some residue of plastique in his apartment."

"Unless he put them together someplace else," Martz said. "Maybe we'll find some more pieces to that puzzle."

Scott nodded. "Or throw out some that don't belong."

"Let's go get that warrant."

"A courier is bringing it to us."

~ ~ ~

As Sabyl boarded the plane for her return flight, she looked at her watch. She would be getting back to D.C. much earlier than she would have on the previous flight she was supposed to be on. She was glad her client had insisted on an early dinner.

The Christmas Party with John Thomas Cantrell, one of her most important clients, had been pleasant but not without stress. All he and his guests could talk about were the bombings. Knowing she would be boarding another plane that evening didn't help. But the flight to New York had been without incident. She prayed the flight back to D.C. would be as well.

A young lady, slim and blonde with freckles, heaved a bag into the luggage compartment overhead and sat down next to Sabyl. She shoved her bulky pocketbook down by her feet and fastened her seatbelt. Sabyl smiled and said a friendly hello and then looked out the window at the young man loading the conveyer belt that carried the passengers' luggage and packages into the cargo hold. Sabyl hoped each piece had been carefully examined.

As they taxied down the runway, flight attendants went through the safety issues and then took their seats in fold-downs in the upper galley. The huge aircraft lumbered to the end of the runway and waited behind several other planes that were lined up, their wingtip lights flashing in the cold December night.

There could be a bomb aboard any one of them, she thought. For that matter, there could be one aboard the plane she was on. One by one the giant birds lifted into the black sky. She tried to think about all she needed to do when she got home. As late as it would be, she still needed to wrap a few more packages for Dotty and Mary. She still hadn't shopped for Frank or Barbara. And she couldn't wait to shop for little Sabyl Lynn. The thought of her brought a smile to her tense face.

The plane moved into position. With brakes on, the engines accelerated like a drag racer before he takes off. It went roaring down the runway and lifted steeply into the night. Several minutes later, after the aircraft reached 10,000 feet, the flight attendant announced, "The Captain has turned off the seat belt sign. You are free to move about the cabin. In a few moments, we will be offering our beverage service. It is now safe for you to use your electronic devices."

Sabyl thought, Safe? Are any of us safe anymore?

Her feet hurt, but she wasn't about to take her shoes off. Not that it would make a difference. If the plane blew up, there would be no need for shoes. She couldn't help but think about the fax she had received with the threat that the next bomb was for her. She closed her eyes and prayed silently, *Lord, please keep us safe. We're in Your hands.*

CHAPTER TWENTY-FIVE

Derrick's face was grotesquely sullen. Scott opened the door to the interrogation room and led him in and removed his cuffs. "Sit down."

He slumped into the plastic chair and glared at the agents. "Why am I here? Why did you take my computers? What do you want?"

Lou Martz said, "We want answers."

"About what?"

"About the bombings."

"The bombings? Why would I know anything about the bombings?"

Scott said, "We want to know about what your relationship is with Professor Hickson."

Derrick's face grew sour. "What about him?"

"We hear you had it in for him."

"You've got to be kidding me!"

Martz squinted. "Not kidding."

"Is that what this is about?"

"How did you feel about Professor Hickson?"

"I hated him."

"Enough to kill him?"

"No!"

"Did you have anything to do with his death?"

"Look, I hated him. That doesn't mean I'd blow him up."

"So what's the big infatuation with the D.C. Snipers?"

Derrick shook his head, slid down in his chair with his hands in his pockets, looked down and said nothing.

~ ~ ~

The young girl sitting next to Sabyl unfastened her seat belt, stood up, and retrieved a laptop computer from her bag in the overhead compartment. She sat back down, lowered her tray table, opened the laptop and turned it on.

Sabyl looked at it and said, "Oh, you've got an Orion. I've thought about getting one of those. How do you like yours? Oh, by the way, I'm Sabyl Martin."

"Amy Holloman. Nice to meet you. It's okay, I guess. It's school-issued."

"School issued?"

"Yeah, all the incoming freshmen at AU got one this year. It's included in our tuition. I like my Apple better, but these are programmed for the students' various academic needs."

"I guess that solves the problem of computer abuse with the school system."

"Yeah, and we can access our professors' classroom agenda—and even get immediate feedback on how we did on tests. But we get email as well."

"So, did they have a training period for you to familiarize yourself with the laptop?"

"Yeah, the University Instructional Tech Coordinator set up two-day seminars for us to get acquainted with the software."

"That's great," Sabyl smiled.

"Tough class, though."

"Amazing. Well, I'll let you get back to your email. I'm going to try to take a little snooze."

"Okay, thanks."

Sabyl leaned her head back and closed her eyes. She was amazed at how quickly technology was invading every corner of life. Imagine, she thought, fifteen hundred computers just handed out.

Suddenly her eyes popped open. What if that's the common denominator? She turned her head and watched as Amy went through her email. Oh, God, what if...? What if there's a bomb in there?"

~ ~ ~

"You've got clippings of them all over the place. Why?"

"I'm writing a novel."

"A novel? About what?"

"About the perfect murder. If John Mohammed and Lee Malvo hadn't gotten greedy, they could have pulled off the perfect murder. His ex-wife would have been considered just another victim."

"I guess that would have worked for Professor Hickson as well, wouldn't it, Derrick?"

"What?"

"You wanted him dead, didn't you?"

"No."

"Then why did you threaten him?"

"I never threatened him!"

"Didn't you tell someone, 'He'll get his'?"

Derrick stared at Scott.

"You said that to Kyle Sloan, didn't you?"

"Maybe I was talking about karma."

Martz got in his face. "Maybe you decided that the bombings would make a good D.C. Sniper scenario and you used that to make it look like Hickson was just another victim."

"I want to leave now."

"We're not finished with you, dude. Didn't you say to Kyle to watch for some major crashes?"

Derrick's face flushed. He felt like his life was going down in descending spirals like those grainy World War II news films of airplanes that had been shot down. "I want a lawyer."

"You're gonna need one, pal."

~ ~ ~

Sabyl watched as Amy hit "enter" to reply to an email. Her fingers flew over the flat keyboard, and then she moved onto the next email. Amy smiled at Sabyl. "Looks like I got an email from my professor."

From her professor? Why would a professor email a student while they're on Christmas break? Certainly, that would be an email that any student would open.

"Excuse me, Amy, I've got to get up."

"Oh, uh, sure." She closed her laptop, stood and let Sabyl out and sat back down.

Sabyl approached the flight attendant, who was preparing the catering cart. "You've got to order all computers to be put away."

"What? Why?"

"There might be a bomb…"

"Now, Ma'am, we're all nervous about the explosions, but—"

"No, you don't understand. There has to be a common denominator and that could be it!"

"Ma'am, I'm going to have to ask you to take your seat—"

"Can't you just ask her to put—"

"Ma'am, take your seat, or I'll have to call the Captain."

Sabyl could feel her face flush. The woman thought she was a crackpot. "I've got to use the restroom."

"All right, but then return to your seat."

Sabyl opened the restroom door, stepped inside, closed and locked it. She sat down and began to pray. "Lord, show me what to do. You're the only one who can help us. Please, do something!" She stood up, splashed water on her face, patted it dry with the small brown paper towels, straightened her clothes and came out.

Amy, slightly annoyed, closed her laptop again, stood up and let Sabyl back to her seat and sat back down. Thankfully, she had been distracted by a good-looking young man across the aisle from her. They had struck up a conversation, and she had not continued working through her emails.

Sabyl pulled out the phone Ron Keefer had given her and started to punch in Scott's number. She froze when she realized she didn't know what to say—and she certainly didn't want to upset Amy. She took a deep breath and instead entered a text message to Scott's cell phone. Amy opened her laptop again. She deftly moved the mouse to the email entitled "AN URGENT MESSAGE FROM YOUR PROFESSOR."

~ ~ ~

Scott pulled out a chair and sat down next to Martz and across the table from Derrick and his lawyer, a slight man of around fifty-something, wearing a gray suit with an overcoat over his shoulders.

"Gentlemen, my name is Stan Worley. I'm Derrick's attorney. Seems there's been a little misunderstanding."

"Is that so?" Martz said.

"Yes. I think you'll understand after you hear his explanation."

"Okay," Scott said. "We're all ears."

Derrick sat up and cleared his throat. "I created software that not only keeps viruses from coming into anyone's computer, but it returns the virus to the original sender and destroys his computer and everything attached to it."

Scott folded his arms. "Go on."

"It keeps a record of the path back to the origin so that when the message is relayed to the potential victim's computer, it practically gives the perpetrator's address."

"What about all the other people it infected?"

"If they don't have the anti-virus software, they're toast. But if they have my software—or what was my software—the virus returns to the origin and—well, you get the idea."

"Pretty clever. So Hickson took your idea. Ideas aren't patentable. How could he have come up with the software if he only had the idea?"

"He hacked into my computer and stole the whole program."

"How do you know?"

"I had a friend of mine, a patent lawyer by the name of Lee Jernigan, to do a patent search. It was already patented and I followed the trail of who did it. It was Hickson. He took it and presented it to Mar-Tech."

"And they bought it and paid him…"

"Millions."

"Well, that sounds like a pretty good motive for killing him."

"I didn't kill him! I don't know anything about bombs. I wouldn't even know how to start."

"Sure you do, Derrick," Martz said. "You know all about the Internet. You just look it up on the web and find a site that tells you how to make a bomb. It's just that simple."

"That's insane."

Worley leaned forward. "You have no proof." He started to get up. "Let's go, Derrick."

"We can keep him and you know it."

"On what grounds?"

"Probable cause."

"Not good enough."

"What about threats? What about his comment about watching out for crashes?"

"Weren't you talking about computer crashes, Derrick?" his lawyer asked.

"Yes."

Scott leaned forward. "Why would Kyle know about the computers of would-be virus senders? They're certainly not going to advertise..."

"Tell them, Derrick."

He shook his head.

"Tell them, Derrick."

He sighed heavily. "I put something into the program that if anyone used my idea without my permission, it would crash their computer."

Scott and Martz looked at one another. "You mean Mar-Tech is putting a product out there that is going to..."

"Yeah."

"So anyone who uses this program, their computer will crash?"

"Without my specific permission to install it, yeah. You might call it a little extra protection on my part."

"Could Hickman override that?"

"He could if he knew where to look."

"Has it been released yet?"

"Yes."

"When?"

"Yesterday."

Keefer walked into the room. "Scott, Martz, can I see you for a minute?"

They opened the door and walked out into the hallway. "What's up?"

"His apartment's clean. Nothing. Oh, and we just got word that all of Mar-Tech's computers have crashed, and some others in the industry."

Scott and Martz looked at one another. "Looks like Hickson failed to override the part that the program installation needed Derrick's specific permission," Lou said.

"Looks like it and, of course, they installed it into their own system first."

"And already downloaded it to others in the industry."

Lou said, "There go some of the pieces that didn't fit."

Keefer frowned, "What are you talking about?"

"It's a long story."

"Fill me in."

~ ~ ~

Sabyl sat with her arms folded tightly across her chest. She had attempted to distract Amy from further computer use, but it only annoyed her. She closed her eyes and began to pray silently, *"Lord, I don't know if this is the cause of these explosions, but if there is a connection, if there is a bomb in that computer, please, God, do something."*

Just as Amy was about to open the email, the plane began to shudder and bounce. The laptop almost flew out of her lap. The seatbelt sign came on with a noticeable "dong." The Captain's voice came over the speaker, "Folks, we've encountered some—uh—unexpected turbulence. Please keep your seat belts fastened the remainder of the flight."

Amy sighed and closed the laptop and put it away.

Sabyl leaned her head back and smiled. *Thank You, Lord.*

CHAPTER TWENTY-SIX

Scott saw a signal on his cell phone that he had a message. He walked over to the corner of the room and opened it and read the text message from Sabyl. "COM DENOM. AU ISSUED LAPTOPS."

Scott turned to Keefer. "AU issued laptops!"

"What?"

Scott walked over to Derrick and bent down in front of him. "These students. They all use laptops, right?"

"Sure. In fact, all the incoming freshmen were issued laptops."

"How many?"

"Fifteen hundred freshmen, fifteen hundred laptops. We ordered them in February and they came in June. They were in the warehouse until school started in the fall."

Scott looked up at Keefer. "The common denominator." He motioned for Keefer to step aside with him. "Ron, we may have another situation. I just got this text message from Sabyl." He showed it to his boss.

"The only way she could know that is if she's up close and personal with one of them."

"I'm heading for the airport. She'll be approaching National about now."

"Go. And hold that plane until it's been swept!"

~ ~ ~

The turbulence continued. The flight attendants quickly picked up all remaining cups and mopped up a couple of spilled drinks and then took their seats.

Suddenly, the turbulence stopped. Everyone seemed relieved. Amy reached down and pulled her computer out again.

Once again, Amy opened her laptop and got online and opened her email.

~ ~ ~

Derrick looked shocked. "You mean somebody put bombs in the laptops?"

"You tell me. Who else had access to them?"

"Kyle, myself, Abdul."

"The Instructural Tech Coordinator?"

"I guess Kyle told you his theory about him."

"Yeah. Might be more than a theory." He spoke into his radio. "Get Agent Carl Riddick on the phone." He turned back to Derrick. "Where is Abdul?"

"Not sure."

"Where does he live?"

"He has an apartment in Georgetown."

"I wonder how he can afford that."

"No idea."

Keefer got on the phone and ordered more agents to look for him.

~ ~ ~

Amy's email opened. She clicked on the one from her professor.

Sabyl, once again, began to pray. Lord! Please! Do something!

Her finger was about to hit "enter" to open the message from her professor when the Captain's voice came over the speaker, "Ladies and gentlemen, we are now approaching Reagan National Airport. Please put away all electronic devices. We'll be on the ground shortly. Thanks."

Amy's finger hovered over the "Enter" key that would open the email. She fought the urge to go ahead and open it anyway but decided she would comply with the captain's orders. She sighed with frustration once again and reluctantly closed her laptop and put it back in its case.

~ ~ ~

In the UATF Strategy Room, an agent entered the room and announced, "Carl Riddick, sir."

Ron Keefer greeted him with a handshake. "Carl, come in. We need to pick your brain."

"Yes, sir."

He turned to the other agents and introduced him. "Carl is one of our best forensic scientists. He's forgotten more than most people will ever know about forensics."

"Thank you, sir."

"Carl, how long would it take to make an undetectable bomb and put it in a laptop?"

"A while. You'd have to have the right tools. The material—I'm assuming you're talking about something like Plastique or Sentac—would have to be placed perfectly so that it could be closed up again and made to look like it had never been tampered with. I'm sure it would be a long process because it could interfere with the computer's components. He would have to work it and make sure nothing was disturbed and—"

"How long?"

"It could take a week or two to get one just right. Maybe longer."

"So within a period of, say two months, how many do you think?"

"He could have done five or six. But again, it depends on whether or not he had enough of the materials to work with one after another. And that stuff is hard to come by."

Keefer sighed. He liked less ambiguous answers.

"And sir, there is something else to consider. Maybe some of the bombs were in the chargers. No one ever checks those."

"That's a thought."

"And it wouldn't take as long to put one together and place the materials in them. And just imagine the magnitude of a bomb in one of those. There's much more room to place materials in a charger than the new thin laptops."

"So he could have made ten?"

"Depends on how good he is. Also, for these kinds of materials, most manufacturers are voluntarily tagging their materials with chemical markers among international explosive suppliers. If the markers are present, they'll lead us to the origin of sale. But I'm not sure we're looking at either of those materials. They can be detected by dogs."

"Of course, there were no dogs at any of the airports of origin until after the bombings started happening."

Riddick continued, "We're not even sure it's the laptops themselves. There are new kinds of bomb-making devices that can go undetected through even our most recent and sophisticated screening techniques."

"What are they?"

"A new generation of liquid explosive devices called LXD's are a new tactic where the bomb maker can dip ordinary clothing or some kind of material into the liquid that makes the cloth itself into an explosive after it dries. It was the brainchild of the notorious bomb-maker Saudi born, Yemen-based Ibrahim al-Asiri."

"Kind of like the underwear bomber?"

"Not exactly, although that was his idea as well. There were actual plastic explosives sewn into his underwear that he tried to ignite but failed to do so, and was tackled and detained by a passenger. I'm talking about a liquid bomb substance that is actually in the material itself."

"So are you saying it could be in the laptop covers? All the laptops came with covers made of some kind of strong polyester and nylon materials with the AU logo on them. Is that what you're saying?"

"Yes. Or it could even be the padding on the inside."

Martz blurted out, "That's ingenious!"

"Yeah. Evil genius."

Keefer continued, "But how are they detonated?"

"Not sure. The students themselves certainly aren't going to detonate them like Umar Farouk Abdulmutallab did when he tried to ignite his underwear. Again, we're not sure if that's what we're looking at or if the explosives are in the laptops themselves or in the chargers."

"Or all the above."

Keefer rubbed the back of his neck and turned to the agents. "Whatever it is, gentlemen, we're still dealing with explosives, and they're out there on planes and trains and homes. We've got to stop them. Let's get to work."

"Keefer looked at Derrick. Do you have one of those computers?"

"Yes, sir."

"And the cover?"

"Yes. Your people confiscated them."

Carl said, "We've got them in forensics."

"Have you checked out your LXD theory on the laptop cover?"

"Not yet, sir."

"Get on it."

"Yes, sir."

~ ~ ~

The aircraft followed the river at 1,800 feet at Chain Bridge, 1,200 feet at the Georgetown Reservoir, and 900 feet at the Key Bridge and lined up with runway 19. Landing at National was, as the locals put it, a "slam dunk" due to the shortness of the runway; less than 7,000 feet. When they touched down, everyone on the plane let out a collective sigh of relief.

Amy was still thinking over what Sabyl had told her. She handled the computer with care as she lifted the black case with the AU logo on the front. "What should I do?" she said nervously. "I'm afraid to carry the thing around with me now."

"I know," Sabyl said, "I'm sorry, but you can see why I was…"

"I'm scared. What should I do? Hand it over to security?"

"We don't know if there is a bomb in there, but I couldn't let it go if there was even a possibility. Look, let me make a quick call. I know someone with the Secret Service. He'll know what to do. He's investigating the bombings."

Amy sighed. "Absolutely."

Glad she didn't have to join the stampede to the baggage claim area, Sabyl followed Amy off the plane, up the ramp and exited the gate.

The two women were met with airport security. They quietly asked them to step into a side room behind a nondescript door. Sabyl pulled out the special cell phone Scott had given her and called him. He answered just as he and another man walked into the room.

Sabyl looked up. "You're here!"

He took her hand. "Thank God you're safe."

"Scott, this is Amy Holloman. I take it you got my message."

The man with Scott, a bomb expert, looked at Amy's laptop case. "May I relieve you of this for a while, Amy?"

She handed it to him gingerly. "Gladly."

He turned and headed out the door.

Scott walked Sabyl and Amy to Sabyl's car. He turned to Amy and asked, "Why are you returning to D.C. here at Christmastime?"

"I live here. I was just up in New York for dinner with my brother. He's a lawyer there."

"Okay. I hope you have a nice Christmas with your family."

The three of them walked toward the parking garage.

"It's nice of you to give me a ride," Amy said.

"Glad to, dear," Sabyl said as she punched the unlock button on her key ring. The Murano's light blinked and the doors unlocked.

Scott said, "Just a minute, honey." He took out a small LED flashlight, got down on the cement and looked under the car.

"Oh, Scott, you don't think…"

"Just checking."

He got up, opened the driver side door and checked under the dash.

He stood and straightened his coat. "All clear."

"Thanks, honey," Sabyl said, hugging him. She got in and closed the door, started the car and rolled down the window.

Amy cautiously got in the passenger side. When Sabyl saw the look on her face, she assured her it was fine.

Scott bent down, his arms resting on the open window and said, "I'll call you as soon as I know something."

"Okay," she said. "It may be nothing, Scott, but…"

"You did the right thing. We'll check it out."

Amy asked, "When do you think I could get my laptop back? I have homework to do."

"Yeah. So do we."

Scott pressed his finger to his ear. He was getting a message from Keefer. He stood up straight and frowned deeply. "Oh, my G—!" He rubbed his forehead. "Yes, she's safe. She's here with me now. Okay, I'm on my way."

He put his phone away and looked at Sabyl with sad eyes.

"Scott, what is it?"

He hesitated a moment and then said, "The original flight you were supposed to return on tonight just blew up."

CHAPTER TWENTY-SEVEN

Frank worked diligently to secure the new car seat properly in the back seat of their Volvo. "There! I got it in. Man! I didn't know these things were so high tech!"

Barbara smiled as she handed their newborn daughter to her husband. He gently placed her tiny body in the seat and fastened all the belts, hoping he had done it right. Barbara got into the front passenger seat and fastened her seat belt. Frank got in, buckled up, started the car and the radio immediately came on with the news of the plane that went down last night.

"Oh, my God, I think that was Sabyl's plane!"

"No! It can't be, Frank! Someone would have called us if anything had happened to her...wouldn't they?"

Frank sat staring out the windshield. He then reached for his phone. "I've got to call and make sure she's all right." He punched in the speed dial number for Sabyl and it rang and rang. "Something's wrong. She usually answers right away."

"Maybe she's on another line. Oh, Frank, you don't think..."

"I have to know she's alright. I'm going to call the office." He dialed again and Dotty answered. She sounded like she had been crying. Oh, God, no, he thought.

"Martin Transportation Group," Dotty answered, wiping her nose.

"Dotty, it's Frank. What's going on? Is Sabyl...?"

"She hasn't come in yet, Frank."

"You heard about the latest plane explosion, right?"

"Yes. She was on another plane. Scott made her switch flights."

"Oh, thank God." He looked at Barbara and nodded. "She's okay."

"Frank, when are you going to bring Barb and the baby by so we can see her?"

"We're in the car now and heard the news on the radio."

"You mean no one called you to tell you that Sabyl's okay?"

"No. It nearly scared us to death!"

"Well, that's just the pigs. I guess I thought…"

"Never mind, it's okay. We're just glad she's safe."

"Yeah. Scott saved her life! He's the man!"

"Yes, he is."

"Hey, Frank, are you and Barb coming to the Christmas party? Or are you going to be up to it?"

"I'll have to get back to you on that one, Dotty. Let's see how Barb feels and how little Sabyl Lynn does her first few nights home."

"Copy that. Can't wait to see her."

"I can't wait to show her off. She's beautiful."

"She must look like her mother."

Frank chuckled "You got that right. Okay, we're going to take her home now. I'll get back with you about the party."

"Gotcha. Tell Barb I said hi. And congratulations, Frank. I'm proud of you."

Frank laughed. "I didn't do anything. Be proud of Barb. She did all the work."

Barbara smiled and nodded and looked back at her sleeping infant.

Frank pulled out of the parking lot of the hospital and headed home.

~ ~ ~

The interrogation room was once again filled with agents of all persuasions. Scott and Lou Martz stood to the left of Keefer. Derrick sat slumped in a chair, a half-empty diet drink in front of him on a marked-up table, his face displaying a thick five o'clock shadow that was progressing toward 9 o'clock.

Keefer walked around the table and leaned on it. "Has anyone broken into the storage area where the computers were stored?"

Derrick straightened. "The silent alarm went off one night. The police called—we met them there. We looked through the area. Nothing was missing—nothing was harmed, so we concluded the alarm had malfunctioned."

"Was there a surveillance tape?"

"Yes, one on the outside and it was so dark, nothing could be seen."

Scott asked, "What about the inside?"

Derrick took a sip of the diet drink and set it down. "There is one on the inside."

Scott turned to his boss. "Has anyone looked to see if there was anything on it?"

Keefer answered while still staring at Derrick, "We have it but haven't heard back from the lab." He scratched his cheek and continued. "Something isn't adding up. Someone has a key—goes in and takes some laptops out of the storage area—sets off a silent alarm, but nothing's missing."

An FBI agent offered, "Maybe something was missing, but replaced with something else. Maybe x amount of computers were removed and x amount put in their place."

Keefer looked at him. "That's the only thing that makes sense." He turned back to Derrick. "Did anyone check the serial numbers?"

"No, we just counted cases. None were missing."

"If someone had a key, would it still set off the alarm?"

Derrick folded his arms and sat back. "Yes, unless they decoded it."

"So anyone with a key would know about the silent alarm. Correct?"

"Yes. Unless someone unauthorized stole a key and somehow got the code to the alarm system."

"How would that be possible?"

Derrick cocked his head to one side and replied, "Anything can be hacked into."

Martz asked, "Who all had keys to the storage room?"

"Hickson, Kyle, Abdul and myself."

Keefer asked, "Abdul?

"Yes. He's the Instructural Tech Coordinator."

"We'd like to talk to him."

Derrick sniffed. "He might not be very cooperative."

"Why not?"

"He was detained earlier this year; accused of being an Al Qaeda benefactor because he had given to a charity that turned out to be an advocate to terrorist organizations. He claimed he didn't know that it was. They finally released him. It embarrassed him and his family. Some of the students started talking about him and avoiding him.

"I remember reading a report on that," said Martz.

"Abdul's a good man," said Derrick.

"And a computer whiz, right?"

Derrick hesitated. "Right."

"Got his phone number?"

"Sure."

"Can you tell me the names of the students who harassed him?"

Derrick's face froze.

"What's wrong?"

"Most of them are dead."

~ ~ ~

"Sit over there, Mr. Arib¬," said Fred Causewell, the FBI agent who was very good at interrogation.

Abdul moved clumsily over to a chair against the wall. He couldn't believe he was back in custody again. What if they didn't let him go this time? Sweat beaded on his smooth forehead. He pulled out his handkerchief and mopped his brow.

"Just be straight with us, Abdul, and it will go much faster," said Ron Keefer.

Causewell leaned into him. "And it will be much better for you."

"Why am I here? I have done nothing wrong."

"We want to talk to you about the bombings, Abdul," Causewell said tightly.

Abdul's eyes widened. His anger was beginning to turn into cold fear. "I had nothing to do with the bombings. I am not a violent man."

"According to some of your recent emails, you're pretty unhappy with America."

He spread his hand on the table. "Yes, I confess that I have been hurt and embarrassed with the arrest that took place back in August, but I am not a murderer. And how did you get those emails?"

"Mr. Arib, we have confiscated your computer and some other equipment you had in your apartment. We'll be looking very deeply into what you've been doing on your computer." The interrogator watched for that glimmer of fear he had seen so often when the reality of possible damning evidence was imminent. All he saw was displeasure that his personal property had been touched.

"When will I get my property back?"

"That depends on what they find."

"They will find nothing because I have done nothing wrong."

"Then you have no need to worry."

"Don't I? When innocent people are arrested just because they are of a particular…"

"Don't play the race card, Abdul. We've got more reason to believe you're a part of this than the fact that you're a Middle Easterner."

"And what would that be?"

"Hickson."

"Because I worked with Professor Hickson? I liked Professor Hickson. He taught me a lot and I respected him."

"No, as a matter of fact, we know you did not respect him, Abdul. You hated the fact that he was messing around with another woman."

Abdul swallowed hard. "I did not approve of…"

"That's a real crime in your culture, isn't it, Abdul?"

"As it should be in all cultures."

Causewell's neck swelled like a cobra. "Oh, so now you're the Taliban all of a sudden? You're going to preach to us…?"

"That's enough, Fred," said Keefer. He turned to Abdul. "You haven't learned yet that you can't legislate morality? Many people have tried and they ended up hateful dictators."

"Your free speech has turned your once great country into a place of degradation."

"And that's worse than murdering people that don't follow your rules?"

They had hoped by allowing Abdul to vent his antipathy might lead to a loose enough tongue to condemn himself, but instead, he folded his arms and crossed his legs in a defensive manner. "How long must I be here?"

"We're not sure yet, Abdul. Just relax. You won't be detained any longer than is necessary."

"I assure you, my being here is completely unnecessary."

"I hope you're right."

In the meantime, the other agents were running his I.D. through their new International Crime Information (ICI) computer. It showed only the arrest and brief detainment at the beginning of the school year.

Keefer looked into Abdul's eyes. Does he look like he would have a passion for killing? But he knew that he could not go by his gut. He needed hard evidence.

Abdul wanted to call a lawyer, but he didn't know who to call. He didn't trust them. Not any of them.

~ ~ ~

Candles, tiny American flags, flowers, and teddy bears made up the makeshift memorials that gathered beside the doors at Dulles and Reagan National Airports and at Beltsville, MD where the Amtrak bomb went off.

Many reporters stood outside the area hospitals where the injured Amtrak passengers were being treated. The death toll from the bombing of the train was now up to 35 with 19 still in serious condition.

Journalists across the nation, indeed around the world, were writing about the same subject in one way or another, each account covering the same topic. Quite a task for those who had little facts to go on except that planes were being blown out of the sky, and now a train, a limo, and a cabin, with still more questions than answers.

Working diligently to find those answers, forensics had gone through the apartments of Derrick, Abdul, and Kyle. So far it turned up nothing solid on any of the three.

At UATF HQ, Keefer pulled his chair out ⌐and sat down. "So far we know who it isn't. But we still don't know who it is that is doing the bombings." He turned to Scott. "You know, Scott, you'd better talk to Sabyl. It looks like the terrorists are back for..."

"Yeah, so it would seem with that fax threatening her. But why Sabyl?"

Keefer took a deep breath. "They always want to finish what they started. Just like when they bombed the World Trade Center in '93. It took them a while, but they came back to finish the job."

"Even though it was eight years later," Martz said in a low voice.

"But why are they threatening Sabyl?"

"She kept them from killing the president."

"So, they want to kill her?"

"Yeah. And him." Keefer shoved his hands in his pockets and walked over to the window and looked out.

Martz leaned forward in his chair, his forearms on his thighs. "But why all the bombings? It doesn't add up."

"Who knows? Maybe it's their way of retaliating since we ruined their little payback game last year."

Keefer turned and looked at Scott levelly. "You'd better talk to her about letting us put her in protective custody."

"She'll never go for that."

"Talk to her anyway. Oh, and Scott, you'd better not let her go again. She's pretty special."

Scott smiled. "Don't worry. I won't," he said, meaning it.

~ ~ ~

Kyle stepped out of the shower and grabbed a towel and dried off. He put on his underwear, shaved, and got dressed. Unzipping a plastic bag, he gathered his toiletries, put them in and placed them in his suitcase. The feds had not told him he couldn't leave town, so he was packing in hopes they were done with him. At least until after the holidays.

His cell rang. He stared at it and thought about not answering but changed his mind. "Hello."

An unfamiliar voice asked, "Is this Kyle Sloan?"

He hesitated. "Yes. Who's this?"

"I'm Darrin Foust. I'm a student at AU."

"Okay."

"I need to talk to Derrick Blake or somebody about my laptop."

Kyle hesitated. "I work at the Tech Center. You can talk to me. What's up?"

"I, uh, loaned my AU issued laptop to my girlfriend and..."

"Uh, you know you weren't supposed to..." Kyle could hear a quiet sob at the other end of the line.

"I know but...anyhow, she's...she's dead."

"What? Who?"

"My girlfriend...she's...Merriweather's daughter."

"Oh, wow, man. The private jet that...?"

"Yes. Anyhow, I know this sounds cold, but I wondered if I can...get a replacement. I have homework and...I thought I was going to join them in Vermont as soon as I could get off work and..."

Kyle rubbed his forehead. "Not sure I can answer that right now, Darrin. Are you calling from your cell?"

"Yes."

"Okay, I have your number in my phone and I'll call you as soon as I find out, okay?"

"Okay, thanks."

"And Darrin...I'm sorry about your girlfriend."

"Thanks. Me too."

Kyle resumed packing. He couldn't do anything at this juncture for Darrin. As far as he knew, there were no extra laptops for replacements.

He went over to a pile of clothes he had left on the floor and pulled up a pair of jeans and dug in the pockets, extracting a card. He went over to a chair, sat down and stared at the number on the card. He put the card down and decided to finish packing.

CHAPTER TWENTY-EIGHT

Finishing up an email to his mother, he sent it and then closed that site and quickly opened another to check all the news report. He knew the last of the bombs had gone off and was delighted that Sabyl Martin's plane was the final one. Well, almost. He scanned the headlines of the major newspapers and then turned off his laptop and sighed in relief. He could now focus on what he had come here to do. And he felt honored that he would be the one to pull it off.

With a satisfied smile, he got up, pushed the desk chair back in its place, and settled into a large, comfortable lounge chair, propped his feet up and picked up the remote and turned on the TV.

News of the flight out of New York heading for Reagan National airport was being reported on nearly every channel. It had exploded in midair and was lying in fragments on the cold ground just south of Philadelphia. All passengers were believed to have perished. Along with the deaths of the victims on the Amtrak bombing and Rufus Merriweather's private jet, the death toll now had reached 1,719.

"He smiled and whispered, "Good riddance, Sabyl Martin!"

~ ~ ~

Scott and Lou Martz sat across from Sabyl in her office. Dotty brought them each a fresh cup of coffee. She patted Scott on the shoulder and said, "You the man!"

He smiled, "I am, eh?"

"Yes, you are. You made Sabyl change flights. You saved her life. You're definitely the man!"

Scott smiled. "Thank the Man upstairs, Dotty."

"I do. Every day. He's the main Man."

"You've got that right."

Martz rubbed the side of his nose and smiled.

"Okay, I'll leave you alone." Dotty went out the door and quietly shut it.

Sabyl leaned forward, her elbows on the desk, her hands folded under her chin. "So what did you want to tell me, Scott?"

"I just wanted to tell you that the guy with the D.C. Sniper fetish is not our man."

"Derrick? Are you sure?"

"We're sure. That whole thing with the D.C. Snipers was some sort of research for a novel he's writing."

Martz spoke up, "Yeah. We checked it out. The book, or what he's done with it so far, is there...in his computer."

"But what about Hickson?"

Scott looked at Martz and back at Sabyl. "We're pretty sure that bomb was meant for Rudy, not Hickson."

Sabyl gasped, "Rudy? Why?"

"The same reason they've threatened you. Their work is not finished. You and Rudy stopped their main goal last year..."

"Oh, Scott! That's...that's so..."

"I know. Look, honey, we're still dealing with someone who wants to hurt you. I'm afraid it's the same kind of terrorist ploy as last year."

But Endicott is dead. He..."

"He's dead, but what he came to do was not finished."

"So the fax I got in Pennsylvania was not from Derrick?"

"No."

"Then who?"

"We don't know."

Sabyl was stunned.

Scott's cell rang. "Sorry, babe." He answered, "Terhune here."

"Agent Terhune?"

"Yes."

"This is Kyle Sloan. You gave me your card and told me to call you if I learned anything new?"

Scott sat up straight. "Yes, Kyle. What is it?"

"I got a call from an AU student, a freshman, who told me that he loaned his laptop to his girlfriend."

"Yes, go on."

"It was Merriweather's daughter."

Scott snapped his fingers at Martz and made a signal to give him something to write on. Sabyl quickly handed him a post-it note and pen. "Do you have his phone number, Kyle?"

"Yes, sir."

Scott quickly wrote it down. "Thanks, Kyle, that's a big help."

"No problem."

They hung up. Martz looked at him quizzically. "What was that?"

"The missing piece of our puzzle. Or at least one of them."

Sabyl looked confused. "What?"

"Merriweather's jet that blew up?"

Martz asked, "What about it?"

"The only one that didn't have an AU student on it?"

"Yeah?"

He explained what Kyle had just told him.

Martz leaned back. "Whew. Now we know the laptops are definitely the common denominator."

Scott turned to Sabyl. "This doesn't mean that you're safe, honey. Please let me put you into protective custody. I won't rest until I know you're safe."

"What does that mean? That I have to hide out in some sort of...boarded up place like a frightened little girl? No way. I've got too much to do."

"But honey..."

"I'm not going to hole up in some...some..."

Scott put up his hands in mock surrender. "Okay."

"I don't mean to be difficult, Scott, but..."

"I understand, honey."

"Good. Look, I have a ton of work to do. I'm not even going to ask if you think you can make it to our Christmas party."

"At this point, probably not, but you never know."

She sighed, "That's for sure." She stood, walked around her desk and kissed him on the cheek and said, "Call me when you can."

He squeezed her hand. "I will."

She headed for her car. When she got in, she noticed she had an unanswered text on her phone. It was from Rebecca.

"MAY I COME BY TONIGHT? I HAVE SOMETHING TO TELL YOU."

Sabyl replied, "SURE. WHAT TIME?"

"AROUND 7:30? I'LL BRING DINNER IF YOU DON'T HAVE PLANS. PIZZA GOOD?"

"ABSOLUTELY."

Sabyl smiled and wondered if she and Paul were getting engaged. He seemed nice but...she let the thought drop as she wondered if she would get a ring for Christmas. Yet she still wasn't sure they were ready.

~ ~ ~

Rebecca greeted her with a kiss on each cheek. "You liked that white cheese and sun-dried tomato pizza that we had at the pub on Wisconsin Avenue, right?"

"Love it!" Sabyl took the square box from her and took it into the kitchen. "Thanks for getting this, Bec. I'm starved!"

Rebecca helped her get the plates and napkins on the table. They sat down, and Sabyl prayed a small prayer of thanks.

Rebecca could stand it no longer. "Sabyl, I can't wait to tell you my news."

"I can't wait to hear." She looked at her and smiled. "My goodness, Bec, you look like you swallowed a light bulb!"

"Do I?"

"Yes, have you fallen in love?"

"As a matter of fact, I have. And it's your fault."

"Mine? How? I've not introduced you to anyone."

"Actually, you have."

"Who?"

"The one I've been looking for all my life."

"Please tell me about it."

"It started with what you shared with me that night at your home in Pennsylvania last year. Sabyl, my life has…changed."

"In what way?"

"I have a strange peace residing in me now."

"Bec, that's wonderful. Tell me about it."

"That night you told me how that Gideon Bible had spoken to you in that hotel room in L.A. when you flew out to meet with a client. I felt almost jealous at the hope it gave you. And as soon as we got back to town, I went out and bought a Bible of my own. Funny, my passion for reading

220

and my love of writing, yet I had never read the best-seller of all time. Never even owned one."

Sabyl sat quietly, waiting for more.

"I'm not usually one to start a book from the middle, but for some reason, I felt compelled to do as you did...to let it open for me, so to speak. It fell open at John chapter one. I began reading and I couldn't stop. It was as though the words were burning straight into my heart."

Sabyl sat forward, smiled and listened intently. "Go on."

"I...realized for the first time that it's...that He is real. It's not all just a nice story, but it's...it's the truth."

"Yes, Bec, it is...He is."

"And I remember what you said to me. You said you would find the truth and then you'd be free. Sabyl, I know what that means now. I have found the truth, and I am free. He...Jesus...is the truth!"

"Indeed He is."

"How could I have been so blind?"

"We're all blind until He opens our eyes." Sabyl smiled and reached over and hugged her friend. "Oh, Bec, I'm so happy for you."

"Thank you, honey." They took their paper plates to the trash and went into the living room and sat down.

"Sabyl, I nearly died when I heard the plane you were supposed to be on went down. I'm so glad you took the time to email me and your other friends that knew you were flying that night. Thank you so much for that."

"You're welcome, honey. I knew you all would figure out that was the plane I..."

Rebecca reached over and took her hand. "I was praying for you but I sure didn't expect anything like that to happen!"

"I know. I'm just so grateful that Scott made me change flights, but I can't help but think of all those poor people on that plane…"

"So many have died. It's just so sad. And right here at Christmastime too. Think of the families…"

"I know. Let's just pray they catch whoever is doing this and that it will stop once and for all."

"Yes!"

"Scott told me that he thinks Rudy and I are being targeted again."

"What? Why?"

"He thinks because Rudy and I kept them from, you know…and now they're back to finish what they started."

Rebecca's face flushed. "Oh, Sabyl, how awful! But why all the bombings? What does that have to do with what they came to do last year?"

"I don't know, Bec. Maybe they just want to show that they can. You know, to terrorize us into somehow submitting to their crazy ideology."

"You would think they would see that after Nine Eleven that Americans bow to no one."

"You'd think but…"

"I'll be praying even more for you and Rudy."

"Thanks, honey. We need it."

"I read the most wonderful Psalm last night. Psalm 91. I'm going to pray that one for you. Then I know you'll be safe."

~ ~ ~

His apartment was dark except for the light from his computer and the small lamp on his desk. The smell of General Tso Chicken was in the air, the small cardboard boxes the Chinese dish had occupied sat to one side, a plastic fork stuck in the uneaten rice.

He sat back, folded his arms across his chest and reread the email he had just composed. He read it again and again. Confident that his words were well articulated and arranged to make the best impact, Derrick's fingers flew over the keyboard like birds in flight. He was careful not to miss one name on the list. Satisfied, he punched in the words, "AN URGENT MESSAGE FROM YOUR PROFESSOR" in the subject line. He punched "Send," and sat back, content with what he had accomplished.

~ ~ ~

Dotty tried Sabyl's cell again. Nothing. Her brow drew up in a knot. That's not like her to not answer.

Derrick opened the door and carried the computer into Martin Transportation. Dotty looked up from her desk. "Well, it's about time! Take it in there," she said, pointing to Sabyl's office.

"Here, let me get the door."

"I got it."

"So what took so long?"

"There was more to it than I anticipated."

"Well, as long as it's fixed."

Derrick took Sabyl's computer into her office, sat down at her desk and turned on the monitor and the computer. "That should do it."

"Okay, what's the verdict?"

Derrick handed her a bill. "Hey! You're pretty reasonable! But slow. Very slow." She turned to go back to her office. "I'll cut you a check," she hollered over her shoulder.

"Jenny around?" he said as he followed her into her office.

Dotty sat down with a thud. "No, she's running an errand for me." She quickly typed in the amount, punched "Enter" and the printer did its thing. Dotty tore it off, signed it and handed it to him. "Here you go."

"Is Ms. Martin around?"

"No, she's at a meeting." She wasn't about to tell him she had no idea where she was.

"Is the laptop I loaned her here?"

"Oh, sure. Let me get it for you."

"Thanks."

Dotty got up with a grunt and went back into Sabyl's office. She opened the door to her credenza and pulled out the laptop. "Don't think she ever used it."

He left and she tried to call Sabyl again. Still no answer. That's it. I'm calling Scott.

~ ~ ~

Sabyl's phone still didn't answer. Scott wondered why she didn't return his call. She hadn't even told Dotty where she'd be, her cell phone was off, and Beau was still with George. Was he too premature in telling her that the terrorists might be back? No. She was in danger and she knew he had to warn her.

Scott got in his Camry and set out for the one place he knew she always went when she wanted to think. He crossed Memorial Bridge, circled around to the narrow road that led to the Iwo Jima Marine monument. He turned into the parking area and saw her car. At first, he was relieved and then wondered if he was intruding.

A handful of tourists stared at the bronze memorial, the floodlights causing the giant Marines' shadows to deepen and seemingly come alive. The flag flapped and the grommets gently hit against the metal pole causing a quiet ping, ping, ping.

Sabyl gazed at the city spread out before her. From there she could see Washington D.C.'s famous monuments, the Lincoln Memorial, the Washington Monument, and the Capitol. Such a beautiful place; home of the most powerful government on Earth, yet it seemed powerless to stop the madness. She watched the movement of tiny headlights along the ribbons of streets, parkways, and bridges, people peacefully going about their lives, or at least most of them were. Among them were also those who wanted nothing more than to bring death and devastation to our great nation. To think that such evil lives among us; that they spend their time and brainpower scheming, contriving, plotting and, building bombs.

The famous site never ceased to amaze her. She never tired of the spectacular view.

It seemed incredulous to her that lurking among the symbols of freedom were those who sought to destroy them and those who defended them. Why can't we all just live in peace? The devil comes to kill, steal and destroy. Why can't they see that's who they're following?

Scott spotted Sabyl sitting on the ground at the edge of the hill that overlooked Washington. He quietly sat down next to her and wondered how long she had been sitting on the cold ground.

Without looking, she knew it was Scott. She felt his presence and knew his scent before he sat beside her. She looked at him with profound sadness in her eyes. He thought his heart would break.

She turned from him and stared at the sight below. "Scott, what makes people so full of hatred? Why can't people be satisfied to let others live their lives in peace?"

"I don't know, honey. Only God knows."

"These people are supposed to be religious...they claim to be doing it for God."

"I know..."

"Not much has changed in two thousand years, has it? When God sent His own Son to bring peace on earth, it was the most religious ones who hated Him the most."

"Seems like they still do."

"Yes, they still do."

"Look, honey, I'm sorry if I frightened you by telling you..."

She turned to him with tears in her eyes. "I don't know if I can go through this again."

"You can't be running off by yourself like this and not tell anybody where you are. Dotty's worried sick and so is Rudy and so was I."

"I'm sorry. I didn't mean to cause...I just needed some time alone to think. And I always do my best thinking up here."

"I know. That's how I found you."

She smiled. "Oh, you didn't find me because you're the best Secret Service agent in the whole world?"

It was good to see her smile. "No, just the one who loves and knows you best. Sabyl, I love you more than life and I don't ever want to let you go..."

She looked at him through a cascade of tears. "Oh, Scott, I love you too. But..."

"But what?"

"Scott, you know we've talked about this before. I'm a Christian and..."

Scott looked deeply into her eyes. *I know you are, honey. That's one reason I love you so much.* "I want what you have. I just don't know how..."

"I'll help you, honey. It's not that hard. It's just a matter of believing..."

"But I do believe in Jesus."

"It's more than that, Scott. It's not a matter of mental assent or just believing that He existed. The devil believes! It's believing with all your heart that He paid the ultimate price for our redemption."

"But what about all those other religions? It's confusing."

"All those other "deities" are created, sons…flesh and blood, just like you and me. Their bones are in the ground; they can't help us. Jesus is the only begotten Son. He's alive because of Easter."

"Begotten."

"Yes, darling. Begotten of God through his Holy Spirit. And when we ask Him to forgive us of our sins and accept Him as our Savior, His Spirit literally comes into us, and our spirit is birthed alive, and we are made brand new."

"Nobody has ever explained that to me before. I need to think about this." He squeezed her hand. "Can I get back to you on this?"

"Yes, of course. I'm praying for you, Scott."

He swallowed hard and looked down. "Thanks, honey. I need it."

CHAPTER TWENTY-NINE

The time for the grand finale was here. The patent information on Ted's software that he had stolen from Derrick Blake had been hacked into and it was now in the name of Eva Thornburg. As soon as the money came into her account, she could leave the U.S. and return home to Great Britain. It had been so easy to maneuver her way into Ted's life. And now he's dead and his program is hers. He had not only gladly willed it to her, but she, with the help of her son, Jeremy, would be set for life. Not that she had not been well taken care of by her late husband, but he was now gone, and no more money would be coming in. Assassins rarely had a retirement plan, although he did have a significant insurance policy that she was already spending lavishly and he did buy her a villa in southern Italy where she planned to live out her days. How nice of Ted to put me in his will and now I'll get the two million for finishing the job John had set out to do. The pain of losing her husband still stung. She seethed with rage as she thought about how Sabyl Martin had caused the death of her husband. And how she had somehow escaped dying in the plane that exploded…That's okay, she thought. I still have plans for Ms. Martin.

Something else was on her mind. She had become concerned about Jeremy. He had changed in the last year. His demeanor had grown cold since he befriended a young man at the university. Jeremy had become intense and had been attending a mosque with him and she was worried that he was being radicalized. Surely he won't do anything stupid, she thought. We've gone over the plans again and again. He had better come out of this alive. I have big plans for that young man.

Tonight would be the most wonderful Christmas ever. Not that she believed in Christmas or what it stands for. She enjoyed being lavished with gifts from her husband in years past. She stood and walked to the window, staring out into the gathering night. This would be her gift to him. She would put the finishing touches on what her husband had begun, plus the massive fee for the contract with the ones who had hired him in the first place to do their little payback game. She was still amazed and a bit amused that they had agreed to let her finish the job. But when she joined her husband on a trip to Dubai, she had made quite an impression on his contacts there, especially after he had bragged on her that she was as smart, maybe smarter than he and much more lethal. She smiled at the thought. He taught me well.

She looked at her watch. They should be arriving any time now. Good luck, son.

~ ~ ~

The roar of the 3,000-horsepower engine of Marine One alerted the staffers at Camp David that POTUS was here. The grass was covered with frost when the powerful green and white Sikorsky VH-3D gently touched the ground. The force of the rotor-wind threw tiny crystals of ice in the faces of the staff that was standing by. The short half-hour, 70-mile ride from the White House had been one of perfect precision operated by the HMX-1 "Nighthawks" squadron. Marine One always traveled with one or two identical helicopters serving as decoys for would-be assassins. Every member of HMX-1 is required to obtain a top secret "Yankee White" security clearance before they can even come near any of the nineteen helicopters in the fleet.

Before the sophisticated variable-chord rotor blades came to a stop, the door was opened, the stairs let down, and two Marines in crisp full dress blue uniforms and spit-shined shoes stepped out of the aircraft and stood at attention on either side of the door.

After the traditional "thank you" handshake to the crew chief, the President of the United States, Byron William Anderson and his wife, Jane, stepped out and waved to the awaiting staffers. Both Marines executed in unison a sharp salute to their Commander-in-Chief. He returned the salute and the Marines conjointly snapped back to attention.

"Merry Christmas, Mr. President," offered the head staffer.

"Merry Christmas, Charles."

After the First Couple descended down the steps, their daughter Allyson followed, carrying her white miniature poodle, Dolly, complete with a red bow on her head.

Behind her, stepped out a young man whom the president introduced. "Charles, this is Jeremy Stallings. Please take his luggage to the guest cabin."

"Yes, Mr. President. Welcome, Mr. Stallings."

"Thank you. Please call me Jeremy."

~ ~ ~

"We got something," Martz said to Ron Keefer as he entered his office carrying a file. He handed it to him and sat down. Scott followed him inside and stood across from them and folded his arms.

"What do you have?" Keefer asked, opening the file.

230

"That laptop of Amy Holloman's. It has a bomb in it, all right. The techs say that it has a mechanism to go off if she opens an email that says, 'AN URGENT MESSAGE FROM YOUR PROFESSOR.'" He whistled softly. "What student wouldn't open that one?"

"Oh, man!" Scott said, "That's the message Sabyl said she saw Amy trying to get into."

Martz shook his head slowly. "If Amy had opened it, it would have been all over."

Scott tightened his fists. "That's just too close to home!"

"They're all too close to home," Keefer interjected.

Martz folded his arms. "But is that what has set off all these explosions?"

Keefer drew a deep breath. "Don't know yet."

"So they may have done some of them by other means."

"Yeah, as we've discussed before, maybe he used a timer on them that could have been set off by the X-ray machine in security before boarding the plane."

"Or they were set to go off when they hit a certain altitude."

"Our guy's pretty bomb and computer savvy."

"Yeah. Most terrorists aren't. But, unfortunately, it looks like they're getting better at it."

"Okay, so we've got a computer geek that's doing this. Now what?"

"We need a geek to catch another geek," Keefer said.

"Derrick?"

"Maybe he can help. The agency's got its own geeks. We'll put them all to work. We've got to find them before they can kill again."

"You got that right," Martz and Scott said in unison.

~ ~ ~

Camp David rests atop Catoctin Mountain outside Thurmont, Maryland. The retreat, which comprises a scenic mountainous thick forested area of 200 acres, is enclosed by maximum security fencing. A short flight from Washington, Camp David is a quick getaway, should the president need a break from the grueling pressures of the office.

President Franklin Delano Roosevelt used the retreat home frequently before his death and named it Shangri-La in 1942. Eisenhower later renovated it and renamed it Camp David in honor of his grandson. The Aspen Lodge was initially called "The Bear's Den" by FDR. The cabin was renamed "Aspen Lodge" in honor of Mrs. Eisenhower who was born in Colorado.

Jeremy and Allyson were the last ones to leave the dining table. He stretched his long frame. "That was a wonderful dinner."

Allyson smiled. "Yes, the food is really good here. Those Navy chefs are awesome. They'll fix anything you want if you get hungry later."

"Do they have popcorn?"

"All you want."

"Your dad said something about watching the Redskins and the Eagles. Do you like football?"

"It's okay. I prefer hockey."

Jeremy pulled back and looked at her in surprise. "Really? I wouldn't have guessed that of you." He bent down and whispered, "What time do your parents go to bed?"

Allyson giggled, "Early. Why?"

He looked at one of the Secret Service agents standing by the door. He leaned over and whispered, "Do these guys watch your every move if you decide to stay up a bit later?"

"What do you think?"

He put his arms around her. "Wish we could have some alone time tonight."

She snuggled up to him. "Me too."

"They won't let me bring my laptop in, or we could play "Dhako's Empire.""

"Oh, I love that game!" She lowered her voice. "Maybe we can sneak it in."

"Are you serious?"

"What do you think?"

He grinned at her and said, "Let's go into the living room before they wonder about us."

~ ~ ~

The family of Vice President Carl Bridges family was relaxing with hot chocolate and popcorn while they watched The Grinch that Stole Christmas on Air Force Two heading for their home in Indiana.

Air Force Two is the air traffic control call sign held by any U.S. Air Force aircraft carrying the Vice President of the United States. The Boeing C-32, a sleek 757 modified to comfortably accommodate the Vice President, the Second Lady, a term the VP loathed, their family, staff and other traveling dignitaries. The forward area was the communications center which featured an advanced communication suite, including state-of-the-art telephones, satellites, television monitors, fax and copy machines.

The Bridges family was comfortably ensconced in the second section, a fully-enclosed stateroom, which included a private lavatory, separate entertainment system, two first-class swivel seats and a convertible divan that seats three and folds out to a bed.

"May I get you anything else, ma'am?" the Marine sergeant asked Mrs. Bridges.

"No, thank you, Chris."

"And how about you, Danny?"

The VP's son ignored him, entirely enthralled with the green creature from Whoville.

Ellen Bridges smiled. "He's fine. That'll be all, thanks."

"Will the Vice President be joining you, ma'am?"

"No, he's resting. Let's just let him sleep."

"Yes, ma'am."

CHAPTER THIRTY

A large screen TV was turned down low as the sportscasters called the plays for the Redskins and Giants game. The President's eyes drooped shut. The First Lady elbowed him gently, "Dear, you're falling asleep. Let's go to bed and leave these two to cheer the Skins on."

He sat up and said, "You're right, as always, my love." They stood and the President of the United States and the First Lady said goodnight as they walked through the wide door that led to their bedroom. "Goodnight, sweetheart. Don't stay up too late. Goodnight, Jeremy."

Jeremy stood. "Goodnight, sir, ma'am." He sat back down, looked at Allyson and whispered, "Alone at last."

"Well, not entirely," she said, nodding toward the front door.

He could see the outline of an agent's head through the small window on the door. "Man! They're everywhere!"

Allyson smiled, "Mr. Sanders is nice. He'll let us have some space."

"How much space?" he said, pulling her to him.

"Not that much," she said, giggling and pulling away.

Jeremy sighed, "Ah, well, that's what I get for falling in love with the President's daughter. A thousand eyes are watching every move I make."

"It's not quite that bad," she smiled.

"So, what do you want to do?"

"We can watch the rest of the game, if you want, or shoot some pool."

"Wanna try to get my laptop so we can play Dhako's Empire?"

Her eyes brightened. "Sure," she said. "But how will we do it?"

"We'll just go for a walk, and I'll run in and get it and put it under my sweater."

"That's not going to work."

He frowned thoughtfully. "I'll figure something out."

"Did you bring a heavy coat?"

"Yeah. It's at the cabin."

"Well, they shouldn't be able to see it if you have it on over your sweater."

"My, what a sneaky little thing you are."

Allyson smiled, "Let me get my coat and we'll just tell them we're going for a walk."

He helped her with her coat and they went out the front door.

The Secret Service agent, Sandy Sanders, standing at the front door, greeted Allyson and Jeremy as they came out. "Good evening Miss Anderson, Mr. Stallings."

"Evening, Sandy. We're going for a walk. Be right back."

"Would you like for me to take you somewhere in the golf cart, miss?"

"No thanks, we need to walk. We've been sitting all day."

Sanders spoke into his radio. "Snow White is on the move."

"Sandy, please. I'm just going a few yards from here. Let us have a few moments alone, okay?"

Sanders looked at her hesitantly. "Yes, Miss."

They walked hand in hand toward the cabins, careful not to look anxious or nervous. Approximately a hundred yards to the east of Aspen Lodge, Jeremy quickly took out his key and opened the door to his cabin. Allyson was quite impressed when her dad told her that Jeremy would be staying at the famous Birch cabin where many dignitaries had visited, including Israeli Prime Minister Menachem Begin in 1978 at the invitation of President Jimmy Carter to negotiate a framework for peace in the Middle East with Egyptian President Anwar Sadat, who stayed in the Dogwood cabin. Jeremy was amazed at the size of his guest quarters. He had expected a small, rustic cabin with limited furnishings, but instead was surprised that the Birch had two bedrooms, two baths, a spacious living room that opens out to a patio and a sizable stone fireplace. Upon his arrival, he frowned when he saw the framed photograph of the Israeli Prime Minister but decided he could live with it for a few hours.

"Hurry," Allyson said. "We don't want them to get suspicious."

He quickly went inside, pulled on his heavy overcoat and put the laptop under his sweater and came back out. Allyson took his arm and said, "Did you get it?"

"I did," he whispered back.

She chuckled and held his arm with both hands, and they ambled along the winding path. A few minutes later, they stepped up on the porch of the lodge and greeted Sanders. "See? We weren't gone long."

Agent Sanders nodded. "I see you got your heavy coat."

Jeremy smiled. "Yeah, it got a little nippy."

Sanders frowned guardedly and opened the door to the lodge for them. They went inside and closed the door.

~ ~ ~

Sabyl pulled out of the parking garage, turned right toward the traffic light and then left onto Connecticut Avenue and headed for the office. The back of her SUV was loaded with gifts. Beau sat on the seat next to her and panted contentedly. She turned onto Rock Creek Parkway and joined the traffic heading south into the District.

She had an incoming call and punched the button on her steering wheel and answered.

"Hi, babe."

"Scott! Are you okay?"

"Yeah, I'm fine. Look, I may not be able to come to your party with all that's going on."

"I figured as much, honey."

"I'm so sorry, babe."

"That's okay, I know you can't help it. We'll have our own Christmas party when this is over."

"I'm looking forward to it," he said, meaning it.

She came to a red light and stopped. "Is everything going okay with the investigation? I mean…"

"Yeah, as much as we're…"

"Are you getting any sleep at all?"

"Not much, but I'm not the only one."

"I'm praying for you, sweetheart."

"I know. I can feel your prayers." He paused a moment. "And I've been thinking about what we talked about the other night at the Iwo Jima Memorial."

"You have?" Her heart rate quickened.

"Yeah. I want to talk to you more about it…you know, later."

"Of course. I love you."

"Love you too, babe. Look, I gotta go. I'll call you when I can."

They hung up. Sabyl smiled and whispered, "Lord, please help him to understand and accept Your grace. Please open his eyes." She sat at the traffic light and watched the people as they went about the business of life. She breathed a prayer for them, for the investigators and for her nation.

~ ~ ~

Jeremy peeked out of the blinds and saw that Agent Sanders was standing with his back to the door. Good. He doesn't seem to be concerned that we're in here alone. He turned and smiled at Allyson, then walked over to the sofa and carefully pulled the laptop out of his sweater and sat down. Allyson pulled the blinds closed and sat down next to him.

"Just a minute," she said as she got up. "I'm going to ask the chef to make us some popcorn."

"Perfect!"

She walked into the kitchen and gave her request to the chef.

Jeremy turned on the computer and they smiled at each other as they waited for it to boot up. It whirred to life and he hit the app that brought up Dhako's Empire and they began to play the game.

~ ~ ~

Director Ron Keefer sat facing the agents of UATF. As he looked closely at the file just handed him by Agent Scott Terhune, he frowned and said, "What am I looking at?"

"The serial number on Amy's laptop doesn't coincide with the serial numbers of those ordered by AU."

"So this one wasn't part of that order?"

"No."

"Who ordered them?"

"You're not going to believe this."

Keefer leaned forward. "Tell me."

"They were bought with a credit card."

"Whose?"

"John Endicott."

Keefer stood up quickly. "John Endicott? The hitman who orchestrated those assassinations last year?"

"The same."

"That's unreal! The man's dead!"

"Tell me about it."

"So who..."

"Someone who came to finish the job, no doubt."

"That proves they're back to finish what they started."

"So they're after the President."

"And the Vice President. The only two who survived their attacks last year."

One of the FBI agents reminded them, "The president's daughter is a freshman at AU."

"Yeah, we already checked that out. She wasn't allowed to have one of their laptops. She has a secure laptop."

"But what about her boyfriend? He's an AU student. Isn't he spending Christmas with them at Camp David?"

The agents looked at one another. Keefer quickly radioed the Secret Service agents there to warn them that POTUS was in potential danger.

~ ~ ~

Allyson laughed as she tapped the keys, trying to catch Jeremy's king in the game. Jeremy hit her player, which ended the game.

"Oh, Pooh! You beat me again! Can we play another?"

"Sure, but how about letting me check my email real quick?"

"Sure, I'll just get us some more popcorn."

"Great!" He deftly moved the mouse, clicked on the icon that took him to his email.

CHAPTER THIRTY-ONE

The night sky was strewn with glimmering stars. The cockpit of the sleek Learjet 85 brought a smile to Colonel Hassan Farage. What fine craftsmanship, he thought. Having taken off out of Chicago at 21:20, and sure that he was far enough from the Class B airspace at ORD, he adjusted his heading to 155, which would take him to the vicinity of the Indianapolis airport (IND) where the Vice President's plane was scheduled to touch down at 22:00. He would have to remain in clandestine mode until the timing was right. Being in a private plane made that possible. Once out of Chicago airspace, he would be able to fly unnoticed and could dip under the radar for the last of the short 155 nautical mile trip to Indianapolis and would prowl above the Indiana cornfields until the VP's approach into IND. He would make his move quickly to come from beneath, pull up and ram Air Force Two's underbelly. Even the F-16's escorting the VP would not spot him in time. Corn farmers might have a question or two.

It was a clear night and flying VFR (Visual Flight Rule) would not be a problem. He would not be able to pick up transmission between the Air Traffic Controllers and Air Force Two, as the famous plane had an encrypted Mode-S transponder. It was going to be tricky, but he would be able to spot the aircraft with its escorts easily.

Colonel Farage was the highest rated pilot in the Syrian Airforce, one of the largest in the Middle East, with 30,000 service members. Although he was trained in the MiG-29 combat aircraft and SU-35 fighter jets, he had no problem handling the nimble Lear, primarily made of composite material rather than metal, making it more durable, lighter and easy to maneuver.

Hassan had been handpicked for this particular kill. He had been carefully brought into the United States through high-level contacts in Venezuela that arranged for him to be taken from Caracas to Mexico. He was able to easily cross the border into the U.S.A, albeit at a high price. But money had been no problem. Not even for the twenty-million-dollar Lear with all its add-ons. Wealthy Iraqis were bent on getting the job finished; a payback that had been started a year ago.

Colonel Farage's heart swelled with pride that he had been chosen for this mission and he would not let anything keep him from his target.

He repositioned his headset and sat back and stared up at the stars. What a perfectly beautiful night to die he thought. And what a grand entrance I will make into paradise. He smiled at the thought of the virgins awaiting him there.

~ ~ ~

Agent Sanders stood with his hands in his coat pockets, wishing he had a hot cup of coffee. His warm breath blew little vapors out of his mouth. Suddenly, a message came over his earpiece.

"What guests are with POTUS?" Keefer asked.

"Jeremy Stallings, Allyson's boyfriend. He's been cleared."

"Obviously, but does he have a laptop with him?"

243

"Yes, but we told him he couldn't use it and it's in his cabin."

"Get that thing out of there! He may be a Jackal!"

Sander's head shot up when he heard the message through his earpiece. "Yes, sir!" He sent Harris to Jeremy's cabin. "Go now!"

Harris jumped in the golf cart and sped over to Birch Cabin. He tried the door. It was locked. He took out a master key and opened it, searched and found the empty laptop case with the AU logo on the cover, lying on the bed. He radioed Sanders. "It's not here!"

~ ~ ~

The neighbors in the farming community had gone from curiosity to anger as they fumed among themselves over their rotary phones about the loud ruckus that was upsetting their dogs and keeping their kids from hearing their favorite TV programs. These were mostly peaceful folk; the kind that tuned in daily on their radios to the farm bureau reports at noon. During the boring winter months, they mostly listened to get caught up on new research, new ideas, and new production techniques. Some people called them the salt of the earth. Right now some of their saltiest words were being hurled at the noisy hot-rod pilot that seemed to be loitering overhead for the past several minutes.

The Lear lurked low over the dormant cornfields of Indiana and slid through the night, now with its heading fixed toward the airspace east of IND. Farage would engage the Vice President's plane just before it began its descent into the Indy airport. The surprise of coming from behind and beneath was his goal. He didn't want to be picked up on radar and tried to avoid small towns southwest of "Circle City." He was sure several farmers were shaking their fists at the low flying aircraft and wondering what the Sam Hill he was up to.

Col. Mac McLain focused on the green radar screen to his right. The odd turn and velocity of the blip below him, and the fact that he was flying unusually low, got his attention. Something's not right. He's flying too low to be coming out of IND. He slowed his speed and descended to take a look at what this guy was up to. He spotted the Lear flying directly toward AF Two. Is that a predator or some hotshot showing off his flying skills for his girlfriend? He could take no chances. He had to join up and see what kind of reaction he would get.

~ ~ ~

Jeremy quickly clicked on his email app. The familiar home page came up and he saw that he had an email from his mother. He ignored it and instead, opened an encrypted one from his friend, Abdul. The content was congratulatory words from his mentor who had taught him "the way to paradise."

"MY BROTHER, YOU WILL BE COUNTED AS THE GREATEST OF ALL OF ALLAH'S SERVANTS FOR WHAT YOU WILL ACCOMPLISH TONIGHT. MY CONGRATULATIONS TO YOU AND MAY YOU PROSPER IN YOUR ENDEAVOR FOR IT BRINGS GREAT GLORY TO ALLAH, MAY HE BE PRAISED."

He answered the email with a simple, "THANK YOU, BROTHER, FOR SHOWING ME THE WAY. IT WAS MY PLEASURE TO BRING REVENGE TO AU FOR THEIR CONDUCT TOWARD YOU. I OWE YOU THAT MUCH. MAY ALLAH BE PRAISED."

He then deleted his friend's email and scrolled down until he found the one he was looking for that said, "AN URGENT MESSAGE FROM YOUR PROFESSOR."

But then he saw another one with the identical words in the Subject box. He frowned warily and opened it and found it was a warning from Derrick Blake to all the freshmen not to open any email with that heading. Jeremy smiled. "Too late, pal. You should have sent your 'Urgent Message' memo a little sooner." He deleted it and went to the one that would soon be known to the world. "Goodbye, mother," he whispered.

~ ~ ~

Sanders tried the front door. It was locked. He took out his gun and shot the lock and went inside.

Allyson screamed at the sound.

Jeremy sat with his finger poised over Enter. "Too late, guys."

Just as he was about to hit Enter, Sanders shot him in the arm. Jeremy jerked back and howled in pain.

The startled President and First Lady jumped out of bed and came through the living room door. "What the...?"

"Get back, Mr. President!"

Jeremy moved his other arm and just as his finger touched the Enter key, Sanders shot him in the head.

Allyson and her mother screamed. The laptop teetered on the edge of the table. Sanders rushed and grabbed it just before it fell, careful not to touch the keys.

Allyson sobbed, "Why did you kill him?"

"He's a Jackal!"

"Oh, my God!"

Allyson, hysterical, was led out of the room by her mother while Sanders explained everything to the President.

~ ~ ~

Col. McLain knew that the best basic fighter maneuvering (BFM) was to fly at a higher altitude and behind the opponent. But tonight that would not be the case as this joker could not be allowed to come near Air Force Two. Plus, it appeared to be a Learjet, not a fighter jet that he was joining on. It appeared to be an unarmed corporate jet. Or was it? Could it have been rigged to carry a weapon? Certainly not missiles, but what about some other armament? He would find out soon enough. If he's a fighter pilot, I'll know by his maneuvers. If he's on a suicide mission to take the VP down, he'll try to avoid me. He'll go for the big enchilada.

~ ~ ~

Sabyl had taken Beau out for a walk and then finished getting dressed to join Rebecca, Dotty, and Mary at the office and then Lawrence would drive them to dinner at the Trump International Hotel in the newly transformed iconic Old Post Office Pavilion on Pennsylvania Avenue. Then they would head to Union Station after dinner to enjoy the Christmas decorations and especially the Norwegian Giant Model Train exhibit on display in the West Hall at the famous railway transportation building. The trains, hand-made replicas of real Norwegian trains, are set in a Norwegian landscape of mountains and fjords. Mary looked forward to seeing the amazing display every year.

She got off the phone with a driver who had gotten a ticket and was complaining of the problem of parking in D.C. She calmed him down and assured him the ticket would be taken care of. It's always something, she thought as she put the finishing touches on her makeup, a quick spritz of hairspray and she was ready to go. Beau looked at her with sad eyes, knowing she was about to leave. She gave him a treat, patted him on the head and said, "I'll be back soon, buddy. You be a good boy." He looked at her dolefully as she headed out the door.

The heels of Sabyl's boots echoed in the cavernous parking garage. As she approached her SUV, she thought she heard a cry for help. It sounded like a woman's voice. Looking to her left, she saw a woman wearing a long coat leaning on a car and crying out in pain. Sabyl approached her quickly and asked, "Are you alright?"

The dark-haired woman turned and looked at her and said, "Please help me! I think I sprained my ankle."

There was something about the woman that seemed familiar. She must have seen her in the lobby or on the elevator at one time or another. "Do you need to go to the hospital?"

"I'm afraid I might. It may be broken."

"Here, let me help you. I'll take to the ER."

She put her arm around her and helped her hobble over to Sabyl's car and opened the door for her. The woman thanked her and got in, and Sabyl quickly got in on the driver's side.

"This is so kind of you," the woman said as she fastened her seat belt.

"Not at all. I'm glad to help." She started the car and headed toward the garage exit. Just as she maneuvered her car out onto the street, she pushed the "Call Button" on her steering wheel to call Dotty to tell her she would be late.

The woman pulled out a gun and aimed it at Sabyl. "Don't do that."

Sabyl's heart felt like it would stick in her throat. "What are you doing? Who are you? What do you want?"

"Just drive where I tell you and you won't get hurt."

Sabyl hesitantly obeyed, praying with all her heart.

~ ~ ~

The Secret Service hurried the shaken first family toward Marine One to take them back to the White House and away from the horrific scene at Camp David. They boarded the helicopter and settled into their seats. The president held his daughter tight. Allyson buried her face in her dad's shoulder and whimpered quietly. "Daddy, I'm so sorry. I—I didn't know…"

"Shhhh. It's okay, honey. Of course, you didn't know. None of us knew."

The agents sitting across from them winced at the thought that a jackal could come that close to POTUS and his family.

Marine One gently lifted into the clear night sky and turned toward Washington.

The bomb squad was on its way to take possession of Jeremy's laptop and all of his belongings.

The rest of the protective detail stayed behind to begin their investigation. They started by interviewing the chefs and servers while others gathered up the gifts, the First Family's belongings and luggage and would follow shortly to bring them to the safety of the White House.

It was going to be a very tense Christmas.

~ ~ ~

After a little more than a half hour's drive, Sabyl's SUV pulled up in front of an abandoned warehouse in the boonies somewhere between Rockville and Gaithersburg, Maryland. No amount of questioning would bring an answer from the kidnapper to her victim. The woman ordered Sabyl to get out of the car. With her gun still leveled at her, she led her to a nondescript door, told her to open it and pushed her inside.

Sabyl felt dizzy and sick to her stomach and thought she might pass out. *Lord, please help me! I don't want to die here!*

A dim motion light came on. The woman pushed her along. They walked several yards into the cold, dank structure, turned right and walked along a wall that led to a large opening. There Sabyl saw someone tied up and sitting on the floor, gagged and bleeding. She couldn't believe her eyes. It was Rudy.

Armed guards stood on either side of him, their stoic faces hard without demonstration of any human attachment.

Sabyl ran over to Rudy, but they grabbed her and threw her onto the concrete floor alongside him. She fell awkwardly on her right arm. The crack of a broken bone was obvious. She screamed in pain.

Rudy's eyes looked pleadingly at them. He pulled forcefully at his restraints to no avail.

"So at last I have the two of you," the woman said, her lips drawn in a caustic curl. "The ones who are responsible for my husband's death. I've waited a long time for this moment." Her face was set in an expression of pure hatred.

Sabyl, wincing in pain, struggled to sit up, holding her arm tightly against her. "What are you talking about? Who are you?"

At that moment, Sabyl's phone chirped. She tried to grab it out of her pocket with her good arm, but the woman beat her to it. "Oh, no you don't." She grabbed it and threw it across the room. She squatted down next to Sabyl and sneered. "You have caused me excruciating pain and now it's my turn to bring it back to you." She stood up and ordered the men to set Sabyl in a chair and bind her. They grabbed her by the arms, ignoring her cry of pain, and dropped her in a chair and tied her to it.

CHAPTER THIRTY-TWO

Mac radioed the other F-16 escorting AF2 piloted by Lieutenant Colonel Dan "Tex" Marshall and got him up to speed.

"Tex, I may need a wingman to help me locate this guy if he starts defensive maneuvers."

"Roger that."

The Lear turned and seemed to be changing course.

"Looks like he's bugging out," Mac said.

"Yeah, maybe," answered Tex. "You staying with us or you gonna chase him?"

"I'll just stay with him and watch for a while." He adjusted his headset and called Indy Approach Control to see if they had a flight plan on the aircraft he was chasing. The response was negative.

Col. McClain joined on the Learjet that had now changed his heading away from AF 2, but in the back of his mind, Mac thought it a bit unusual that a Lear that was built for high and fast would be wandering around slow at low altitude. Maybe he was a rich farmer out for a joy ride in his new toy?

Hassan Farage took note of the fighter on his wing and wondered if the purpose of his mission had been compromised and if he was about to be shot down. The F-16 was heavily armed and he was not. He frowned deeply. *I've* got to remain calm. I don't want to miss my one chance to complete my mission. I have to make this work! I have to!

~ ~ ~

Dotty looked at her watch again. "This isn't like Sabyl not to call if she's going to be delayed. I just know something's wrong."

Lawrence frowned deeply. "I'm sure she's okay. Maybe she got caught up in traffic."

"But she would have called," protested Dotty. She pulled her phone out and called John, the night dispatcher. "Have you heard from Sabyl? She was supposed to pick us up over an hour ago."

"No, haven't heard from her."

"Okay. Call me if you hear anything."

"Will do. Same here."

Mary came out of the restroom. "When can we go? I'm hungry!"

"I know, honey. I'm sure it won't be long now."

"Okay," she said, plopping down in her mother's desk chair, resigned to wait a while longer.

Lawrence looked at his watch again and blew air out of the side of his mouth. "I wonder where she can be."

His ringtone sounded. He answered, "Lawrence here."

It was Layla asking if he had heard from Rudy. "He should have been home two hours ago."

Lawrence tried to assure her that everything was all right. After he hung up, he asked Dotty, "Do you have Scott's phone number?"

"Yes, I do. Why?"

"I think we'd better call him."

~ ~ ~

The woman sat in a chair across from Sabyl, leaned back with folded arms and smiled evilly. Sabyl, almost faint with pain, looked at her in complete confusion and then she recognized her. She was Eva Thornburg, the woman she saw with Ted Hickson at the Sequoia that Sunday she had lunch with Rebecca and her professor friend.

Seeing recognition in Sabyl's eyes, Eva pulled off the dark wig she was wearing, and her blond hair tumbled down onto her shoulders.

"Who are you? What do you want?" Sabyl asked, perplexed.

"I am the widow of the man you killed!"

Sabyl shook her head in confusion, staring at her. "What are you talking about? I've never killed anyone in my life!"

Eva pulled her long neck back and raised one eyebrow. "Does it mean so little to you that you don't even remember it?"

"Remember what?!"

"You caused the death of my husband, you idiot!"

Sabyl just stared at her. "I have no idea who you are talking about!" Suddenly, she frowned and said, "Do you mean John Endicott the assassin? You're his wife?"

"Was his wife! You killed him, or don't you remember?"

"Yes, I certainly do remember it."

"Well! Maybe you're not such an idiot after all!"

"He was a killer! Ever hear of 'Thou shalt not kill?'"

Eva stood up so quickly her chair toppled backward. She slapped Sabyl so hard, she thought she had dislocated her jaw. "So you will preach to me? You think you are better than me?"

"Those are God's words, not mine. Your husband was an assassin. Why is it okay for him to kill and not be punished for it?"

"So you are his judge?"

"I'm no judge. But I do believe in justice and obviously, you do not."

Rudy looked at her with worried eyes, fearing the woman would harm her again.

"Well, this is my justice, Miz Martin." She turned and gave an order in Arabic to one of the men. She then turned back to Sabyl. "There's another old proverb. An eye for an eye. Ever hear of that one, Miz Martin? You hurt the one I loved. I will hurt the one you love." She looked at Rudy and smiled a particularly wicked smile.

Rudy could only think about his wife and son. He looked at Sabyl with excruciating pain in his eyes as if to say goodbye.

~ ~ ~

A coroner was brought in to Camp David. Jeremy Stalling's body was transported to an undisclosed location. The bomb squad arrived and carefully took Stalling's laptop along with his other items left in Birch Cabin. Keefer and his team were notified immediately.

"I hope that was the last bomb," Martz said.

"You got that right." Scott's phone vibrated. He answered, "Terhune here."

A frantic Dotty explained what was going on. Scott frowned deeply as he listened. "Rudy too?"

Martz and Keefer looked on with intense interest.

Scott thanked her and assured her he would take care of it. "Yes, Dotty, I promise I'll let you know as soon as I can." He put his phone away and then told Keefer and Martz what he had heard. "Not only is Sabyl missing, but Rudy's wife, Layla, called and said he was missing too."

Keefer whistled and said, "We were right. They're back."

~ ~ ~

The press had begun to get bits and pieces of news that the president and his family hurriedly returned to the White House. They wasted no time contacting their sources to find out as much as they could. Some had already begun writing stories based on conjecture, which was not unusual for some news outlets.

The president's personal doctor gave Allyson a sedative and put her to bed. Her mother sat in a chair next to her daughter. She was in a daze and would not move until she knew that Allyson had fallen asleep. The doctor tried to assure her that she was fine but she would not leave her side and sat and watched her child's breathing slow to a restful, normal rhythm.

Finally, First Lady Jane Anderson got up, walked over to a large chest, took out her journal and sat down and wrote an entry that she thought she would never write.

~ ~ ~

After several minutes, since the Lear was no longer on a course that would intersect AF2, McLain decided to break off and rush back to resume his primary mission: to protect the VP and his family. Mac was thrilled to see the bright lights of the city below, which meant they were close to a landing, and time was growing short to complete his mission. After detaching from the Lear, even though they were approaching the city, in the back of his mind was the nagging thought of the unusual flying pattern of the unidentified jet.

Col. Farage reached over and turned off his transponder and turned cautiously to follow the F-16. He knew that any pilot worth his salt would not relax, especially if he is defending one as important as the Vice President of the United States.

The intense flashing strobe lights on the fighter greatly simplified the task of following it.

Once again, Farage went over his plan in his mind. He would drop much lower, speed up and then, with the element of surprise, approach from below and behind with maximum speed, head straight for AF2 and pull up directly into the massive plane's belly. He figured by the time the two escorting F-16's saw what was happening, he would be so close that it would be too late for them to fire a missile at him without endangering the VP's plane.

Farage pushed the throttles full forward to attain max speed and started his approach. He checked again to make sure the aircraft lights were off. He was not concerned about any conflict from incoming flights heading for Indy. The sixty-mile restricted perimeter no-fly-zone around the executive plane would give him plenty of room to maneuver without having to worry about hitting a commercial airliner.

By now, in keeping with the planned attacks at Camp David, Farage knew that the president was surely dead, along with his family and their protectors. Now it is up to me to bring Allah praise.

~ ~ ~

In a raspy voice, Eva said something in Arabic to one of the men that sounded like an order. The man nodded and pulled another chair over, and the two men pulled Rudy up off the floor and shoved him in the chair and tied him to it. One of the men walked over to a darkened area of the building, looked around and then picked up something and began dragging it over toward them.

Sabyl stared in horror as the man approached Rudy with a long orange extension cord. Is he going to strangle him? Oh, God, help us!

The man smiled viciously and grunted as he threw it down at Rudy's feet and then turned around to get something else. He walked over to a large wooden box. It creaked eerily as he opened it and pulled something out. Sabyl watched him closely but could not make out what was in his hands. He turned and walked back to where they were, his yellow teeth showing like a rabid dog.

She couldn't tell what it was until he got closer. It was an electric drill.

~ ~ ~

Countless thoughts were going through Colonel Mac McLain's mind as he watched and waited, keeping an eye on the skies around him and on his green radar screen. The lights of the city suburbs below had greatly enhanced his ability to see around him. He clearly saw the wing lights and bright strobes of AF2 and his wingman.

Was that Lear the predator? Or is there another? Are there more than one? He doubted it. Shooting down an unarmed, civilian aircraft is relatively easy. But, he had to know for a fact that this guy is the enemy and is going after the VP. He knew that if the Lear were the predator, he would most likely turn off his transponder, but thought, We should be able to get a radar paint as long as he approaches from ahead. And if he turns off his exterior, he'll be able to see us, but we won't be able to see him. His brow furrowed deeply at the thought. There would be a full moon tonight which would enhance his ability to see around him. He looked to his left and saw the glow of the moonrise coming over the horizon. He hoped it would ascend in time to be of some help.

His mind raced back to the attacks of Nine/Eleven; back to the orders for the F-16 crews launched out of alert that day. They were instructed to ram the remaining high jacked airliner if they could not get in position to fire a missile. His military code of dedication, to protect the VP at all cost, in a similar fashion, flashed thru his mind. But they were near the IND airport and close to completing this escort mission. He looked forward to landing and relaxing at the club after a long day. A thought that would be short-lived.

Within seconds, he saw a flicker of a fast moving shadow below in the lights of the suburbs in his left peripheral vision. He peeled away from AF2 to get a better look. He thought he saw something at 9 o'clock low. He rolled over hard and lit the burner to check it out. He saw what appeared to be the shadow of a darkened aircraft heading straight for AF2. He radioed to the other F-16. "Bandit. Nine o'clock low. No lights. Closing fast. I'm rolling in."

Mac went after him. The Lear was indeed closing fast. Mac quickly realized that with the high closure rate, he had no time to get into a missile firing window behind him. His mind raced at speed seldom experienced before. The VP was in immediate danger. Air Traffic Control was squawking in his ear for some answers regarding the radical maneuvers in their airspace. Mac was doing his best to keep communication going between him and Tex and AF2. But right now, he had to concentrate on the predator.

As he closed on the Lear, he ordered the pilots of AF2 to abandon their approach, go to full power, and pull up immediately. Mac then told his wingman that unless he could get in a position of advantage, the only way to save the VP was for him to attempt to ram the unlit jet. He knew he couldn't use a missile. If the bandit maneuvered too close to AF2, the heat-seeking missile might go after the VP's plane. If he shoots with bullets, he has to be careful that the shrapnel from the plane doesn't hit him. Then I've killed my target and myself. I have to get a position of advantage.

Tex was startled by the imminent danger to the VP. Crap! Why would he get behind us if he's not armed? Are we fighting just the aircraft itself or are we fighting a hidden weapon?

When Farage saw the afterburner light up, and the lights of the F-16's approach aimed directly at him, he knew he had been spotted. Could it be that this crazy F-16 pilot is going to ram me? He is not in position to shoot at me. Farage instinctively pulled up and into the F-16. This resulted in a high-speed rolling dogfight at night. His only chance was to avoid the attacking fighter jet and use the high overtaking speed he had to get to AF2.

Mac was amazed at how nimble the pilot of the Lear was and knew he must be a veteran fighter pilot. But how could a Learjet be a fighter? How could it be armed? Was it armed? Whether it was or not, he needed to keep him away from AF2.

My plane is an instrument of war built to destroy an enemy and their equipment. This guy is in a private plane, probably on a suicide mission, most likely unarmed. Probably going to use his plane as the weapon of choice...just like Nine/Eleven.

~ ~ ~

The President, still in his bathrobe, sat at the head of the large conference table in the Situation Room in the White House. He had called in his staff. The ones who were able to get there on such short notice, all looked deeply concerned; some were visibly shaken at the news of what had taken place at Camp David.

The Director of the Secret Service was there, his head down, no doubt disturbed that a jackal had gotten through their primarily impenetrable hedge of protection around the

President of the United States, but thankful that those agents who were there to protect him, had done so with courage and excellence.

The President assured everyone that he and his family were alright. "Allyson is distraught and shaken, of course, but she's resting now, and I'm sure she will come through this just fine."

His National Security Advisor handed him the phone. "It's the Vice President, sir."

POTUS grabbed the phone and said, "Carl, are you where you can talk? I don't want your kids to hear this."

He told him he was in his office on Air Force Two. "What's going on, Byron?"

He filled him in on what had happened at Camp David. "We think the terrorists are back to finish what they started last year, Carl. You and your family are no doubt on their hit list."

Looking out the window, Vice President Bridges noticed that one of the F-16 escorts was missing. When he mentioned it to the President, he said, "Get me your pilot on the phone!"

"Yes, sir."

Within a minute Air Force Two's pilot, Colonel David Fleming was on the phone. The president exclaimed, "Dave, what's going on?"

"We may have a predator stalking us, sir. One of our escorts is taking a look."

The president briefed him on what had happened at Camp David. "Dave, you're the PIC (Pilot in Charge), it's your call, but you might consider an alternate course."

"Yes, sir! Already on it, sir!"

Colonel Fleming's crew acknowledged the new heading to turn the VC-25 around, its four General Electric CF6-80C2B1 jet engines responded with gusto. On heightened alert, the crew of Air Force Two quickly flipped on the switches for the plane's decoy settings, sending radar pulses that would simulate a false target in case of an incoming missile. They were not sure what they were facing, but their training kicked in with intensity and complete confidence.

He briefed his crew on what had taken place. They sat in silence.

CHAPTER THIRTY-THREE

Sabyl began to plead with Eva to stop the man with the drill. "Please don't hurt Rudy. He didn't cause your husband's death. I did!"

"Oh, so now you admit it! And now you are feeling the pain of watching a loved one suffer? How does it feel, Miz Martin?"

Rudy tried to cry out, but the tape over his mouth kept him from being able to make any noise other than a muffled, "Mmm...mmmm!!!"

Eva told the man to take the tape off his mouth. "I want to hear him scream just as I am sure my dear husband cried out in anguish as his plane fell from the sky."

The man ripped the tape off of Rudy's face. He looked at him gleefully as he cried out in pain from the tape tearing at his skin. "You think that hurts? Just you wait, Rudy, you haven't felt pain yet."

Eva folded her arms and watched Sabyl's face contort into sheer terror. "How does it feel, Miz Martin?"

Sabyl cried out, "Please! Please don't..."

The man plugged in the extension cord and turned on the ancient, rusty drill. "Let's see. Where shall I start? Maybe with his eyes?"

Eva spat out, "Yes! An eye for an eye!"

He grabbed Rudy by the hair and jerked his head back and aimed the drill straight at Rudy's right eye.

A violent storm of horror washed over them both. Sabyl screamed and kicked as hard as she could, but the restraints wouldn't let her move enough to do any good.

The man with the drill leaned in towards Rudy and a loud cry of pain followed by a deafening crack and blood spattering all over Rudy's face. The drilled fell out of the man's hand onto his own foot. He screamed and kicked it away and pulled his bleeding hand up and stared at it in shock.

Eva turned and saw several very large men dressed in black, armed to the teeth, coming toward her. She reached for her gun.

"Don't do it, lady!"

She pulled out her gun and they shot it out of her hand. She screamed in pain. The weapon fell at her feet.

They grabbed her and the wounded man, cuffed them and led them toward the exit. As they led her out of the building, she screamed, "You! You've ruined everything!"

The agent ignored her and kept walking.

Rudy broke down in tears, "Thank You, Lord. Oh, thank You!"

"Sabyl!"

She looked in the direction of his voice. "Oh, Scott, thank God!"

He ran over to her and untied her.

Martz untied Rudy. "Man! Are you okay? You've got blood all over your face!"

"I am okay," he said, his voice clearly shaking. "It's not my blood."

Scott helped Sabyl to her feet. "Sweetheart, are you alright?"

"Yes…no…I think my arm is broken."

"Oh, God, babe!" He held her gently then pulled back and looked at her. "What else did they do to you? Your face is all swollen."

"She didn't like something I said."

A vein on Scott's neck began to swell. He grimaced. "We've got to get you to the hospital."

"How did you find me? How did you know I was here?"

"I followed the signal on the phone we gave you."

Tears sprang into her eyes. "I just thank God you found us!"

"Me too, honey." He wiped a tear from her cheek and then turned toward Rudy. "You okay, buddy?"

"Yes, Mr. Scott, thank you. You c-came j-just in time."

"Oh, Scott. I hate to think…"

He brushed back the hair out of her eyes. "Shhh, …it's okay, honey. Come on, we've got to get you two to the hospital."

Rudy was still shaking so hard he could barely talk. "I…I can drive her…"

"No, Rudy, I'll have a couple of agents drive both of you to get checked out. You've been through a lot."

Her legs felt wobbly like walking on a suspension bridge. She looked at her car and then at Scott.

"Don't worry, honey, we'll get it home for you."

Martz asked, "Rudy, you didn't come here on your own steam, I'm sure."

"No, sir, I did not."

Scott said, "After you're checked out, I'll have an agent drive you home. They may want to keep Sabyl in the hospital."

"Thank you, Mr. Scott. I must call my wife. She must be terribly worried."

"Scott, my phone! That woman threw it across the room."

Scott handed it to her. I already found it, honey. That phone led us to you."

She took it and hugged it to her chest with her good arm as though it was her best friend.

"And, by the way, I've already spoken to Dotty. They know you're safe."

A helicopter could be heard in the distance.

"I have to go, honey, there's a lot happening tonight."

Keefer walked up and said, "We'll take good care of her, Scott. Don't worry."

Scott kissed her and said," I'll be in touch when I can."

The other agents began scouring the warehouse for evidence for their investigation. Others helped Sabyl and Rudy into a black Suburban.

The helicopter gently set down in a nearby clearing. Scott and Martz turned and climbed into it. It quickly pulled up and headed for Camp David.

~ ~ ~

Col. Farage continued a series of rolling maneuvers to keep his speed up so he could close in on the VP while avoiding contact with the F-16. The Syrian pilot was very skilled, and in spite of Mac's best moves to impact the Lear or get in position for a close-in gunshot, the wild rolling maneuvers continued as AF2 took evasive action. Tex, by this time, realized that he needed to support Mac and pitched back to get behind the rolling maneuvers.

Mac noted Bandit was close to 400 knots. Try as he may, every time Mac got close to hitting the Lear, Hassan would make an instinctive move to miss the impact. He kept maneuvering to try and close in on AF2, but being heavily engaged with the F-16, he saw his opportunity slipping away. Was his chance to honor Allah slipping away? Was the mission doomed to fail?

To make sure that Tex maintained sight of the dogfight while trying to position for a shot at the Lear, Mac was deploying decoy flare cartridges to clearly mark in the night where they were. Mac was sure of this: he doesn't want me. He wants the VP.

Tex had followed behind the twisting, turning dogfight and was trying to get in position to shoot. The violent movements were more aggressive than a normal barrel roll. Range is critical to the success of the roll. Farage applied hard back-stick pressure, creating the high g-forces and adding hard rudder input to assist the ailerons, rolling the Lear.

As Air Force Two began to open the distance from the engagement, Mac started to gain nose to tail separation on the Lear. He was gaining an advantage and directed Tex to return to AF2.

By now the moon was out in full, making it fairly easy to see the white Lear. Mac knew he had to maneuver as though that pilot was as good as he is. Mac began rolling upside-down, beginning from the inverted position. The high-g barrel roll is an energy-depleting maneuver that rarely causes the attacker to fly out in front, but usually results in a flight path overshoot, which could temporarily disrupt Mac's aim.

He had finessed the Lear away from AF2 and had worked his way into a firing position on the Lear. It had not been easy. The Lear pilot was a skilled and worthy opponent – especially at night in an aircraft designed for transporting passengers. The Lear was now in his gunsight and clearly in the envelope for a shot.

Farage tried to jink right. Too late. It was over.

Bandit barbequed.

~ ~ ~

Sabyl sat up in her bed, her arm in a heavy cast. Flowers that had been sent or brought to the hospital were now placed on her dresser, her bedside table and a lot more in the living and dining room. She had been on the phone with several of her friends and her drivers, all of whom had heard about her ordeal and wanted to check on her. She assured them all that she was fine.

Rebecca came to the bedroom door and whispered, "Are you off the phone?"

"Sure am. Come on in."

"Is there anything I can get you, honey?"

"No thanks, Bec, I'm good. Thank you again for coming over to stay with me. You're a sweetheart."

"What are best friends for?" She fluffed Sabyl's pillows and sat down next to her on the side of the bed. "I'm just glad you're okay. I still can't believe all that you've been through!"

"Me either. It seems like a bad dream."

"More like a nightmare!"

Beau came wandering into the room looking lost. He went to the side of her bed and looked up at Sabyl with worried eyes.

"It's okay, buddy, I'm fine."

He jumped up on the bed, laid down next to Sabyl and began to lick her cast.

Sabyl said, "Bec, look at that. How could he know that's the exact place where my arm is broken?"

Rebecca smiled. "I think they somehow sense these things. God put such love and loyalty in dogs. It amazes me how they can care so deeply for their owners."

"I know. It's pretty remarkable. They both petted his soft ears.

Rebecca stood, picked up Sabyl's empty glass and said, "I'll get you some fresh water. Are you getting hungry? You haven't eaten much."

"Is there any of that wonderful quiche left?"

"Absolutely! I'll warm you up a piece. Would you like some toast with it?"

"That would be great. Thanks, Bec."

"I'm glad you've got an appetite. Be back shortly." She walked out of the room toward the kitchen.

Sabyl sighed deeply and thanked God for how He had spared her life once again. She thought of Scott and how God had used him to rescue her. She wondered if he had gotten any rest. He felt with the arrest of Eva and her thugs that they had the main perpetrators, but there were still many unanswered questions. Scott didn't say it, but she knew it was on his mind as it certainly was hers. The terrorists still did not get their targets. Would they be back? She sighed and prayed, "Father, I can't worry about this. I have given You my life and I trust You to do Your perfect will. And please guide Scott to come fully to You. Show us what You would have us do. Thank You again for your mercy. Amen."

~ ~ ~

The tradition of decorating the White House for Christmas started with President Benjamin Harrison in 1889 when his family decorated the first indoor Christmas Tree in the Oval Office. Since 1929, it has been the responsibility of the First Lady to oversee the holiday adornments, aided by hundreds of craft people from all over America. This year, they had done a magnificent job turning the mansion into what could only be described as a winter wonderland. Dozens of white heavily flocked trees trimmed in silver adorned all but a few of the 132 rooms with matching wreaths on each door. From all of the 147 wreathed windows, a white light glowed warmly and flocked greenery was carefully placed on the 28 fireplace mantels and the banisters of each of the 8 staircases.

At the main entrance were two enormous white swans made of feathers and white flowers from the tropics that were guaranteed to make it through the holidays before showing signs of fatigue.

The more than 90 White House service staff members were made up of chefs, butlers, valets, maids, doormen, plumbers, and a florist. They all prided themselves on excellent service and devotion to the First Family. After the news of the horror that happened to them at Camp David and their return to the Residence, many of the White House staff canceled their own family time to be on hand over the Christmas holidays. They even came together with special gifts to be a further blessing to them.

Allyson had a cousin who was her best friend from childhood. The First Lady invited her sister and her family to spend Christmas with them along with other close friends who were more than happy to be among their special guests.

The Vice President and his family were able to continue on to Indianapolis for the holidays. The local newspapers and newscasters were full of articles and reports of the dogfight that occurred over their city. The farmers had their answer as to the ruckus that had played out over their farms. They were just glad the Lear didn't land on one of their barns.

~ ~ ~

The Marine helicopter set down with a slight bounce on the helipad on the roof of the building that housed the Unified Agency Task Force. Scott, Martz and four other

UATF agents climbed out and headed for the door that would take them to the control center, now buzzing with activity.

As they entered the massive room, Director Ron Keefer walked over to them. "Well?"

Scott handed him a folder with several photographs and statements from the Camp David staff. He and Martz filled him in on the information they had gathered.

They walked over to the conference table. He took the pictures out of the folder and spread them on the table. There were photos of the would-be assassin, Jeremy Endicott aka Jeremy Stallings, his body still on the blood-soaked sofa where he and Allyson had played Dhako's Empire, a photo of the weaponized computer, and photos of his other belongings.

UATF agent, Tommy Reid, sitting at one of the many computer terminals, called out to Keefer. "Sir, I have something you'll want to see."

Keefer got up and walked over to him. "What have you got?"

"I hacked into Abdul Arib's computer and managed to retrieve some of his emails. I'm printing them out now."

Keefer walked over to the printer and picked up several of the pages and began to read them carefully. After reading a few of them, he walked over to Scott and Martz and dropped them in front of them on the table. Scott quickly picked them up. Martz moved his chair closer, and the two of them began to peruse them.

Keefer folded his arms. "I still don't get why Thornburg or Endicott or whatever her name is, wanted to target all those AU students. It still doesn't add up."

"Maybe this will help clear it up, sir." Agent Reid hit PRINT on the keyboard and sat back looking satisfied. "This is the last email he wrote."

Keefer picked it up as soon as the printer released it. It was the last email between Jeremy and Abdul that was sent from Camp David.

"There's your answer, sir."

"It definitely is." He picked up the phone and sent several agents to arrest Abdul Arib. He then turned to his aide and said, "Get the President on the phone."

CHAPTER THIRTY-FOUR

Dotty and Mary finished putting the finishing touches on the happy business of wrapping their gifts. Mary gleefully clapped her hands when she heard the news that Sabyl would be arriving at the office party shortly. Rudy had just called and told them that he, Layla and David would be pulling into the circle drive at Martin Transportation at any time.

The drivers, still in shock about what had happened to Sabyl and their fellow driver and friend, Rudy, had talked nonstop about it ever since. In between rants, they had managed to decorate the lounge area with an eight-foot tree, decked to the hilt with lights and multicolored ornaments. The Muslim drivers excused themselves from attending the party and left to go home to be with their families.

Burt's wife, Phyllis, walked in wearing her faux fur and earrings shaped like little Christmas wreaths. Burt, wearing a Santa's hat, followed with an armful of gifts. Dotty helped him place them under the tree. She had on a red Christmas sweater with sparkly sequins on it spelling out, "Nice until Proven Naughty."

Frank and Barbara were next to arrive, towing the baby carrier Sabyl had given them in which little Sabyl Lynn was sleeping. Barbara had been out of the hospital only a couple of days and looked tired but strong. She wore a black sweater with a red reindeer on it and white glittering sequined snowflakes scattered on the front. Dotty squealed with delight when she saw the baby. Frank let her take the carrier and went back out to the car for the gifts.

Stubby and George brought in their gifts just as Rudy, Layla, and David walked in the door. Dotty greeted them warmly and said, "Hey Rudy! Boy, are you a sight for sore eyes! Uh, no pun intended."

Rudy grinned at her and gave her a hug. "I'm glad to see you too, Dotty. Or anyone, for that matter!" They all laughed.

David had two large shopping bags full of gifts that he let Mary place under the tree.

Layla brought homemade Baklava and set it on the table the drivers had set up for the food at Dotty's request.

Karen came in carrying a load of gifts and a Bose CD player, and after placing the gifts on the floor next to the tree, immediately put on Christmas music while Dotty poured the punch.

Lawrence's car pulled up into the bricked circle drive. He got out and opened the door for Rebecca and then went around to the other side and opened the door for Sabyl.

Frank stood with the heavy glass office door open for them. Lawrence came in behind them with Beau.

Mary cried out "Yaaaay, Sabyl!" Her employees applauded as she walked in, smiling warmly and happy to see her crew.

"Hi, Everybody! Merry Christmas! Boy, are you all decked out! And look at all the gifts!"

Lawrence led Beau in and handed the leash over to George, who unfastened it and hung it on the hook just inside Sabyl's office door. Beau had on a red knitted sweater with a bell around his neck.

Frank hugged Sabyl, careful not to squeeze her arm, now in a cast and sling. Having been a fan of her books for a long time, Frank was a bit star struck to see the famous author Rebecca Carriere in person. "Let me help you with your coats."

Rebecca helped Sabyl off with her cape and handed it and her coat to Frank. "Thank you so much, Frank."

He grinned sheepishly and took them into Sabyl's office and hung them on the coat rack.

Everyone was talking at once, the music putting everyone in the mood with Brenda Lee belting out, "Rockin' Around the Christmas Tree."

Jenny walked in with Derrick. He walked over to Sabyl. "Jenny invited me. I hope that's okay."

"Of course it is, Derrick. I'm glad you came."

Jenny hugged Sabyl and smiled. "Sorry we're late. He wanted to come to my apartment tonight to use my phone to call his mom. He's flying out the day after tomorrow to go home to Ohio to spend Christmas with her."

"That's great, Jenny."

"He let me read the first draft of his book. He's really a good writer."

"That's wonderful, Jen. I'd love to read it myself."

Rebecca shook his hand and said, "Let me know if I can be of any help, Derrick."

He stood stunned in silence meeting the famous author. "Are you serious?"

"Of course," she replied. "I'd love to read your manuscript. I hear it's a suspense novel. I love a good thriller."

"Wow! I'd love for you to read it! But I'm not quite finished with it."

"Well, when you're ready, I'd love to take a look."

Sabyl walked over to Frank and Barbara and looked down at the beautiful little infant. "Barbara, how are you feeling?"

"I'm fine, Sabyl. The doctor said I just need to take it easy for a while. What about you? Frank told me what happened. I just can't believe it! I'm so glad you and Rudy are safe."

"Thank you, dear. We're all going to be fine." She looked down at little Sabyl Lynn. "I wish I could hold her, but I guess I'd better wait till I have two good arms."

Barbara smiled up at her. "There'll be plenty of time for that." She touched her broken arm gently. "I'm just glad you're okay."

Frank had tears in his eyes. "I, uh…we've been praying for you."

Sabyl said, "Frank that means more to me than anything. Thank you. Thank you both."

Dotty bellowed out, "Well, this food isn't going to get eaten by itself! Sabyl, why don't you sit over there by Mary and I'll fix you a plate."

Lawrence said, "I'll be right back." He went back out to his car to get the rest of the gifts that were in the back seat.

Sabyl sat down, and she and Mary began to chat. "I'm sorry we didn't get to go together to go to Union Station to see the trains, honey."

Mary grinned, "That's okay. Dan took Mom and me."

"Dan?"

"Mom's boyfriend."

Sabyl smiled, and looked up at Dotty. "Boyfriend?"

Dotty handed her a plate of food. She turned nearly as red as her sweater. "Yeah, the boss guy that did my floors. He'll be here shortly…oh, wait, here he is now." She moved swiftly over to the door to open it for him. "Everybody, this is my friend, Dan."

Mary belted out, "Boyfriend!"

Everybody laughed and welcomed him heartily. Dan stood there grinning and gave a little wave as he came in. "Hi, folks."

"Here, let me take your coat," Dotty insisted. "Help yourself to some food. There's plenty!"

Sabyl noticed a silly grin on Mary's face. "What are you smiling about, Mary?"

"Look!" she said, huskily and pointed to the door.

Sabyl turned and saw Scott coming in the door, his arms full of gifts that George had commandeered him to help bring in. "Scott! You're here!"

"I'm here, angel face." He handed the gifts to Dotty and walked over to Sabyl.

"I thought you had to go to Camp David."

"Just got back. Looks like we might have a merry Christmas after all."

"I've already got mine," she said as he took her in his arms.

Mary blurted out, "Guess what!"

Rudy answered, "What's that, Mary?"

"I have a new name!"

"You do? What is it?"

"Mary Christmas!" She clapped her hands and laughed like a child at play.

"Mary Christmas?" Frank went along, grinning. "I guess you've been hearing your new name a lot these days."

"I have! I like it a lot!"

Scott asked Sabyl if they could slip out for a minute. She said, "Sure. My office, okay?"

They stepped into her glass-enclosed office. He closed the blinds and kissed her. "Babe, it's over. I can't go into details yet, but we got the bad guys."

"Oh, Scott, that's wonderful news! Thank God!"

"Yes. Speaking of...uh...I have something to ask you."

"You do?"

"I've been thinking a lot about what you said at the Iwo Jima Memorial the other night. You said that God...or Jesus...makes us a brand new person. I want that...I need that. I keep thinking how I abandoned you three years ago when you needed me the most. I've changed a lot, and I would never leave you like that again, but I'm not the man that I should be or that you deserve...and I want what you have." He rubbed his forehead. "Will you tell me how to...how to meet your friend Jesus?"

Her eyes welled up with tears. "Oh, honey, of course, I will. All you have to do is ask. He's already drawing you to Himself. Just open your heart and ask him to come in."

He searched her face. "Is it really that easy?"

She nodded with tears in her eyes. "It really is. But you must ask Him to come live in you so He can do His redemptive work in your heart."

"I think I understand."

She said, "Are you sure?"

"Yes. I know He's alive and I know I need Him."

She whispered, "Then just pray this prayer with me, Scott."

He held her hand and followed in prayer.

"Father God, I confess that I have sinned against you. I know that Your Son Jesus took the punishment on the cross that I deserve so that I can be forgiven. Please forgive me for all my sins. I place my trust in you and ask you to come live in me. Help me to become the man You want me to be. Thank You for the gift of eternal life. In Jesus' name, Amen."

"Amen." He looked at her and exhaled. "I feel like a thousand pounds has been lifted off me!"

Sabyl wiped a tear. "I'm so happy for you, sweetheart. So very happy and grateful."

Scott looked at her with wonder in his eyes. "I just want to know all about Him."

She touched the Bible on her desk and said, "This book will teach you everything about Him…and about you." She reached over and pulled a tissue out of a cube-shaped box on her desk and blew her nose softly.

He lowered his head and said, "I don't know why I waited so long."

"I guess it just wasn't your time yet, honey."

He cupped his hand under her chin. "I saw something in you that I knew I had to have but I didn't know how. I didn't know it was this easy."

"I know. We are complex creatures, so we try to complicate everything. But it's not that hard. Just let Him take control."

He cleared his throat. "I, uh, I have something for you. A little gift. May I give it to you now or do you want me to give it to you later?"

"Now would be lovely."

He reached into his pocket and pulled out a small velvet box and opened it. In it was an entirely different ring from the simple solitaire he had given her before.

Sabyl put her hand over her mouth and she began to tremble.

"Sabyl, I love you with all my heart, and I can't imagine life without you. I want to live the rest of my life with you. Sweetheart, will you marry me?"

She fanned her face and said, "Yes, yes, YES!"

He slipped the ring on her finger.

"Scott, it's beautiful! How did you find time to…?"

"I had it made special. The diamonds are from my mother's engagement ring. I wish you could have met her. She would have loved you."

"That...that's so wonderful. It makes it even more precious. I love you!"

He kissed her and held her gently in his arms. He pulled back and looked deeply into her eyes. "You do know what you're getting into, don't you?"

She looked up at him and said, "You mean...your work?"

"Yes. You've already got a pretty good idea of what it can be like."

"I know."

"There will be days that you won't see me at all; won't be able to get in touch with me..."

She put her fingers on his mouth. "There are many wives whose husbands are far away on the front lines getting shot at every day. If they can do it, so can I."

He hugged her again and whispered, "That's my girl."

A few minutes later, they came out of the office. All eyes were on them. Scott announced, "Folks, it's over. We got the bad guys!"

A huge cheer arose from the Christmas party attendees.

"Thank God!" Rudy exclaimed.

"Yes, thank God," repeated Frank. He looked at his newborn and thought, maybe she has a future after all.

Barbara squeezed his hand, looked into his eyes and beamed.

Sabyl said proudly, "Everybody! We have a little announcement." She held out her hand to show off her ring.

Everyone applauded and yelled "Congratulations!"

Dotty hollered, "Well, it's about time!"

They all laughed and gathered around them and, one by one, hugged Scott and Sabyl.

Mary smiled and yelled, "Merry Christmas everybody!"

THE END

ABOUT THE AUTHOR

Tempe Brown is a native of Oklahoma. She is a former magazine editor and is the author of an enhanced historical novel entitled, The Seed, a children's book called The Little Dirt People (What it Means to be Born Again) and a suspense thriller, The Payback Game (Sixteen Days of Terror). She has gained recognition as a speaker for the Gideons International and Stonecroft Ministries. She currently resides in Greenville, South Carolina.

Made in the USA
Columbia, SC
16 April 2019